Beneath the Image

Vanessa Pearse

V

PRESS

PRESS

Published by Vulpine Press in the United Kingdom in 2021

ISBN: 978-1-83919-150-3

Cover painting Fiona Walsh

www.vulpine-press.com

To my wonderful family Brian, Sarah, Naoise, Fionn and Martha,
May we always be kind to each other and to others.
And may we be there for each other through the highs and the lows.

Also by Vanessa Pearse:
Deniable Memories

Acknowledgements

Writing is such a solo process yet it takes an army of people to take a novel from an idea to publication. *Beneath the Image* or my first novel, *Deniable Memories*, would never have come to fruition without the support and encouragement of some of my great friends and tutors, especially my friends: Fiona Tierney, Suzanne O'Connell, Marion Roche, Pauline Brennan, Ita Hicks, Eimear Shanahan and Eimear Gallagher and my writing tutors: Magi Gibson, Claire Hennessy, Lisa McInerney and Conor Kostick. Thank you one and all, and a special thank you to my wonderful, inspiring friend Fiona Walsh who painted the powerful cover image.

I still pinch myself to think that *Vulpine Press* believed in my writing enough to want to publish my work. I am forever grateful to them. Sarah Hembrow, my editor at Vulpine, was a joy to work with on both of my novels. Thank you, Sarah, for all your wonderful, wise and thorough editing and feedback that always feels as if it is done with a smile, even when I think I must be driving you scatty!

Without the support of my husband, Brian, I could never have written one novel, never mind two. I suspect friends will tease him about what traits he and the fictional Patrick have in common. The answer is little else apart from being middle-aged men with wives who don't share their passion for golf! Ours is a marriage of equals and joy in shared experiences and we take great delight and wonder at each of the four unique, beautiful adults we have created together.

Chapter 1

The Dinner Party

Late June 2018

Nobody could drive a nail home quite like our youngest daughter. Once, she had diagnosed me as *hysterical without the laughter* and that became the retort of choice that thundered off her lips every time we clashed – she liked to hit deep into what remained of my ego.

Honestly, as a young woman I had been no more unreasonable than the next person. The highlights of my social life were long nights of food, drink, talk and laughter served by me in a bedsit that boasted a nylon patterned carpet in various shades of dirty brown, a single bed, a wardrobe, a rickety table, three chairs, a two-ring cooker and a two-foot-high fridge. Those nights of food, talk and laughter continued when I moved to an apartment with a separate kitchen and a proper cooker and fridge. They remained my preferred choice of a good night's socialising all the way to my current house. But something changed. A night with more food, drink, cutlery and crockery and less laughter became a *dinner party*.

I looked around the large open-plan space of our kitchen-dining-living room and wondered when did it all get so complicated?

I straightened the shiny Newbridge silver cutlery – two knives, three forks and a dessert spoon per person. Three hours of elbow grease I had spent to work the years of tarnish off them. As if it mattered.

I ran my finger around the smooth silver edge of a Wedgwood side plate and considered how the white china sat well beside my otherwise blue on blue theme. Nearly twenty-five years since our wedding and the plates had barely seen the light.

The Dublin colours were for me. I'd lived most of my life in Dublin and most of what came before was best left where it happened, in a place well west of the pale, a house devoid of maternal love that was never a home to me. Dublin was the only place I had ever called home; the blue table cloth and darker blue serviettes combined were my symbolic comfort blanket. I needed comfort.

I had been planning the dinner party down to every detail for months, but as I stood leaning against the island unit a salesman in a kitchen showroom had told me no home should be without, my stomach was more jittery than ever. The menopause and multiple sources of anxiety hadn't mixed well. I was stuck on a downward spiral of sleepless nights, endless sweats and tears, a brain on go-slow and a body that bumped into things. I consistently had the urge to tell everyone who looked twice at me to take a long running jump, preferably right out of my life. It appeared some people had decided for themselves that getting out of my life was a good idea. I couldn't blame them. I no longer liked myself either. I could barely feign some level of sanity with the help of daily naps and the more than occasional sleeping tablet.

On a rare good day, I'd revert to my old self. I'd had the last good day just before Matt left for a summer in Canada. He had answered the door to a courier.

"Just a delivery of golf clubs for Dad, Mum. Don't get excited now," he called to me.

"Fecking golf," I responded as I came down the stairs. Golf was a dirty four-letter word in my books. Golf was all-consuming. I hated it. Matt knew my feelings and he knew that I had been screaming for overdue blinds for the kitchen. I'd been about to go on a rant along the lines of *what would Patrick need more new golf clubs for, isn't the house creaking under the weight of a tonne of them* when I spotted my blinds and I laughed. That was a good day. On a bad day I'd have spotted the blinds and then given Matt an earful for winding me up in the first place. I hoped Canada was going well for him. He deserved it.

With my malfunctioning brain and my big plans for the dinner party that night, I remained determined to leave nothing to chance. I had showered earlier and put on a light touch of foundation trying to fool myself that I could hide the age spots on my face and the black circles around my eyes. I stood at the mirror and put a brush through my shoulder-length hair, freshly dyed mahogany-brunette at the hands of my local hairdresser and friend. I carefully applied mascara to compensate for my fading lashes, waterproof, in anticipation of both sweat and tears. Before it had time to dry to the promised waterproof, tears appeared in each eye and ran down my face. The earlier careful camouflage of my black circles was wasted – I now had black circles with long tails. I cursed and rubbed the worst of it off with a tissue creating what might, in another life, have been regarded as a seductive smoky look. I pulled on a new turquoise dress. As I struggled to squeeze into its figure-hugging fabric, I reminded myself why I had chosen it. Patrick would like it because it was sexy and showed off my still good knees and slender calves.

I hadn't married him for the frequency with which he whispered sweet nothings in my ear. But there had been some tingling occasions when he had surprised me. Years ago, as I was walking on a beach in Portugal, enjoying the cooling waves at my ankles, he had come up behind me.

"Those legs, Martha. They're dangerous. They could drive a man to distraction," he'd whispered, wrapping his arm around my waist.

I had turned, raised a doubting eyebrow at him and smiled.

"I'm telling you, Martha, it was those legs that persuaded me to ask you out. I dreamt of running my hands the length of them."

"And so you have, more than a few times…"

I'd laughed and we had fallen into a long lingering kiss that quickly came close to becoming an indecent public display of more than affection.

It had been a long and varied journey from then to now.

I patted my exercise-defying muffin top, grateful for the advantages of stress-induced weight loss which had reduced me to a passable size 12 as long as the waistband was forgiving; the stubborn menopausal middle remained but, ironically, the love handles had shrunk.

Standing in our eldest daughter's room in front of the only full-length mirror in the house I tried to convince myself that at fifty-three, I'd do for an auld one; I wasn't looking too bad after three children.

"You look amazing, Mum." I looked at our eldest daughter's reflection in the mirror and made a sceptical pursed-lipped expression in her direction and mine.

"Thank you, Fiona. You really think so?" I asked as I pulled the dress down my legs as far as it would stretch.

"Yeah, you could pass for forty easy. Dad had better watch out tonight."

"Yes…Yes, indeed he'd better watch out." I sighed and hugged her tight, savouring the solidity of her body and spirit. "See you tomorrow evening for dinner, yes?"

She nodded.

"You look great too, Fiona."

"Cool. Yeah Mum, and Matt might ring us from Canada tomorrow night." Her phone beeped. "Daniel's double-parked outside. I gotta go. See you." She kissed me lightly on the cheek, grabbed her overnight bag and breezed out the door.

4

"See you tomorrow night, Dad. Don't forget to look over Daniel's CV for him please. It's due in on Monday."

I went into my bedroom and struggled to get the spike of my silver long-drop earrings into my ears. I uttered the F-word under my breath as I almost snapped a spike clean off. They were too new to break; I had bought them at a craft fair just over six months previously, just before Christmas. I had fallen for their classic modern design, clean lines with a defined twist. Everything has a twist these days, I sighed to myself just as Patrick walked into the room with a towel around his waist. Despite my mood I caught myself observing that his strong legs and body looked as good, if not better, than when we had married. I moved my focus to the scowl on his face, certain it was a reasonable reflection of the scowl on my own.

"Dad rang," he said. "He wants to know if you're still okay to bring him to the doctor on Monday." He turned towards me. "I said that you probably were but that I'd let him know…"

"I told him only yesterday," I snapped. "He's not processing things these days…"

"So I gathered," Patrick said.

Makes two of us, I thought.

Patrick stopped and looked at me. His hand reached out to within a foot of touching me.

"Wow…Martha, you look great!"

"Thanks. I guess I'll do," I said, turning quickly away from him and stabbing my earring finally into my ear. Was he teasing me? I was in no mood for it. I meant to say no more but, as I looked back at him, my thoughts floated unexpectedly out of my mouth. "You still look fecking good too, Patrick," I said. If anything, his now short, but still curly, salt-and-pepper hair added to his sex appeal. I wished it was otherwise.

5

There had been times when a more sincere exchange of compliments had us falling into bed together, later laughing as we rushed to get our clothes on in time to answer the door to our guests. Back then we thought that we would be young and giggly forever. I wondered if Patrick thought back to those times. Maybe he deserved better than the menopausal maniac I had become. Only maybe.

He released a barely audible grunt, plonked himself on the side of the bed and sighed. I felt his eyes resting on me. For all his size and muscle, he looked vulnerable. Part of me wanted to go over and take his head in my arms and hold him tight to my chest, claiming him as my own. Another part of me wanted to slap him across the face and then run down the stairs and knock back a strong gin and tonic. But I did neither. I cleared my throat in an effort to clear my thoughts and then made myself walk slowly and purposely down the stairs, holding the handrail and putting one foot in front of the other. I reiterated a promise I had made to myself. I would not drink until all the guests had arrived. I made a lot of promises to myself. It helped me to deal with anticipated tricky situations. At least I used to think so. Now I realise that some of those promises were ill-founded and cost me far more than they saved me.

The doorbell rang and I jumped. Don't let them be early. They are never early.

It was Celine, arriving at her appointed hour. She had had her dark grey hair cut surprisingly short and it revealed her petite face and almond-shaped dark eyes.

"Celine, you look amazing. I am so glad you've decided to come out from under that mop of hair of yours."

She gave me a warm hug, the top of her head barely reaching my shoulder. She stepped back and nodded. She had tried to persuade me not to go ahead with the night as I had planned it, but I had insisted that I was doing it my way for my own reasons. So she had resolved to be there for me, to give me moral support.

"That wee dress looks even better on you tonight than it did in the shop. Ach, you're going to steal the show, my dear."

I coughed, acknowledging the ambiguity of her statement.

In true Northern Irish fashion, Celine rarely said a sentence without the word 'wee'. This often made me smile. But not tonight. I gave her a warning look.

"I'm just sayin'. I'll hould my whisht, don't worry," she said touching me gently on my arm before throwing her vibrant stole over her shoulder.

"Thank you, Celine. You really are a Trojan."

"What now, sure you were there for me, Martha, I'll be there for you."

"Still, thank you. Come on. Let's have us each a glass of water. I've gone posh and bought you Pellegrino."

"You're so kind, as always."

If only that was true, I thought.

Celine was lighting the candles and I was sweeping the already clean floor when the doorbell rang, this time for longer than was necessary.

"Oh shit...here goes."

I felt my heart accelerate. I closed my eyes for a moment and took slow, deep breaths. I plodded my way to the front door and positioned myself firmly behind it as I opened it. Across the threshold came Isabel; the large solid door felt an insufficient protection against her forward march. In the forty plus years that I'd known her I'd never found a shield that could withstand her.

She stormed through with her upper body and face camouflaged by a bouquet of pink lilies in full bloom. I hate pink lilies. Their sickly scent repulses me. Their ochre stamens were aimed at my dress as she pushed them towards me. I resisted them with force and directed them back towards her crisp white blouse. She withdrew and whacked her back off the corner of the hall table.

"Fuck," she said.

As she stumbled, I retreated and manoeuvred myself around her to plunge the pink weapons into a large empty vase on the table.

"Perfect. Thank you, Isabel." I smiled. Dusty ochre stains were sprinkled on her designer white top. Stains of your sins, my dear Isabel.

"Martha, it's been forever. How are you?" She air-kissed me. I didn't return this customary act of insincerity. I should never have let her back into my life all those years ago. I had experience of her going back to our days in boarding school and that should have been more than sufficient warning for me. I should have learned then that she and her gushy groupies were best left to their Oh My God selves.

"Grand. And how are you two keeping?" I said, looking to her relatively demure husband, Gavin, as he followed her in the door.

"We are just great. We'd a fabulous holiday in South Africa. Saw all of the big six and the weather was *so* perfect," Isabel said, displaying her chunky arms and legs, expecting me to admire her orange tan. I didn't think nature made it in that shade so I said nothing.

"Oh my God, Martha. What have you done? The hall, stairs and landing look totally…totally different. Patrick said that you were getting some work done but I'd no idea it was going to be so…transformative. It must be Farrow and Ball. Such loud colours, they can work in old houses, I suppose. They'd look awful in ours. The new tiles…and the old rug…it must have cost a fortune."

"Not really actually."

The colours were Dulux, admittedly inspired by the Farrow and Ball blues range. The tiles were an end-of-line bargain. The rug Celine

8

had given me, old and more beautiful for it. I wished that age and wear and tear had done the same for me.

Isabel continued her march down into the kitchen-living-dining room which I usually referred to as the extension. I had recently taken considerable time and energy giving the entire room a fresh look, kitting it out with second-hand bargains bought online. For the ready availability of almost-new furniture at knock-down prices I was grateful to the Isabels of the world who always had to have the most up-to-the-minute fashions, be it in clothes or furnishings. A friend's husband, who was forever between jobs, had done an amazing job fitting the barely pre-used kitchen cupboards which came complete with a shiny cooker and hob and the de rigueur island unit.

"It looks great, Martha, and so do you. Well done." Gavin pushed his sandy hair back from his forehead and gave me a warm kiss on each cheek. Then he hugged me tight. I returned both the kisses and the hug with more protracted enthusiasm than was decent. I was acknowledging that he had to put up with actually being married to the woman.

"Isabel could learn a thing or two from you."

"Thank you, Gavin. You're such a pet. And I love your vibrant waistcoat. You must have quite a collection of them," I said, thinking it was really a bit too loud.

"Perhaps ten or so, but building." Gavin smiled and winked at me as he ran his hand down his red waistcoat with its large buttons and strong navy stripes. "Isabel hates every one of them. But there you go."

Gavin's minor act of rebellion.

"Oh my God, Martha. You must have spent an absolute fortune. Where did you get the money?" Isabel stopped. "And who are you? Should I know you?" Isabel pointed her finger at Celine's small chest.

Isabel looked Celine up and down, trying to put a price on her dress and shoes, I imagined. They were both designer vintage and the scarf, handmade felt and silk, was a work of art, a present from Celine's friend from college. I loved Celine's style. To me it was wonderfully free and expressive. It wasn't either when I first met her.

"This is Celine, a good friend of mine from down the road. Celine, this is Gavin and Isabel." They shook hands in turn.

"And is your husband, partner or whatever here?" Isabel looked around as if he, or perhaps she, might be hiding somewhere.

"Can not you find him? He could be under the table, ready to pounce at any minute now," Celine said, looking in that direction.

"Long banished. The bastard," I declared. Isabel looked at Gavin and rolled her heavily made-up eyes.

A whiff of Patrick's musky aftershave caught me unawares just before I felt his arm take possession of my waist, stirring butterflies in my stomach.

"Patrick, perfect timing," I said, spinning across towards the fridge. "Drinks anyone?"

"Hello Celine, Isabel, Gavin." Patrick smiled and nodded in their direction as he spoke. "Celine, you look great." He kissed her on the right cheek with genuine affection. She gave him a distinctly cool, uncertain smile which I'm sure he did not notice. To another onlooker she would have seemed to have his undivided attention.

"Martha, allow me to do the drinks. What will you have, Celine? First come, first served."

"I'll stick with Pellegrino, thanks Patrick."

"Isabel, Gavin, glasses of sauvignon or beer for you two?"

"Ice-cold sauvignon for me, Patrick darling," Isabel said, gnawing her words with an unnecessarily wide-open mouth. Her teeth, gums and tongue were displayed like a horse in full neighing.

"Beer please, Patrick," said Gavin, pushing his spectacles up his nose in that way that spoke of intelligence; an intelligence that ran deep but not the full bandwidth. He could give an in-depth talk on the economics of shopping local vs online, or capitalism as seen through Shakespeare's plays, but he could be pure ditsy in his grasp of everyday things. He spent half his life looking for where he had left his wallet, his car keys and even, often his car.

"Sauvignon for you, Martha?"

"Yes, *not* ice cold. A glass of water too please."

"At your service, as always!"

"Lucky me," I mouthed towards Celine with a roll of my eyes.

Celine touched me gently on the small of my back and nudged me towards the lounge chair. Gavin sat down on the couch beside it. Isabel took up position at the far end of the coffee table, opposite me, on what was normally Patrick's chair. Ever the diplomat, Celine sat at the end of the couch nearest to her. Isabel's large diamond earrings sparkled against the backdrop of her heavy Oompa Loompa make-up. The holes in her earlobes had long since stretched to near Maasai proportions. The accountant in me calculated that her many earrings, together with the diamonds that invariably dipped into the depths of her cleavage, equated to the value of the average punter's mortgage. She had proudly told us that when she moved through the corridors of SIB, the bank where she once held sway, she had heard her colleagues remark, "Here comes the crown jewels on heels."

I had never aspired to such bling and I wondered why, over recent years, Patrick seemed to have started to think otherwise. He had taken to presenting me with some outlandishly expensive pieces of jewellery. For our twentieth anniversary, he had given me a necklace with a large square diamond surrounded by small sapphires and a matching tennis bracelet with alternating diamonds and sapphires. For my fiftieth birthday he had given me large diamond earrings. They were all beautiful but just not for me. I preferred relatively inexpensive one-off pieces that I could choose to match or to lift my sometimes dark moods.

I had bowls of tortillas, olives and stuffed peppers dotted on the large coffee table. I bent forward to bring a bowl of olives closer to me as much for something to distract me as for want of an olive; my hand collided with Isabel's.

"Oh, I'm so sorry Isabel. You have a bowl of olives all to yourself right there, darling. Do you need more?"

"Martha. Don't be so silly. I don't need more. I just didn't see them."

I can do gush too on occasion. It comes to the surface when I'm nervous, or in Isabel's company. It is another one of those things I don't like about myself. I had never managed to crawl out fully from under Isabel's put-downs going back as far as when I was the vulnerable teenager and she was the popular girl whom nobody liked but everybody feared falling out with.

Patrick served the drinks and sat down on the couch between Gavin and Celine. As he made himself comfortable, I gazed up at the large volcano triptych that hung above him. The first image was of a peaceful snow-covered mountain with a hint of white smoke spouting from its crater; the second was the same mountain with a massive flame of red-hot lava spewing high into the sky and running down the sides of the entire mountain, leaving a vibrant red-and-yellow trail of destruction in its path; the third image was the same mountain barely visible behind a dense smouldering grey cloud of ash; images of before, during and after. I considered the ambient temperatures of each image, from cold, to terrifyingly hot, to what?

My thoughts were interrupted by a guffaw of laughter from the ever-polite Gavin as Patrick was giving him a loud and entertaining account of his golf that day. I had already heard it twice in phone calls to two of his fellow golf enthusiasts, something Gavin was not. Patrick didn't let truth get in the way of a good story and the story was becoming more embellished with each telling. I could learn from him.

My stories can fall flat because I tend to stick to boring facts. I'd learned to tell them fast to try to finish them before I lost listeners' attention, but even this often failed when Patrick was present. Patrick's stories soon become unrecognisable from the reality of what actually happened. But I am convinced that whatever version he tells, it is the version that he believes at that moment. It is not therefore lying as such. In each version the coup de grace always comes at the end, after a big build-up. In a golf story that normally means the eighteenth hole.

When Patrick was on the twelfth hole, I was setting out the selection of starters. When he was on the seventeenth hole, I called everyone to the table. A younger, kinder and more patient me would have let him get to the eighteenth hole.

I took my usual place at one end of the oval table. I directed Gavin to sit beside me. Celine sat opposite him with Isabel beside her, and then Patrick at the other end of the table some distance from Gavin. It was an almost circular arrangement, perfect for intimate dinner parties of six or so.

"Martha, you've outdone yourself tonight. All my favourite starters on one table. I am impressed." As Patrick spoke, he rested his elbows on the table and held one hand in the other, twirling his wedding ring. He caught me observing him and gave me one of his encouraging affectionate smiles from behind his hands. I looked away, feeling tears pushing their way to the surface.

"Indeed," said Isabel, observing our interaction. She picked up a slice of my homemade sourdough, her nose twitching as she looked at it. She bit hard into it, adding venom to a good but distant memory that came to me. In bed one night, after a not so quiet night in when we had munched our way through more than half a loaf of bread, also in bed, and Patrick had joked that I was like a good sourdough with an appealing outer crust and a firm but soft centre. My scent, he said, demanded that I be eaten slowly and with deliberate appreciation. It

13

sounds corny in the telling but it, and what preceded and followed it, was delightfully romantic at the time. In recent times, I tended to mostly forget his romantic side. Perhaps it was better that way.

"Patrick darling, I see, yet again, the table is all Dublin. Your beloved Mayo doesn't even get a look in," Isabel gushed and put her hand on his lower arm in sympathy.

Patrick shrugged and lifted a piece of courgette and almond bread to his mouth, causing her to remove her hand from his arm.

"And Martha doesn't even follow Gaelic football…or hurling," she added.

She had a point. I never went to a GAA match unless Matt was playing in it, and I barely knew the name of a single GAA county player. Patrick, by contrast, would follow his Mayo team to the ends of the world, bringing some of his fellow county men and clients with him. They all live in eternal hope, with annual interludes of deep mourning when, yet again, Mayo suffers a bruising defeat just when the All-Ireland Cup is within their grasp. Time and again Dublin snatches it from them. Next year is always going to be Mayo's year. This year I'd no idea what had happened. It had all passed my befuddled head by.

"There's more to Dublin than Gaelic games you may not have noticed," I said. "There's its architectural mix from the Georgian to the modern, the increasingly eclectic mix of the people – thank goodness – not like years ago when everyone wandering the streets had white skin and wore navy, brown or grey. Now we have a city filled with people of every colour, race, creed and culture. There's its museums and galleries that are easily accessible and free—" I stopped abruptly, surprised by my pedantic monologue. What was that about, I asked myself. Nerves. I spout on when I'm nervous. Shut up, Martha, I said to myself. I hadn't even been into a museum or art gallery for well over six months.

14

"Well said," said Gavin, slapping me on the shoulder.

Celine smiled.

"Thanks, I guess," I said.

"And you forgot to mention good food and company…This looks delicious. Tell me what it is?"

"Sorry, Gavin. I was distracted. It's a family favourite, sweet and savoury courgette and almond bread. You could say an unlikely pairing that has a surprising spicy kick at the finish."

"Sounds tantalising, and these?"

"Homemade duck and orange pâté for the carnivores and goat's cheese and asparagus loaf wrapped in blanched leeks for the vegetarians," I said, looking Isabel's way. "There are fresh mixed green leaves from the garden there too. Slugs are extra." I forced a smile, hoping she might get a stray one.

"Wonderful. If these are just the starters, I can't imagine what the main course might be."

"You might well be surprised, Gavin. Best to enjoy what's in front of you at the moment. The main course might disappoint."

"Don't worry, I intend to savour every bite," Gavin said, touching the bare skin of my upper left arm gently causing me to shiver slightly. The words *please don't touch me or I might hit you or break out in an unwanted sweat,* materialised in my brain, immediately triggering my sweat glands to do what they continuously insisted on doing. I got up to get some tissues to mop my brow. Celine watched me from her place at the table. I felt her support and concern.

As I went back to my place, I noticed a generous portion of each of the starters neatly arranged on Patrick's plate. Fresh green leaves beside a goat's cheese and asparagus loaf beside a portion of duck pâté with a slice of orange on top. I wondered if he had created the Irish flag deliberately. He was systematically working his way around his plate. A mouthful of leaves with goat's cheese, a bite of courgette and

15

almond bread, a mouthful of crusty sourdough and pâté…his focus was entirely on his food. He lifted another slice of courgette and almond bread, brought it up to his nostrils and sniffed. The ginger tickled his nostrils and he sneezed.

"Bless you," I said in spontaneous response. Patrick smiled my way again and then resumed giving all his attention to his food. A love of food had been one of our shared passions for many years.

I could see Isabel getting agitated. Her earrings were in full erratic flight. "Patrick?" She prodded him in the arm. "So, what do you think?"

"About what?" he said.

"The current cost of city centre office space."

"I have no thoughts on the cost of office space. City centre. Southside. Northside. Or Timbuktu."

"The pâté's good, isn't it Isabel? We must get the recipe," Gavin chirped.

"Yes, Gavin. You must. I don't cook."

"How could I forget," Gavin said. "Safer that way," he said for the benefit of Celine and me.

With the starters cleared away, I set down a large warm plate in everyone's place and put a bowl of baked potatoes, a dish of gratin dauphinoise and large casserole of coq au vin on the table. The garlic aromas filled the air, reigniting everyone's appetites, or so I imagined.

I opened my mouth to suggest that everyone might serve themselves, but Isabel liked to be heard and we all heard her.

"Well Patrick, I can see where Martha's time and your money have been going over the last while. The house has had one hell of a revamp, hasn't it?" Her horse of a mouth released each word with exaggerated emphasis.

Patrick held his breath and looked at me as I nearly choked with fury at her choice of phrases, 'Martha's time', and 'your money'. The bitch. I reminded myself that I had anticipated such Isabel comments. Where Isabel went, snide comments had always followed. Deep breaths, Martha. Deep breaths. Choose your moment.

"I'm glad you like it," I said.

Patrick's face relaxed a fraction but I was only warming up.

"But I'm sure, Isabel, it is in the ha'penny place beside what you spent on your bedroom, let alone on anywhere else in that house of yours."

"And your point is?"

"Last year, wasn't it?" I said, ignoring her question.

"And your point is?" Isabel repeated her question, louder this time.

"I'm wondering how much quality time you spend there; in your own bedroom, for example?" I paused briefly. "And our house needed a revamp, before I put it on the market!"

Isabel shot out of her chair, spoiling my immediate view of Patrick. "What I do in my bedroom is none of your business."

I wanted to yell back at her that some of what she did in other bedrooms was my business and I would effing well prefer if it wasn't. A lump lodged in the back of my throat and I swallowed so hard that it hurt.

Patrick took her arm and abruptly pulled her back down. "Leave it go, Isabel. Leave it go."

"I'll not leave it go. Who are you to tell me to leave it go?" Isabel spat her words out and glared at him through her overly dark false eyelashes.

"Is that a lover's tiff?" I asked.

Celine's jaw dropped and she darted forward in her chair as she heard my words. She had known what was coming but she seemed startled now that it was actually happening.

Patrick was on his feet this time. "Martha, please. What are you doing? First you're selling the house and—"

"And what? And now I am looking at you having a lover's tiff with Isabel?"

"Martha, what are you saying?" Gavin grabbed my arm.

"I'm sorry, Gavin. I came close to telling you a hundred times…Patrick and Isabel have been…have been…you know…with each other." I looked at Gavin's horrified reaction and I turned quickly away, accidentally banging my elbows hard onto the table as if demanding all the very attention that I did not want. I felt their eyes and ears on me and I put the palms of my hands over my face and eyes, trying to shut them all out. I'd promised myself that I would say it. I'd said it. It was over. Now I wanted them to go away and take all the shit with them. Thump. Thump. The volume had been turned up on my heart. Thump. Thump. The sound banged off the inside of my head. I moved my hands up my face and pressed the heel of my hands tighter into my sockets.

Gavin's hands prized mine from my face. "Martha?"

I nodded. "Yes. Ask them yourself?"

His face was bursting with fury. His neck stretched out of his yellow shirt and a tide of redness rose up from under his collar to his cheeks and nose. There was a pregnant pause. He lifted out of his chair, turned towards Isabel and roared, "For feck's sake, Isabel. For feck's sake. I forgave you once…you promised that was it. And this time…this time with Patrick…you're a selfish slut…what the hell, Isabel!"

I was shocked. I didn't think he was capable of such a show of anger. It jolted me to silently cheer for him. *Give it to the bitch,* I thought. I looked at Celine and imagined that she was thinking something similar. Her eyes were on Isabel. There were so many things that I wanted to say to that witch. Most of them I should have said years ago.

Isabel stood back up to respond to Gavin. Her chair fell back with a clatter onto the tiled floor. Her mouth opened. And shut again. And opened again. A bleach blonde goldfish, I thought. She stared at Gavin with beads of spittle running down from her lower lip to her miserable chin. Then she turned and looked to Patrick imploringly.

I looked from her to my husband. His expression was beyond me. Emotional turmoil tinged with relief maybe? I used to think I knew him well but I could not read him at that moment. There were so many emotions going on inside me that I couldn't name them all: confusion, frustration, hurt, anger, hate, love. They were all there inside my head, banging into each other but I couldn't see any of these emotions on Patrick's face.

"Patrick, I…We agreed…we always said there could be no coming back from an affair. Any affair. I get the message – you want out. I get that. But Isabel of all…of all people…" My voice was not loud. On the outside I was not hysterical. On the inside it was a different matter. I spoke in a level voice. I had been thinking about it for a long time. Patrick had an affair. He had had enough of me. I could understand that. I had become an unlovable demon. I often had enough of me. But an affair. The ultimate painful breach of my hard-earned trust. But an affair with Isabel, that took the pain to an unbearable level.

"Martha. Listen, please…it's not how you think it is…"

"Really, Patrick. Please. Just go. Pack and be gone. There are suitcases in the spare room. Take whatever you think you need, and after tonight, if you need me then contact me through my solicitor." I was raising my voice. I wanted this bit over with. I wanted to get on with finding out what came next.

"Your solicitor?" Patrick's face showed shock.

"Yes, my *new* solicitor. I've fallen out with my old one, in case you haven't noticed! She, Sandra MacDonald, is not an old classmate of yours – although, as you know, you've crossed paths before in the legal domain. You said she was very impressive; so, thanks for the recommendation, Patrick!"

Patrick looked at me quizzically as I mopped the inevitable sweat off my brow and neck.

"You've known for months, haven't you? That explains why you've been avoiding me. You've been planning tonight for ages?" In true Patrick fashion, his voice was only slightly raised.

"Yes, Patrick. I've known for months. I needed to wait until after a little thing called Zara's Leaving Cert exams. You've no idea how lucky you are that I had to wait." I caught myself speaking through gritted teeth and I paused. "When I first found out I thought of selling your golf clubs on eBay, handing out your precious wine collection like a milk delivery to the neighbours, painting something damming on your beloved but aged car..." As I spoke, I remembered that at first I had considered smashing up his car and record collection with said golf clubs, but the worst I had done was smash a few wine glasses and plates on the kitchen tiles and I'd hated the tedium of cleaning up the pieces of glass and crockery all the way from the far end of the kitchen to the door into the hallway. I swallowed down the memory. "Now, I am hoping reason will prevail. I am hoping that, despite everything, we can do this amicably, for the children's sake."

He gave me a slow nod. I couldn't decide if his expression was one of relief, pain or guilt. If it was pain, was it his own pain or the pain of having hurt me? We had been good, very good. How did we come to spoil it? There was no easy answer. He stood up, walked out the kitchen door and along the hall. I listened to that familiar sound of him going up the stairs. My heart remembered the times I sat or lay in bed and welcomed that sound.

Gavin's mouth was stuck on half-open.

"Gavin, I'm sorry," I said.

"Gavin"—Celine put her hand on his—"would you like a wee drink, aye?"

Gavin shook his head. Shock and fury were written in every line of his face.

"Shall I call a wee taxi? One or two?" She looked at Isabel and then back to Gavin.

He held up two fingers and turned them towards Isabel as if the gesture was meant for her.

"You bitch. You absolute selfish bitch. You stay in your sister's house. I'm going home to Meath."

"I'll book the taxis," I said, reaching to take my phone off the nearby counter and going into the taxi app.

Isabel was still standing.

"Gavin, Gavin, it's not…It is…but it's not. Don't listen to her. Patrick told me she's hormonal. She doesn't know what she is saying."

"The word is *hysterical*. I am absolutely off the scales hysterical. So Zara tells me!"

Isabel looked at me with disgust, her nose twitched upwards as if I was no more than a bad smelling piece of dog dirt.

"Isabel, listen to yourself. You had an affair with Martha's husband and you want to make it her fault? Are you for real?"

She ignored Gavin and turned towards me with the ugliest expression I've ever seen, even on her. Her mouth was open in a seething snarl and her tombstone top teeth were firmly biting down to meet her uneven bottom teeth. Botox and make-up could not smooth over the cracks and crevices caused by her inner poison.

"Martha, you don't know what you've done? You think you've it all worked out. Just you see. You haven't got a fucking clue. You know nothing. Nothing at all. You'll regret this. That I guarantee you."

The way Isabel said 'fucking' with that pseudo-posh accent of hers made me laugh.

21

"You're right, Isabel," I said, "I should get back in my little accountant's box. I should be grateful to bask in the light that's reflected off your obscene diamonds. But FUCK YOU, Isabel…" I said, rising out of my chair. And fuck me too, I thought, losing a good husband to you of all people. Until my discovery six months previously I had thought that despite my menopausal rough patch, we would pull through and that before the end of the year Patrick and I would be celebrating our twenty-fifth wedding anniversary. So much for that. I sniffed loudly.

Celine's hand touched my wrist, reminding me I had promised myself not to give Isabel the pleasure of seeing me lose the plot. Celine's touch pushed my tears nearer the surface. I did not want Isabel to see me cry. I looked down at my plate. I picked up a slice of sourdough bread and dipped it into the coq au vin. I took a bite and concentrated on tasting each morsel, naming the individual flavours as if I was going to write a review on it. There was a pause in proceedings.

"Isabel, it is a mild evening, would you like to wait outside?" Celine looked at my phone. "It says your taxi will be here in two minutes. I guess you might like to wait in the front garden. Aye? Shall we?"

Celine directed Isabel out the door. Watching them both, I marvelled at how far Celine had come, from the nearly slaughtered lamb I had befriended two and a half years previously to the shepherd leading a ewe to what I hoped would be a metaphorical but imminent slaughter.

"Gavin, you see Celine there?" I said.

"Of course. Why?"

"She has been through hell and back more times than I will ever know. Look at her. She gives me faith. If she can deal with all the shit that has come her way, we can deal with ours."

"I hope so, Martha. I do. But it's going to be one hell of a battle."

Chapter 2

Celine

Late 2014 – Early 2015

I had often seen Celine making her way slowly, and I thought painfully, down the path from her house, through the overgrown grass in her front garden and out her rusty gate to her car parked on the side of our road. For years I saw a woman bent double to the point that her knees rose to meet her lowered chest. Behind the curtain of grey, unkempt hair I imagined an old, wrinkled face. I saw a walking foetus, a woman edging towards Shakespeare's seventh and last stage of life; second childishness and mere oblivion, without teeth, without everything.

Before I met her, I had read somewhere that if you get someone to smile then you are doing yourself and them a good turn. Smiling stimulates the muscles in the face which in turn stimulates serotonin, the happy hormone. I had resolved to smile and say hello to everyone I met walking towards me on my daily walk. This wasn't easy, it meant continuously pushing myself outside my comfort zone, especially as many people out walking rejected the very possibility of eye contact.

One clear, crisp autumn morning, as I took my regular walk along the promenade at the end of our road, I saw a brightly dressed, diminutive woman of maybe sixty walking towards me. I looked at her and she looked at me. I smiled and said, "Hello." A warm smile appeared on her face.

"Hello, how are you?" she said. As she spoke, she bent forward and looked down at her shoes.

I stopped.

In that gesture I recognised her as the woman whom I had decided was entering her last stage of life.

"Grand and how are you?" I said.

"I am well actually." She nodded as if surprised at her own assessment of herself.

"You live on our road. Don't you?"

She nodded again.

"I'm Martha from number fifty-two."

"Aye. I'm Celine from number thirty-one." She straightened up, revealing large, deep dark eyes on a petite face. The face was that of an antique porcelain doll, peeping through a curtain of grey hair; a delicate beauty with cracks of ill-treatment or poor ageing, I wasn't sure which then.

We walked together, taking in the changing sky as it made a colourful backdrop against the tall chimney pots of the long-decommissioned power station, the large cylindrical oil storage tanks and suspended containers moving along the gantries of Dublin Port.

"It's a great wee view, isn't it?" she said with enthusiasm.

"You like it! Most don't. They dismiss it as too industrial and think the chimneys should be blown up. I love the ebb and flow of the water, the birds feeding on the grey sandbanks, the movement of the docks, the solidity of the mountains…and I love the ever-changing sky…" I opened my arms towards the sky and inhaled its beauty. I stopped and gave a silly laugh. "I'm spouting on. Sorry. It's just something I've been thinking over many walks for too many years." And never got to fully express before, I thought, and as usual, when I'm nervous, I'd spouted out more than was appropriate.

"Ach, spoken like an artist. I love it too. I like that it is always changing and yet remaining the same. I like the honesty of it." She smiled warmly. "Do you paint?"

I laughed at the thought of such a thing as me painting anything more than emulsion on to the bedroom walls. "I wish. You?"

"I did once."

I sensed a sadness in her words.

In the months that followed, autumn faded into winter and we had often met each other out walking. Our communal constitutional became a firm arrangement every Tuesday and Thursday morning, normally including a stop for coffee. I told her about my best friend who had died too young, leaving a gaping hole where a friend should be. I did have other good friends, especially the O'Reillys who had been neighbours when I was growing up. But I never had another friend to equal the bold and blunt Trish. Celine told me that circumstances meant that she hadn't had a good friend in years. I wondered at that comment and assumed that she must have spent too much time painting alone to have time for friends.

We found that we shared more than a passing interest in art, culture, current affairs and politics. We had varying opinions on everything but we both fell politically and in other respects into the middle ground despite our backgrounds; hers being Northern Irish Catholic and mine Southern Irish Protestant. We were amused that our divergent paths had brought us to similar positions and passions. We both had travelled for a few years before settling down and perhaps this had played its part in shaping our perspectives. Our common interests kept us animated and her Northern accent and expressions added extra spark.

We talked about our children, at least I did. All our three were living at home so they were very much part of my life. Fiona, our eldest, was in the final year of her degree, studying English and history. Our second child, Matt was in his last year in school and facing into his Leaving Cert. He was so laid back he was horizontal. Zara, our youngest, was doing her Junior Cert on her terms which meant sport, party, study, sport, party. She was generally giving me hell! Poor Celine had to suffer my rants about the younger two in particular.

I learned that Celine had two adult children and I was curious about them but she rarely gave much away. I gathered that her daughter, Karen, she saw occasionally, while her son, Shane, she never saw.

"Our eldest gave me hell too, especially as a wee teenager. Nothing I ever did was good enough for her. She said it was best if I stayed indoors where I wouldn't be out 'n' 'bout embarrassin' her!"

I burst out laughing. "How did they ever understand you when you lived away?"

She laughed too.

"Aye. It had its situations. I near landed myself in some trouble alright. I offered a fella a lift home one night and he thought that I was going to kill him!"

"Because you were from the North?"

"No, because I told him 'I'll run you over...' you know like give him a lift?"

I looked at the laughing Celine beside me and I remembered the small mousy woman I had seen for years coming and going from her front door to her car. I wondered what her story was, but I didn't ask.

"I seem to say the wrong thing too, especially in front of Zara's friends. Afterwards I tell her it's my job to embarrass her, which makes her even more angry! Why can't you be like everyone else's Mum? Blah de blah de blah. Because I'm your Mum, Zara, and you're stuck with me…" I rolled my eyes to heaven. "Does it get better as they get older?"

"Truth is Martha, it's complicated. But, aye, since they moved out of home, it's better."

That was the end of that conversation.

A month or so later, we sat down in our regular coffee shop on the promenade. We had arrived after a shorter walk than usual as the wind had been whipping over the grey, churning sea and carrying sprays of icy salt water into our paths. It had both thrilled and frozen us. The thought of the heat radiating from the café's stove drew us in and the eclectic mix of framed old advertisements and quirky cartoons that hung from its walls added to the welcoming feel of the place.

It had been my fiftieth birthday at the weekend and I was geared up to give a small tirade about Patrick wasting more money on extravagant diamond jewellery that I no more wanted or needed. But, contrary to her norm, Celine jumped in first.

"I need an accountant and you're an accountant Martha?"

"Yes. Semi-retired a few years though. Now I'm primarily a mother, a carer, a housekeeper, a taxi…and the pay is lousy!" Celine knew the story. I'd got bored with accountancy and I had no interest in doing any more of it than I felt I had to.

"But can not you still understand things that I don't?"

"Perhaps." I smiled, still not fully used to Celine's habit of slipping in the occasional Northern Irish turn of phrase. "I still do some work for Patrick so I guess the brain can still compute! Why?"

Celine lowered her head and shrunk into her seat. "Ach you've surely gathered that my family life's a bit of a mess."

I nodded.

"A year or so ago, I got a barring order against my husband. And 'tis time now that I go for a full legal separation."

"Oh God, Celine, I'm sorry." I swallowed down on a gasp of shock.

"He was, and is, a wee bastard. A proper wee bastard. And fool that I was I let him dictate my life, day in day out, for close on thirty years. Thirty long feckin' years. Martha, I was a qualified art teacher. I was a successful artist. I travelled the world. And I let him dictate my life until I had no life." Her voice grew smaller as she spoke.

She held her hands together in front of her on the table. She clenched them tight with the fingers intertwined but still they trembled. Her legs shook too and I felt the tremors rising through the table. I reached across and held her elbows. I wanted to anchor her, to hold her firm. I saw the pain and fear in her eyes and I felt them.

"The solicitor says I'll get nothing for the beatings." She sneered. "The law says that I made my choices. I chose to stay with him. I chose to be beaten by him. I chose…Ach, I barely was able to choose the colour of my knickers in all my years with him." Tears flowed from the dark pools of her eyes; they glistened under the stark café lights as they ran down her face. She let them flow.

I turned and gazed out the window struggling to digest her words, wondering how to respond. Rain fell messily on the dark sea, the wind whipping it in many directions. I knew Celine had no more chosen to stay and be abused by her husband than, as a child, I had chosen the abuse Heather, who for nearly half my life I'd known as my mother, had inflicted on me. If I had a choice, I'd have chosen to be reared by my real and loving mum even if it meant being poor as church mice. I would never have chosen Heather, Cruella Deville my friend Trish always called her, for good reason. Nobody chooses abuse. I didn't know any other woman who had been beaten by her husband. At least none had told me that they had been. But how many people had I ever told about my abuse? It's not something you bring up over cocktails or the average cup of coffee.

"The law's an ass, Celine. A total ass. I'm so sorry. I had no idea." I took her hand and I squeezed it firmly. The phrase 'made my choices' was still ringing uncomfortably in my ears. I felt a chill, like a cold hand, run across the top of my head and down the back of my neck.

"It was my art that paid the deposit on the house. It was my art that furnished and renovated it. I don't want to lose the house! It's mine. It's all I have. Please can you help me?"

"Of course, I will. Celine, my friend, I'll do what I can."

"Thank you. I know you will. I'm not used to having friends. Haven't had any in years. My sister tries her best but she lives in the wee North."

"In all the times I saw you, it never dawned on me…I never thought…"

"Aye, sure nobody really knew. I hid it well. Didn't I? Even from myself." She half laughed. "For years the cops didn't want to know. Sometimes the hospital would call them. They didn't like to 'get involved in domestics'!"

"The cops did nothing?"

"For a while amount of time, nothin' useful anyways. I gave up on them years ago. Anyways, when a husband beats his wife, society likes to cover it up…"

"And pretend it didn't happen. Because if people admitted that beatings were happening then they might have had to do something about it." This I could relate to, based on long and painful personal experience…

"And I played my part too you know. My artistic talents stood to me. I hid the bruises…and all the other shit."

"Oh Celine. Don't blame yourself. We all hide stuff, from ourselves and from others. I've done it myself. It's for our own self-preservation, I think."

"Stupid cunt. Stupid fucking cunt. When you hear it often enough, you start to believe it…"

I winced when she said the C-word.

"I've shocked you with that one word, *cunt*. Haven't I?"

I nodded.

"I never got used to hearing it. Each time he said it, it felt like a stabbing." She jabbed hard at her chest with her forefingers as she spoke. "It caused the last drops of my sense of self to drain from me, until I felt like nothing, a nobody. My first counsellor tried getting me to say it over and over again: cunt, cunt, cunt, cunt. Let yourself own it, she said. Give it no power. Give the bastard no power." Her voice was small again. I heard the words 'cunt' and 'bastard' said emphatically but I had to strain to hear every other word. Repeated beatings do that to you, I thought, they make you feel diminutive and inconsequential – a ball for the kicking, a good-for-nothing nobody. I'd worn that T-shirt at the hands of the woman who reared me.

"Oh Celine. I don't know what to say…you are somebody…you are amazing." I wanted to hug her and reassure her but I was stuck to my seat, shoe-horned into the corner of the café. I felt impotent and small against the magnitude of what she was telling me.

"I don't know. I stopped painting. My silent protest at all the money that he was pouring into guitars and drink. I had no money for oils or canvases anyway. It was the start of the end. Even with a small mortgage, we could barely live on his civil servant's salary. He drank most of it. He didn't always drink. But as my sister Jacinta would say, beneath the veneer he was always a wee bastard."

"Celine, how'd you cope? What about the kids? Did he beat them?"

"He rarely slapped them. I could usually keep him away from them when he was in the mood for it. They learned to go up to bed and stay quiet. Ach, they had left home before the slaps became full punches…I was able to say I fell or something, you know if the injuries showed…I know they saw more than was good for them. They were still at home when he shoved me down the stairs and I fractured two ribs. I said I fell. He told anyone who listened, including them, that I'd been drinking. He was the one who was drinking but he was forever tellin' people I was the drinker!"

I watched her twist the hair at the front of her ear around her finger and then take it between her thumb and forefinger and pull it. Four or more strands came out at a time. I could feel each pull. I could see the skin straining from the side of her head and the individual hairs pop out one by one. If she kept going, she was going to have no hair there soon.

"Surely social services…somebody did something then?" I was getting more shocked and unsettled as she spoke. I kept waiting for her to tell me about how someone put a stop to it…people must have known…

"Not at all. Clumsy me. It was I who banged into things. I was that cliché. I was the woman who walked into doors. He liked to laughingly call me the three Cs: Clumsy Celine, the Cunt."

A shiver ran through my body listening to those words. I looked at her and I understood why she had walked as she had. Just as a hedgehog rolls itself into a ball to protect itself, she curled into the foetal position to protect herself. I am often amazed how often I wake up from a bad dream and I am curled in a ball. But we are not hedgehogs, we have no prickles to ward off threats to our bodies.

"I am sorry, Celine."

"He tried strangling me of an evening. I locked myself in the bathroom until he went to work the next morning. I called the guards when he was gone but they pointed out to me that he was at work and therefore not a danger to me at that moment. Unless I wanted to press charges, they said. They mentioned a helpline but I didn't see the point. Where would I go? What would I do?" The size of the clumps of hair that she was pulling out was getting bigger. I put my hand up to hers and brought her hand down to the table, holding it there under my own hand for a few moments.

"You'll be bald soon if you're not careful."

"Does it matter? Who cares?"

"I care," I protested. "I'd have cared sooner if I'd only known…And I was living up the road from you…" I was thinking walls are thin. Neighbours have ears. In our house we can smell our neighbour's dinner cooking. We can listen to their radio. We know what kind of music they listen to. We know when their grandchildren are over…

She told me how he often arrived home drunk, on Friday nights in particular. He would roar and smash furniture or ornaments. Nobody heard. More likely nobody chose to hear. One Friday she'd put the dinner that she had managed to rustle up for him from the nearly empty cupboards into the fridge. He was so late. It wasn't in the oven where it usually was. He marched into the sitting room and pulled her off the couch, leaving a three finger and one thumb bruise on her thin little arm.

"He punched me. I must have fallen backwards and hit my head off the coffee table. I don't remember. I woke up in hospital. I don't know who called the ambulance. Maybe it was me. Maybe it was him. Maybe he got a fright. He told them I slipped. She was wearing her slippers, he said, on a wooden floor, of course she slipped. I was past pretending. When he wasn't there the social worker pointed to the bruises on my arm and face. You didn't get those slipping. What really happened? That was all she had to say. I fell apart. She put me in touch with my local social worker and Women's Aid. I should have done something years ago…what a fool I've been." She spoke without emotion, as if she was telling a story she had read somewhere. As she spoke, she was picking at imaginary fluff on her cardigan sleeve. It didn't matter if her sleeve ended up bald.

"You're no fool, Celine. I'd probably be no different in those circumstances. None of us know until we've lived it." I couldn't imagine how I might be. Perhaps my past would mean that I would react differently. But what would differently be?

"Women's Aid helped me get a protection order against him. He left the house the day before I got home. Then I got a barring order and I haven't seen him since. My sister got on to the local cops and left them in no doubt about the situation. I told her that I had got nowhere with them years before. She said that if they didn't look after me this time, she'd have them all knee-capped! She didn't tell them that though! Thank Christ."

I looked at petite Celine and I was horrified to think of the sort of man who could even consider lifting a finger to her. I imagined she'd shatter into tiny pieces.

"Pity she didn't get *him* knee-capped all the same."

"Oh, she might yet! I live in hope…only joking. More's the pity, but we've no paramilitary connections."

"What's his name anyway?"

"Joseph Mary Murphy, the bastard!"

"And you're what size? Not much over five feet…"

"Five feet and nearly four inches, and I weigh around one hundred to one hundred and ten pounds. I'm getting better though." She picked up her coffee cup and drank the last mouthful of it, looking into the cup as if checking that it was indeed empty.

"And the wee bastard?"

"Six feet three. About two hundred pounds."

"Fuck Celine. He could have killed you." I squeezed her hand tightly.

"I know. He had nearly thirty years of trying. I told you I can do stupid. At first, I denied it. Then I covered it up. Then I told myself I was protecting the children. I suppose the AA would call me an enabler – I was certainly that."

"It's never that simple. Is it? I guess you lived in hope that it would stop."

"It was more that I was scared that if I did something, like try to leave him, it would get worse…"

"I never thought of it like that…but when you say it, it makes sense, you stayed because you were scared to leave."

"It wasn't entirely reasonable, a part of me still thought I loved him! He had been fun sometimes. And even charming…he could make me laugh. Imagine!" She laughed as if at the madness of her having regarded him as charming, or even fun.

"Charming…" I repeated the word, trying to match it to the man in the scenes that she had been describing. "Charming," I said again.

She laughed a smaller laugh. "You'd have found him charming. Seemingly, apparent charm can be a serious part of an abuser's profile. I was a fool. I fell for his charm. I thought his jealous ways were signs of his love for me."

"You are no fool, Celine. Read my lips. You – are – no – fool. I am sure that there are many women like you, doing their best to protect themselves and their children." I stirred the last of my coffee in the bottom of the cup wondering what else I could say to reassure her that I believed in her.

"Huh. You think so? Since I got the barring order the children hate me. They say I'm rewriting our family history. I am making up a Grimm's fairy tale and they prefer to believe in the old happy family tale I had painted for them."

I looked at her in disbelief. "You protected them and they've abandoned you. Here I've been living in my happy family cocoon, with nothing much more than finances and messed-up hormones to worry about and you've been going through all that. Jesus Christ, Celine, I know nothing."

"Ah, that's where you're wrong. You know figures…and I need help putting an Affidavit of Means together to commence legal separation proceedings." She pulled some paperwork out of her bag. "I don't even know what half the language means."

"That's okay. I can help with that. In my past life I helped a client with the finances for a messy break-up."

While I scanned through the key pages, Celine ordered us more scones and coffee, we were going to be there a while; give me something figures related to get my head around and I switch into accountant mode. To me an Affidavit of Means is quite straight forward, especially if it is for someone who leads a simple life…financially speaking.

"Firstly, just list the bigger value items and put the lower end of your best guess value on them. Let's see…I'll make notes in pencil as we go so you'll have a list of what you should follow up on." I quickly wrote brief notes in the margins as we talked, trying to be as clear as possible with my writing.

"'Assets held in joint names of applicant and respondent'. That would normally be things like your house, furniture…is the house in joint names?"

"Yes. If he'd had his way it wouldn't have been, but the solicitor insisted."

"Good. You'll need to get it valued and anything else of significance. Any valuable art or furniture?"

"Aye, but he has no idea that they are valuable and I'd like to keep it that way. When I was successful, I used to swop pieces with other artists, so they could be worth a wee bit now. The furniture is either cheap and cheerful or inherited from my grandmother's house. I'd hate to end up losing my gran's furniture…"

"Let's aim to make that as difficult as possible. You can make notes of how you acquired everything in a way that shows them to be yours by birth or other right. This can influence what a judge might determine if you end up in court, but I stress *can*. Also, be modest in the valuations for the furniture and art. Talk to some friendly auctioneers and get them to value them low and net of selling costs. If you swapped art for your work, list them under the next heading – 'Assets held in sole name of applicant'. Similarly, include your gran's furniture under this heading and your valuable jewellery, car…is the car in your name?"

"Aye, he has his own. Mine is ancient."

"You can value that easily online." I turned over the page. "What about your income?"

"I've been living off the rent less the mortgage payments from a wee house in Drumcondra that I bought thirty-odd years ago, after my first really big successful solo exhibition. Way back when houses were affordable and interest rates were high."

"I am impressed," I said with sincerity, thinking clearly Celine had been an accomplished artist to put a deposit on a house from the proceeds of an exhibition. "Celine, I'd love to see some of your work sometime. Wow. If you bought the house thirty years ago, is there still a mortgage on it?"

"I took out a second mortgage on it twenty-odd years ago to pay the deposit and renovate the current house. The first mortgage is long gone."

"Good. And it's still in your name?" I looked up to see the waiter standing tray in hand waiting to serve us.

"Excuse me," he said as he put fresh coffees and scones on the table. I thanked him and put a few euro onto one of the used saucers for him before he lifted them and the other used crockery off the table. "Thank you," he said with a beautiful young smile that would cheer you on a dull day. Celine smiled and thanked him too.

"Yes," she said. That house is still in my name, and he didn't stop the rent being paid into my account as the mortgage payments were always paid out of it. It wasn't easy I can tell you. There were years when I'd to top up the account to meet the payments. That meant doing without buying paint or canvases, or even food. Now the second mortgage has nearly run out and the rent on it is ridiculously high, God bless the tenants. It feels wrong but I am grateful for the money. The balance left over gets me by. Our cups of coffee are my only extravagance."

"Celine, you're far more astute than you thought you were. Listen to you. Very few would have a second house to fall back on. Thank goodness for big mercies. Any debt on your current house?"

"No, paid off a few years ago. It was fortunate timing. The last mortgage payment went through a week before I got the barring order." She gave a half-smile.

"Well thank God for that. Any other debt?"

"No. Just a wee bit on my credit card."

"Fair play to you, Celine. It sounds like you have your finances under control."

"Martha, when you have lived for nearly thirty years with Joseph Mary Murphy, you learn to make a little go a long way and even how to squirrel a bit of money away for the unexpected."

"I bet you do. I could have done with some lessons from you when the crash hit."

"I never felt the benefits of the roaring Celtic Tiger." She laughed. "And I guess there's a positive side to that, because I never noticed its demise either!"

"The so-called rising tide didn't float your boat so the falling tide didn't slam it into the rocks either. Not like the rest of us eejits." I shrugged.

"That bad so?"

"Pretty fecking bad. Still picking up the pieces. And the aftermath robbed us of some precious years with the children and more. You can never get those back…"

"No. And I can't get back those years of abuse either."

"Too horribly true." I felt immediately guilty for the implied comparison. "Sorry," I added. "That was much worse for you and longer lasting. You didn't deserve any of it."

"Thanks, Martha. I know that now but for years I thought I was the problem."

"Fuck him," I said. It just came out. I hadn't meant to say it. "Sorry," I said again.

"Fuck him is right." Celine laughed and took a large bite of her scone.

"The best way to do that is to hit him where it hurts and make sure that you get the best share of the assets. Let's make that happen." I flattened out the pages of the draft affidavit in front of me and reviewed where we had got to.

Celine sniggered and there was a moment where some of her scone might have made a reappearance out of her mouth.

"This is serious, Celine. This is war." I smiled at her. "Okay. Next. You will need up-to-date credit card and bank statements for all your accounts including your mortgage."

"Fine. No problem. There's only really that one bank account and our joint account. There's nothing in our joint account, he continuously cleared that out."

"'Details of personal weekly outgoings…' dig out all your utility bills etc. for this. They've given you a possible list of expenses there to work with."

"Great. I'll do that. It will be short and bitter."

"Any pension?"

"Aye."

"You will need a valuation of it from the pension company."

"A pension from fifteen years of teaching is all I have. It's not much mind."

I handed her back the paperwork with my pencilled notes down the margins. "Your homework so," I said. "I hope you can read my writing. My kids tell me that a two-year-old would do better…but for you, I've tried to bring it up to a six-year-old's standard!"

Celine laughed again. It felt good to see her laugh.

"I'll manage," she said.

"You will. Though there is a good bit of work in it. Think about any valuables that he might own also. He will have to do a statement too," I said.

"He has some very serious guitars. They must be worth a wee bit. They're his babies. Got more attention than the children. Some of them are still sitting in the music room at home."

"That's good, the more valuable the stuff he owns in his name, the better chance you have of hanging onto your art and furniture… It is best if you can work it out between you and your solicitors."

"That could be fun!"

"Not a word I was thinking! But failing that a judge could tell you to sell the lot and split the proceeds 50:50 or 60:40. Who knows? Depends on the judge and his mood on the day. And it may be a she. And even if it is a woman, they aren't necessarily any more generous than a male judge." As I spoke, I was wondering if many judges might get stuck on the question why didn't she just leave him? I was starting to understand that it was an ignorant question. Ignorant of how complex and horrific domestic violence situations are. Up until two hours previously I had been blissfully ignorant on this front and I was finding the crash course challenging.

"I don't want to sell my stuff! Some of the furniture has been in the family for generations. Most of the art is from friends from college...other artists are dead...I get the Adam's auction catalogues. I can see that some of the art is still popular and is worth a bit."

"Just a random thought, you haven't promised any of the art or furniture to your children?"

"Aye, I have actually. Why?"

"Well you could leave those items off the list and maybe plan to pass them to them sooner rather than later, or just keep them hanging on your walls for giving to them in time. Maybe ask your solicitor about that."

"It could be a challenge to organise actually giving them to the children, as one isn't talking to me at all and the other just about phones me once a month! Shane hasn't forgiven me for kicking his father out. 'Abuse. What abuse? There was no abuse, just normal family rows'."

"Normal? To be beaten to within an inch of your life?"

"Shane didn't see the worst of it."

"So, Shane thought that it was normal that Joseph Mary Murphy yelled endless abuse at you and your face was often bruised and battered back when he was at home?" I was speaking out of turn but I couldn't help myself. I took a massive bite of my scone subconsciously trying to stop myself saying too much.

"I told you. I am an artist. I thrive outside of reality. I primed my life by painting over the truth and from there I painted what I wanted to see. I couldn't handle the truth so I painted over it. I sought colour and beauty. I used to do it on canvas and I learned to do it with a make-up brush. They saw and heard what I revealed to them and now that I want them to see and hear the truth, they can't handle it. I have rewritten the past. I've ruined our family. With my selfish lies…" She was plucking at her sleeve again.

I spoke quietly. "De-nial. The longest river in the world. We all do it. But how could they deny what they saw with their own eyes?"

Celine shook her head.

"You haven't ruined your family. Your husband beat the bejaysus out of you, Celine. He's the problem. Not you." I had raised my voice in frustration at the injustice of it.

"Shush Martha. It's complicated. My counsellor says that she knows plenty of other cases like mine. Some or all the children side with the abuser. Firstly, because the abuser is an accomplished manip-ulator. He colonises your head. Mr Hail-fellow-well-met on the streets shows no signs of the devil he is at home. You'd like him, Martha, if you met him. Secondly, he is inside the kids' heads too. They are sub-consciously scared to fall out with him. They're not scared to fall out with little old me…who would be?" She was sobbing.

"I'm sorry, Celine. So sorry." I reached across the table and put my hands on hers. I willed her to think better of herself but I felt I had so little to offer her.

"Like I said I did a great job covering it up. Made-up excuses and make-up. I thought I was protecting them. More fool me."

I thought of the few stories Celine had shared with me of them growing up and my frustration mounted. "You changed their nappies, wiped their snotty faces, kissed away their tears, read to them, fed and watered them and you protected them. He was at work or in the pub when he was not at home abusing you…and at the end of it all, they take his side?"

"Aye. That just about sums up my sad wee life."

41

Chapter 3

Midlife

Pre-2014 and 2014/ 2015

My married life can be mapped out in hormonal and economic phases. My favourite came first when I had built our nest and filled it with babies. Baby boom brought sleepless nights and colic. I had often fallen asleep babe-in-arms with trails of white baby spew decorating my pyjamas and bed clothes. I was tired, very tired, but happy. The Irish economic boom that we loved to call the Celtic Tiger followed with its distorted values, endless spending and half of any night's socialising wasted on talk of property prices and designer goods. I would have happily swopped these nights for being half asleep in a sea of baby puke. The inevitable crash followed bringing years of austerity when cash was king and we struggled to find enough of it to cover life's bare necessities. There was briefly new light at the end of that gloomy tunnel, only for it to have been followed by the midlife train of hormonal deprivation. Until that train hit me, I had been under the illusion that I could avoid the crisis part of *midlife crisis* with simple things: healthy eating, staying active and having good people in my life. I was wrong.

Before the hormone demons came into my life, I had walked for an hour each day, played tennis at least twice a week, cleaned the house in a whirlwind, kept beautiful roses and grown plenty of the vegetables and fruit that we consumed; I'd cooked and frozen the surplus for the winter months. I got pleasure out of all these things. I had missed them during the years of austerity when I had taken up a more fulltime position in Patrick's office as we desperately fought to keep the business afloat. In those years I powered through tasks. Alongside working in Patrick's office, I had cooked for the family, taxied the children to their matches and to their friends, brought two surviving grandparents and my mother's husband to appointments with GPs, cardiologists, geriatricians, hip surgeon, chiropodists, physiotherapists, looked after the paperwork for both their and our bank accounts, car and house insurance, tax returns. When we emerged out of the austerity tunnel, I kept all these things up but I cut my hours of doing regular accounting and finance work to about a day a week. We were going to get back to being a family. I was going to reclaim my primary role as a wife and mother. But I make plans and the gods laugh – just when the economy was picking up my hormones were crashing.

During the years of financial struggle, Patrick and I had consoled ourselves that at least our love life was good. After a few years of endless grind, we had even learned the importance of stealing off for occasional discount romantic weekends around the country. Mum encouraged us to go. She spoiled us. She'd missed out on so many years of my life and I hers, years when I didn't know she existed. We treasured each other all the more because of all the precious time we had not known each other.

"Keep the romance alive, Martha," she had said. "It will help you get through the rough patches."

"Mum thinks we need more romance in our lives," I said to Patrick, with an exaggerated wink.

"I'll never say no to that," he said, taking me by the hand and leading me willingly up the stairs. "No time like the present."

I suppressed a giggle, knowing that the kids were dotted around the house, doing homework or watching a screen.

43

"I think Mum meant that we should go away for a weekend of romance," I said as we had a quick shower together after our stolen time in bed.

"Sounds like a good idea to me. The more we are together, the better the sex," Patrick said as he drew our wet naked bodies together.

We had previously agreed that for us our love life was more about being at one with each other than keeping up with published statistics for the average weekly frequency of sex for middle-aged couples. After a few weekends away, we reckoned we blew the statistics to a new level. All we needed was good walks, good food and wine and a comfortable bed that didn't creak on impact and we were happy. At home our love making was an embarrassment to our teenagers who, like most teenagers, preferred to think that their parents didn't do that sort of thing. But we hadn't let our children's opinions hold us back.

When I remember those pre-midlife years, I think I am making it up. It must have been someone else, maybe my memory has merged the real me with some dream person's life. It could not be possible that I achieved so much in twenty-four-hour days allowing time for sleeping in between all that coming and going, and still had time and energy for sex.

Austerity had had me working and racing around all my waking hours. Post-austerity I gave my share of lifts to Zara and her friends to and from the various parties but, with improved cashflow and Fiona and Matt over or heading towards eighteen, I felt I could release the reins a bit and I left them to get themselves home by taxi after nights out. All I asked was that they let me know in advance if they weren't coming home or to text me with any revised plans.

On the odd occasions that I woke and was expecting them home, I would check if their shoes were somewhere on the hall floor or if their jackets were on the end of the stairs. If neither were visible, I checked my phone and usually found a text telling me of their change of plan. There was only the odd glitch in the system, such as Fiona's boyfriend, Daniel, making an appearance unannounced and me going to the kitchen for water in a state of relative indecent undress. I got used to encountering Fiona or Matt late at night slightly more pissed than I would have liked. They sometimes woke me as they stumbled around the house banging doors behind them. I accepted the regular late-night visits from Daniel. Sometimes there were no shoes, no coat and no text. But that was rare.

One night, post-austerity but pre-midlife madness, as I was blissfully in the throes of a pleasant dream, the doorbell rang long and loud. And again. I jumped up and out of bed. I pulled on my dressing gown, remembering that Matt was out painting the town after a big match win. I glanced over at the still sleeping Patrick and ran down the stairs, aware as I ran that Fiona was hot on my heels.

I stopped myself just before opening the front door.

"Who is it?"

"It's the guards. It's Mrs O'Sullivan, is it?"

"Yes," I said as I opened the door to face two uniformed guards, a male and a female. A bad sign. I looked behind me into the hall for a pair of shoes, a jacket, any sign of Matt's return.

"We are here about Mathew O'Sullivan."

"Yes." I stopped breathing.

"He needs you to go to him."

"Sorry?"

"Mathew O'Sullivan of 70 Roscarberry Gardens."

"Oh. Thank God. You mean Grandad, Patrick's father. Thank God."

The guards looked at me as if it was I who had a comprehension problem.

"What's the matter with Grandad?" Fiona asked from behind me.

"He can't open the door and he tried calling you and when you didn't answer he called us."

"I didn't hear the phone?" said Fiona.

"Me neither. What's the matter?"

"That's all I know," said Guard 1.

"That's all I know," said Guard 2.

"We better ring him so."

"Yes," said Guard 1.

"Yes," said Guard 2.

"Right then. Thank you."

They turned around and slouched away down the path. I couldn't imagine either of them ever moving fast.

"Good night," I said.

"Good night," Guard 1 and 2 said to their feet.

"That was vague," Fiona said.

"Wouldn't exactly inspire confidence in the old Gardaí Síochána if you were about to be murdered or anything, would it?"

"Then again how were they to know there are two Mathew O'Sullivans in our lives!"

"True."

Grandad answered the phone on the first ring.

"Mathew, what's wrong?"

"I don't know. I don't feel right and I can't move. I was going to call an ambulance but then I thought that I'd no way to let them in so I rang you. But you didn't answer. What could I do?"

"It's okay. Don't worry, Grandad. I'll wake Patrick up and we will be up to you in less than five minutes." I hung up and got Patrick out of bed.

When we got to Grandad's bedroom, he was sitting on the side of the bed holding onto his stick looking not any worse or better than usual.

"I'd no way to answer the door to an ambulance. And you didn't answer your mobile phones…" he repeated.

"Sorry, Dad," Patrick said.

"Mathew, sorry but we don't answer them at night, they are not in our bedroom. Remember that's I why I wrote our landline number here beside your bed and in your phone."

"Oh, yes. I forgot."

"What's the matter, Dad?"

"I don't know. My back. My side. I can't move."

"Okay. Let's see, Grandad, can you lift your arms? Good. Can you smile? Stick out your tongue? Lovely."

"I was worse you know, Martha."

"I know, Mathew. Don't worry. Doctor on Call are on the way. We will see what they say."

"Muscular spasm. I've given him something for it. It's already easing. If he's not better, bring him to his GP in the morning," the on-call doctor said.

Patrick stayed over with his dad and I went home to bed and back to sleep. The joys of an easy peaceful sleep.

Then came the first strike to its pleasures. As hitting the big five zero drew nearer I was still having no problem falling asleep but I'd wake up and the front of my thighs would be below fridge temperature. The rest of my body would be a normal temperature but I had the sensation of little creatures racing around inside my veins, frantically looking for something that couldn't be found. I googled cold thighs and got '0' results. I didn't find anything answering to my invading creatures' problem either. The issues continued. I started to feel sluggish. I was running on dirty fuel that wasn't reaching my legs or brain properly. I had my bloods done. My thyroid hormone levels were borderline but fine. No immediate action required. We'll monitor it. Grin and bear it.

I dragged myself out for a walk every day. A dog is a good incentive. But I didn't have a dog. Fiona always says that if she was a counsellor, her solution to everything would be 'get a dog'. "I'm lonely." "Get a dog." I'm fat." "Get a dog." "I'm depressed." "Get a dog." I should have got a dog then but I couldn't face the added responsibility.

I put dinner on the table. Boring but easy-to-prepare meals. Baked potato, broccoli, carrots, chops. Donegal Catch, chips, mushy peas, more carrots, more spinach, sometimes pre-packed, ready-prepared dinners. The kids were not impressed.

"Oh no. Not Donegal Catch or bought burgers again," Fiona said.

"Yeah, whatever happened to homemade burgers or stir-fry or lasagne or even Thai-green curry? Or those lovely spicy minced meat and vegetable wraps? They are class. I'd kill for one of them," Matt said.

"Kill away. Let me be your first." I sighed, a tired I don't really care sigh. "Or I could write the recipes out for you, you know. You're free to cook whatever you're wanting yourself. I'll buy the ingredients. No problem."

Zara looked up from her pre-packed spinach bites and peas fresh from the freezer. "I'm green with envy. At least you guys have a choice."

"You made your choice. You chose to go green!" Matt brought his face close to Zara's and peered at each of her cheeks, then he pulled up her sleeves and looked at her arms. "You'd want to watch that, Zara. The green is starting to show."

Zara smacked him on his arm. Fiona hid a laugh. Roderic O'Conor's portraits had taught me that green is more naturally part of our skin tone than I had imagined. I pictured Zara's face in one of his portraits of a Breton girl. I started to imagine that Zara's skin was actually taking on a green hue. I even dreamt about it.

Patrick said nothing.

The roses withered with greenfly and rose rust. The vegetables went to seed or rotted from neglect. The slugs were never better fed.

I put things in stupid places. I lost my ability to be always punctual as I'd have to find my phone, my purse or my keys. I made interesting discoveries like that my phone didn't work at fridge temperatures.

I left the groceries in the car, forgetting that I'd been to the shops.

I knocked over things. I broke things. I screamed at these things. Fuck became my word of choice in response to situations. Mostly to myself but sometimes loud enough to startle the others who were used to a mother who only cursed in extreme circumstances. These were extreme circumstances.

I took naps every day. I'd no choice. I couldn't keep my eyes open.

I took the grandparents to their appointments but I resented every outing, especially the afternoon ones when I could barely string two words together. I was still shy of fifty and I felt as if it was they who should be driving me to my appointments.

I brought Grandad to the wrong doctor. He sat in the car and let me reverse cautiously into a parking space. I was conscious that I could be that woman who hit all three cars surrounding my chosen parking spot. I turned and looked at him, half expecting to hear, "Well done, you didn't crash."

"Is this my GP?" he said.

The look of fear on his face lifted me temporarily out of my brain fog.

"Sorry Grandad. I'm not having a good day. It's me who's losing it. Not your GP. Someone else's." I looked at my watch. "Still time to get to yours."

I was in bed before Patrick most nights.

"Can I cuddle up to you?" he'd say sometimes if he got into bed before I'd turned off my light.

"Okay," I'd say in a way that meant, if you must. He got the message.

When he was in a deep sleep and I woke up with my thighs freezing, I'd press my thighs against the back of his, stealing some of his heat. Sometimes he would groan in response in a not unpleasant way. I didn't encourage his groaning. I hadn't the energy for one thing to lead to another.

I tried to tell the kids how I was, but they didn't hear me.

"Mum, I said you'd collect a few us from the party on Friday night. Okay? About two o'clock," Zara more demanded than asked.

"Mum, will you give me a driving lesson later please?" Fiona asked hopefully.

"Mum, we are short on lifts for basketball. We need you to drive five of us to Bray." Zara again.

I had a seven-seater. I used to enjoy giving lifts, saying nothing as I drove so that they'd forget I was present and I could eavesdrop on their conversations. The things I heard I stored up for use as necessary but mostly they just made me smile and gave me insights into how the current generation lived. I was shocked to realise that it was okay to snog several people in one night or even go to a debs with one person and get off with another. Back in my day that made you a slut. Well maybe it made a girl a slut and the guy a lad. Had that changed so much? Don't ask me. I knew nothing.

You could go out a number of times with another person and even "meet" them a number of times, (get with them, it was called way back when) but now you are not boyfriend and girlfriend until one of you officially asks the other to be their boyfriend or girlfriend. As far as I could gather, it is mostly the boy who is doing the asking and is expected to do the asking. So, on the one hand they are more casual and on the other they are more official! And what ever happened to women's lib? Why does the boy have to do the asking? And sometimes I think that blowjobs are now more common than French-kissing was in my day. Don't they know about the warts and other ghastly things you can get from blowjobs? I tried bringing that up in conversation by telling them about a speech therapist I knew who was spending a not insignificant number of her working hours giving speech therapy to girls who had been treated for oral HPV. "Gross, Mum," Matt said.

"That HPV vaccine is all big pharma pushing more drugs on us," Zara said.

And then there was a conversation in the back of the car that went something like this.

"So, James was telling me that his girlfriend isn't a girl anymore and she is – sorry – he is now to be called Harry. And you're still going out with her who is now a him? I said to James." Brian paused and the others in the car giggled. "Yeah of course, James says. So, I say, tell me James, if 'she', Harry, is now a 'he' does that make you gay?" Brian paused again for dramatic effect.

"And?" the others chorused.

"And James loses it with me – he told me I needed to grow up and accept that there is more to gender than being born and being labelled a boy or girl for the rest of your life, just because society likes to fit everyone into one of two boxes and keep them there – like, am I missing something here?"

There was a communal sigh from the back of the car and then the conversation resumed.

"I actually know Harry since primary school," Zara said in a quiet, considered voice, causing the others to become noticeably less noisy. "We were good pals but then she went a bit too wild even for me. I met her...sorry him, the other day and I don't think I've ever seen her, I mean him, happier."

51

I was proud of Zara in that moment. She spoke with compassion for another person, a compassion she normally reserved more for living creatures other than humans in my experience.

"That's good, Zara, but it's still all so confusing. I don't fecking know who is what anymore! Soon we'll have to call everyone 'they'," Brian responded.

"That makes no sense either. They is fecking plural and there is still only one of them!" Josh piped up.

"I don't know about that. Like maybe if you're gender fluid there's two of you!" Brian joked.

"Then would you have to do your Leaving Cert twice?" Zara said teasingly.

"Imagine," came the response with a big groan.

"It's wrecking my head," said Brian. "I mean, you're alright Josh cos you're gay and I can get my head around that but, feck, soon there will be no letters of the alphabet left for us heterosexuals...LGBQRSTUV. We can't even claim H for Heterosexual!"

"Yeah, our Irish teacher is struggling to get her head around it. She was telling us she was teaching Irish dancing to the first years for Seachtain na Gaeilge and she was directing them as usual. You know 'cailíní trasna', 'buachaillí trasna'. Up goes this little guy's hand, 'excuse me miss but I don't think that you can assume which of us are boys or girls or whatever'."

I sat there driving them to their party, not saying a word, fascinated but feeling a little slow as I tried to process what I was hearing.

If the teenagers were struggling to get their heads around it all then what hope had I? I had listened very hard to work the conversation out and then I had to talk to Zara about it. I pretended I'd heard about it from another parent rather than from eavesdropping in the car and that I just wanted to see if 'the other parent' had got the right end of the stick.

52

"For God's sake, don't ask me, Mum. I get confused too. My friends and I were discussing getting our own minority sexuality, you know just so we will be listened too. We might even pick a letter of the Greek alphabet! We fear that we heterosexuals will become the unheard majority!"

I could see where Zara was coming from. Especially in their school, where sexuality seemed to span a lot of letters. Things were definitely simpler in our day, or at least they seemed that way. Ignorance was bliss. But before I got to explore this thought, she jumped in.

"Mum, Friday night, didn't you say that you'd bring the five of us home here after the party…well you'll have to leave Mary and Shana to their houses, because they have a match first thing…"

I paused before responding. I looked at her and thought, *when it comes to me, you're so fecking presumptuous.* Where was the compassion that I'd heard from her in the car? There was a moment of apparent calm. Then I lost it, as my hormones dictated only I could; I could be perfectly civil one minute then something would rock my boat and, in a flash, I could hit you like a freak tornado. Hormonal fluctuations have a lot to answer for.

"Zara, did you happen to notice that I am sick tired? Sick and tired? Exhausted? Wrecked? I've said it a thousand times. I'm done being everyone's unpaid slave, yours in particular. I am an unheard minority of one and I'm taking my minority of one, *me*, off to bed. Right now. Don't anyone dare disturb me, myself or I. Okay! Goodnight." And off I stormed.

Zara said nothing, a rare event. Normally she kept coming back at me until she wore me down.

She was, no doubt, on Snapchat to her friends before I'd hit the bedroom, telling them about her bitch of a mother who had totally lost it this time. She didn't text me to ask me if she could get me anything, like a cup of tea. My exhaustion was one big inconvenience to her. I resented her reaction but I felt sorry too that I hadn't the where-withal to be there for her the way I felt I should have been. I simply hadn't the energy to deal with it.

I heard Patrick open our bedroom door tentatively late that night and close it again quietly without entering. I presume that he slept in the spare room. He tiptoed into our room the next morning to get a change of clothes for work. I ignored him as he felt his way around with nothing but the dim light coming from the crack in the curtains to guide him.

That evening he came home early from work. Another rare event. He laid the table and he and the kids cleared up after dinner. I said only what was necessary. When the clear-up was done the kids thanked me for dinner and disappeared.

"We need to talk," he said.

That was normally my line. My eyes bored into him but my lips were sealed.

"What's wrong?" he said. He put a hand on my knee. I looked at it as I would if a fly had landed there. I was getting ready to pounce.

"Everything's wrong. I'm so fecking tired of it all. I'm sick of cooking, cleaning, doing laundry, doing taxi. I'm just sick of the whole bloody lot of it. It is as simple as that."

"Okay, okay. I hear you. I'll do my best to help more. I'll get the kids to help too. Maybe that will make things better." He looked at me, hoping that I would answer in the affirmative. I looked back blankly. "But do you think that maybe…perhaps you should go back to the doctor?" he added.

"Get real, Patrick, please. How can you help more? You barely make it home for dinner you're so up to your tonsils with work. You're still trying to make good some of those Celtic Tiger nightmare deals. And you're trying to drum up new work which might actually pay.

Tell me exactly *when* you might have more time to be at home, never mind help?"

"I'll work on it. I will do my best. And I will talk to the kids too." He tried to hug me as if to seal the deal but I was having none of it because I couldn't see how he might deliver on his part of it, and I was drowning in hormonal despair.

And he didn't deliver. Nothing seemed to change workwise. And worse, his weekends got increasingly hijacked by golf, all in the interest of building new and existing client relations of course. Saturday mornings and sometimes Sundays too, if he wasn't gone to the office.

The kids did try a bit harder. The dishwasher magically got cleared occasionally or the clothes got hung on the line. I was aware enough to acknowledge these things in the hope that they might continue.

Then the nightmares started. Every time I closed my eyes to sleep, day or night, dark forces took control of my mind; aliens landed outside the bedroom window, they constructed a tall, narrow headquarters in our garden to use as a base from which to conquer the world. I needed to escape to warn the rest of the world but I was frozen immobile between the sheets. Another time, I saw a brute of a man, larger than the door frame break into our house, the dog that we didn't have went to greet him and the man delivered rapid-fire kicks sending the dog up into the air, to fall bloodied and listless to the floor. I hid from the man, I was under the bed, crawling between cobwebs and trails of hairy grey dust, the dust made me want to sneeze but then the man would find me. These endless nightmares were real. I knew because in my head I would wake up and check that they were real. I saw the lights of the alien ships. I ducked down at the bedroom window so they would not find me. I heard the thuds of the intruder's boots. I felt the cold from the broken door.

Still each day I walked. If I had to go to see Mum, to the shop or wherever I would park my car a distance away from where I had to go so I would have to walk there and back. I knew that if I was feeling down, I must exercise.

I got up in the middle of the night to escape the nightmares. Sometimes, I would meet one of the older two in the kitchen, having a cup of tea after a night out or a late-night session on the Xbox live. Sometimes, I joined them but mostly they were just finishing. I wouldn't want to cross me either.

I ate less but my waistbands were getting tighter.

Mum said that I looked tired.

"Are you sure you are okay, Martha?" I could see the concern in her eyes and hear it in her voice.

"Just middle age, Mum. I'll get over it…when I am no longer middle-aged and just plain old, I suppose."

"Maybe get your bloods done again love, will you?" She hugged me. Since we'd first met back when I was in my late twenties, Mum had that way of making me feel loved no matter what. I often felt that I didn't deserve it, that I didn't deserve her or Patrick, or anyone's love for that matter.

I went back to the doctor. Bingo. On the day of my forty-ninth birthday I heard that my thyroid hormone levels had officially crashed. A large daily dose of eltroxin was required, but, he said, it takes a while to kick in. Three weeks later and the sleep monsters were still alive and threatening. I stopped putting on a smile when I met people on the street.

"How are you?"

"I feel awful. And you?"

"Grand."

"I can't sleep. I've terrible nightmares. My thyroid's crashed."

"I must get mine checked…"

The level of disinterest knew no bounds. Asking how are you is just another way of saying hello and the response is heard as hello. Few people, if any, gave a damn about how I was.

Finally, a small miracle happened. My older and wiser friend Máire listened.

"That is horrible. You must be exhausted. Did you try magnesium?"

"No?"

"Well you know between filtered water and mass-produced vegetables many of us aren't getting enough magnesium and minerals…"

"Thank you, Máire. You're a true friend." I hugged her. "I will definitely try it. I've nothing to lose."

I walked to the nearest health food shop. I told the shop assistant my symptoms.

"You might like to try magnesium," she said. "Just stick to the recommended dose."

I had the first nightmare free sleep that night. Within a month I was back out trying to rescue my roses and my vegetable patch. It was autumn. Mum came around to help me. She missed her garden since she moved into the apartment after she and her husband, Fergal, downsized. A heavy pruning of the diseased roses was the best that we could do. The vegetables were beyond salvaging. They had gone to seed from neglect. We cleared the ground and coated it with a layer of homemade compost in preparation for when I might next plant afresh. Zara became more devoted to the vegan cause. No problem. I cooked two meals from scratch most nights, vegan and carnivore. Patrick and Matt didn't feel as if they'd eaten if it didn't include meat.

My bloods had shown a rise in my cholesterol.

"You're heading towards fifty, Martha," Mum warned. "Remember your father died in his fifties from a heart attack."

"I'm only just forty-nine," I said indignantly but knowing that, with my family history, I couldn't afford to ignore my raised reading. I decided that a bit more vegan would do me good.

I regained an interest in sex. I had the energy. Patrick was still working long hours and if golf, under the guise of building client relations, didn't take up most of his remaining waking hours, it seemed to take his remaining energy. When I reached across for him, to rub his back and run my fingers down between his legs, he might respond and take me in his arms and all would be well. He never said it but, on these rare occasions, I sensed that he was glad that I had re-found my libido. I wondered if he had taken it personally. But there were times when I would reach out to him and I could rise from him nothing more than a series of loud snores. He was trying to do too much. While our time together happened in short snatches, I felt that we could get back on track. Patrick just needed to work less and golf less and we'd be fine.

It took another six months for it to fully sink in that Patrick wasn't going to work and golf less and that my crashing thyroid and rising cholesterol was my body screaming 'here comes the menopause'.

In the meantime, I went back to playing tennis and gave my friends and foes a run for their money. It was the following year that I met Celine, by which time I knew the difference between a good sweat and a long hot flush. I called them flushes but most people call them flashes; they were wet and they weren't over in a flash!

By then Patrick had become captain of the golf club. He was seldom at home.

I'm not saying I could have ever done stand-up comedy but before my thyroid crashed, I could raise the odd laugh and most weeks of the month I could laugh at my own awkward self. I'd had a lifetime of burns from the oven and the iron and bruises from bumping into things that I couldn't remember bumping into. If they had been doling out labels back in the day then I'd have been labelled dyspraxic, a term I hate.

Fiona has dyspraxia and dyslexia. She is not dyspraxic and dyslexic. She is far more than both of those. I have often apologised for giving her my gene that carries dyspraxia, if such a gene exists. We have been known to compare and count each other's bruises and burns. It's almost a competition to see who has more.

Menopause multiplied the frequency of my bumps and burns, and the sweats that came with it washed away most of what had been my reasonable sense of humour, not to mention my sense of reason. I have heard of women pleading temporary insanity due to PMT. I wondered if menopause was a more permanent insanity. Menopause did not come gently in the dark night. It came in the day and the night and in a flood of sweat and bad humour.

There was more. At my gynaecologist's suggestion a few years after Zara's birth I'd had a Merina Coil fitted. I'd been pleased with the outcome: only a light occasional period and contraception that I didn't have to remember to take or even think about. And low and behold the Irish Health Board's Drug Payment Scheme covered the lion's share of the cost of it. State sponsored sex I called it. Patrick and I had enjoyed its benefits right through the boom years and the teetering-on-bust years.

My latest coil was coming to the end of its useful life as I understood it so I had it removed and decided it would be my last coil. Three days later I was sitting at our kitchen table reading the paper when I had the sensation that I had wet myself. I was still, as I had reminded my mother nine months previously, not quite fifty. I wasn't expecting to lose control down there for another twenty-five years or so. I stood up and realised that it was a pool of blood that I was sitting in. When I went to the bathroom there was more blood. I was alone in the house and I wondered was this going to get worse. Was I haemorrhaging? I was scared, very scared. The doctor hadn't passed any remarks when removing my coil. I would have called an ambulance for myself there and then if it hadn't been for Doctor Google. Doctor Google told me that this was not an entirely unusual response to the removal of the Merina. My further research – which included joining a Merina Support Group on Facebook – indicated that doctors either don't know about this potential side effect or simply don't see fit to share the information with their patients.

I bled heavily for nine out of the next twelve weeks and for most of the next four months after that. Such was the flow that despite taking iron tablets daily my iron levels crashed and so did I. An abrupt ending came to our briefly resumed sex life. With the blood came the sweats. Calling them hot flushes, hot flashes or royal flushes is to understate them. Think flushing a toilet. My menopause sweats lasted tortuous minutes and irritated my skin especially in every crease and crevice. I had long ago decided that misogyny began with the man above. Look what women have to suffer. Periods, premenstrual tension one week of every month, pregnancy, births. Need I go on? Now I had the T of PMT every day of every month and I was pissed off. My sex drive literally dried up overnight. First, because I was bleeding. Second, because I was exhausted. Third, because I was sweating. Fourth, because I dried up down there and without even being threatened with sex, it hurt. I renamed menopause men-on-pause.

My life became filled with CRAFT moments. Can't Remember A Fucking Thing. I could be driving to tennis and find myself at the supermarket. I nearly gave the epileptic, permanently spaced cat my dinner instead of hers one day. The phenobarbitone crushed into her dinner was tempting. I could have done with its relaxing qualities and maybe I could curl up beside someone on the couch and receive some much-needed pats and cuddles.

These feelings dragging on for torturous months on end. I was struggling but I was determined to get by.

"Martha, you know I hate giving advice but you can't keep going like this. Would you not think about HRT? My friend Rachel's daughter started taking it and she is a new woman," Mum gently suggested, never being one to like to rock the boat but all too aware of how unreasonable I was becoming.

"I'm not going to take HRT, Mum. I'm not because I've had enough artificial hormones to last a lifetime and because HRT only postpones the bloody inevitable anyway…I am just going to have to sweat it out." I raised my voice to Mum, something that I rarely, if ever, did. She didn't deserve that.

"Well pet, I hope that works for you. I really do."

Despite being a tired and bad-humoured sweat-bag, I still thought that a romantic holiday for two to somewhere exotic, but not too hot, would be the ideal fiftieth birthday present for me. I suggested loudly that I had enough 'things' and that it was experiences we should be collecting, such as going to new places. My menopause mood might have played its part in this message going unheard.

When I unwrapped a pair of large diamond earrings on my fiftieth birthday, I decided that Patrick had not been listening and I was furious with him for that. In hindsight I was angry with myself for not spelling it out in black and white or just going ahead and booking a holiday. When he had given me a diamond pendant and a tennis bracelet – which has nothing that I can see that connects it to tennis – for our twentieth anniversary, I had made the mistake of feigning gratitude. I thought that he would notice how little I wore the diamond pieces and therefore not feel tempted to buy me more such expensive bling. He had never been one to tune into what sort of presents I might like. He had history. For example, he knew I liked Clarins skin prod-

61

ucts and for my forty-fifth birthday he gave me Clarins sun-protection…for ageing skin. "Very romantic, thank you, Patrick. Does it come with a sun holiday?" It didn't. I had the full jewellery complement now, the ring, the necklace, the bracelet and now the earrings. The ring had always been enough for me but I had never expressly said so. I should have said it loud and clear, no more diamonds please, and added that the occasional sun holiday would be nice though.

There I was on my fiftieth birthday, over twenty years married, looking at a pair of earrings that my husband had given me. A large square-cut diamond suspended from each earring, each diamond a piece of coal which might never have amounted to anything and which might have been left lying in the depths of the earth forever. But, over thousands of years these pieces of rock had reacted well to inner earth's intense heat and pressure; deep source volcanic eruptions brought them to where each of them was found, possibly not even in the same country; circumstances conspired to bring them together, to be cut and polished to match each other and become a pair. Then, having become a matching-pair, through a combination of luck, hard graft and skill, it was their destiny to always hang apart.

Chapter 4

Celine's Reality

2015

Celine had said that she hadn't had a friend over to her house in years. I now understood why this had been so. She had said it would mark another milestone in reclaiming her true self to cook lunch for me and show me around her home and her beloved art collection. We had also planned to look over her homework on the Affidavit of Means in privacy. A piano exam of Zara's, and Matt's last two appointments with the orthodontist for his front teeth crowns – the broken teeth being one on a long list of his sport's injuries – conspired to give me no expectation of seeing Celine for nearly two weeks between when I had set out what information she needed to prepare the affidavit, to when I was to go to her place for lunch.

I walked down our road of Victorian red-brick houses admiring the various front gardens as I went. I remember feeling good about myself. I was giving help to someone who needed it. And I had the honour of being the first friend to be invited to Celine's house for a long number of years. Her life intrigued me. I had never met an accomplished artist before. I was excited to be seeing her art collection and her own paintings in particular. I believed that they would open another window to the inner workings of Celine. More significantly, I had never before knowingly met a woman who had been beaten by her partner. The key word being knowingly. Celine's story woke me up to the realisation that I had no idea what went on behind other people's closed doors or what ugly secrets a well-painted layer of make-up might hide. This thought led to another and I shivered at the prospect of seeing the stairs that Celine's husband had pushed her down or the coffee table that her head had hit when he sent her flying with such force that she had been rendered bloodied and unconscious.

I could taste the fear of the violence I experienced in the family house where I was reared; the permanent shadow of expectation of the next beating. There was always going to be a next time. No matter how hard I tried to anticipate and deliver her every need or every desire, Heather who reared me always found a reason to beat me. I imagined that Celine too had tried similar avoidance tactics with her husband with equally dismal results. I was glad for her that she was putting that part of her life behind her. I was happy to be helping her to do so.

I smiled when I saw that the brasses of her solid front door were as unpolished as our own. I'd long since given up the repetitive task of keeping them clean. There were always better things to be doing. I pressed her tarnished doorbell with an enthusiastic touch. A shrill sound assaulted my ears and startled my thoughts. It didn't stop. I pressed the bell again, this time with gritted teeth and a punched force that willed its piercing noise to cease. Nobody answered the door. I looked down the garden path to the footpath, expecting passers-by to be staring at me like a thief caught in the act. Two people walked past locked in conversation. Still nobody answered the screaming doorbell. I took out my mobile to call Celine's number. I heard the door creak open. Celine's diminutive head bent low appeared in the crack. When her head lifted, swollen purple eyes looked up at me through a veil of grey dishevelled hair. I slowly reached out to her.

"Oh Celine, Celine. What happened? Dear Celine."

She fell into my arms. I held her like I might a delicate bird, scared that I would crush her damaged body.

"He...came back..." she spluttered through swollen lips.

"The barring order?"

"Expired, he told me."

"How?"

"The two years were up, he said. Time for him to come home, he said."

"Home! Celine, what do you mean?"

"Home here. To play happy family again..." Her voice trailed off as her head sunk low.

"Wow Celine. Shit! Is he still here?"

She gave a barely perceptible shake of her battered head.

I trembled as I gently guided her delicate frame further into the hall. "Let's not stand here, let's get you somewhere warm." I was thinking but did not say, *he has beaten you black and blue, that's assault, what's a barring order got to do with that?* The bastard.

We made our way to the kitchen and I directed Celine towards a large comfy armchair. She resisted.

"His chair," she said, sitting herself painfully onto a small hard chair.

She started to shiver. I took a large towel from a clothes horse and wrapped it around her. I gently rubbed her back, feeling the individual knobbles of her spine through the towel. I cannot describe the extent of my horror. I still feel it when the image of her on that hard chair comes back to me. On the outside, I was cool and practical. Inside, I was trembling. I knew a little of what he had done to her in the past but that knowledge was nothing beside the reality of Celine, my beaten and battered fragile friend.

I filled the kettle and made a pot of tea. There was about an inch of milk left in a carton and I poured that into Celine's mug and handed it to her.

"I'm sorry, Martha. I've no food for lunch. I've emptied the freezer over the last few days. There's still a bag of string beans if you'd like them!" She managed a sort of swollen smile.

"Don't you worry. I'll go to the shops and buy plenty of soup to warm you up. Maybe some lasagne too?" I knew that she liked lasagne and also it would be soft to eat.

"Thank you." She made to reach for her purse.

"I'll get it…you can cook me lunch another time." My words sounded hollow and silly to me.

"I'm sorry."

"Celine, please my dear friend, please stop saying sorry. It's not your fault. He beat you. He's a bastard." I spat out the words with a hatred that I was unfamiliar with.

Celine nodded her battered head. I could sense her pain with each movement.

"Exactly. It's his fault. And your solicitor's fault for not renewing the order."

Celine gave a lop-sided smile.

I smiled too.

"I've gone and brought on a frigging hot flush." I mopped my forehead and took off my jacket. "You should see me when I really rant."

"I'm not sure I want to!" Her words came painfully through her swollen lips.

"You'd be right there! You don't have to speak you know. It looks like it hurts."

She nodded. It looked as if it hurt to nod too. I shivered.

"Do you want to stay in the kitchen or move elsewhere?"

"Kitchen please." No matter what the situation, Celine is forever polite.

"I'll light the stove here so and then I'll be off to the shops. On the way, I'll phone my handyman to come and change those locks to keep the bastard out. If he can't come today, I'll get a locksmith to do it. Alright?" I was babbling on, trying to distract myself from the reality of the damaged Celine before me.

She gave another painful nod. I winced.

I had never seen a real live battered person before and I never want to again. All that I had ever seen on a big or small screen did not prepare me for being in the presence of someone whose delicate face was buried under swollen, multi-coloured bruises. As we sat and sipped our soup, every time I saw Celine's face it came as a fresh shock to me. My instinct was to turn away, the way one might from unnecessary nudity. But nudity is natural, made by nature. A petite woman beaten black and blue by a 200 lb man is not. I wanted to stop looking away. I needed to see it and accept it for what it was. This is the only way I felt that I could be there for Celine. She did not look at me. She raised her head just enough to take slow small spoonfuls of soup. I made myself look at her, make eye contact with her at times even. I considered each bruise and imagined how Joseph Mary Murphy had brought the full force of his fists down onto her china doll face, down onto her fragile head, down onto her frail body. As I looked my anger mounted to the point where I was scared of me. If I had a gun and Joseph Mary Murphy was to have walked in the door at that moment, I knew I would have killed him. I didn't have a gun and, if I did, it would not be the answer. Shooting would be too kind a death for the bastard.

Since Celine had told me some of her story I had googled "domestic violence". I had sought guidance on how to support a friend experiencing it; my anger was not the answer that Celine needed.

"It was Monday night. I was asleep. I heard noise in the box room. I thought it was a burglar. Then I knew it was him. I know his sound. It raises something deep inside me, bigger than fear itself...I once woke up to a mouse that was like a monster on my pillow, right beside my face. It scared me. It was nothing to what I felt when I heard him. I froze at first. Then I forced myself to get up out of bed. I thought that I would lock myself in the bathroom and call the guards. But before I did, he was in my room. He grabbed me. I screamed. He slapped his hand over my mouth to get me to stop.

"Aren't you going to welcome your prodigal husband home? he yelled at me. Then he spat a big gob of spit onto my face." Celine rubbed her bruised cheek with the memory and her entire body tremored.

I felt dirty for her and caught myself as my hand went up to wipe my own face.

"The bastard was drunk," she said as if it provided an explanation. "Welcome home, Joseph, I said. I tried to sound sincere, Martha, I did honestly."

"I know you did, Celine."

"Fuck you, you cunt, he said." Celine stared at the small fire in the stove as she spoke.

Despite her slurred speech the C-word had come out distinctly. I jolted and turned to face her.

"Yes, he still loves that word. Stupid fucking cunt. That's me."

"That's not you, Celine. It's not."

I squeezed my eyes shut trying to hold back tears. I could feel turmoil in my stomach and in my head. There was a battle inside my head, I was listening but I was trying to deny what I was hearing.

"He threw me on the bed and punched me. I didn't fight him. I scratched him on the face once, years ago. He had raised his hand to hit Karen. That time I thought that he would kill me. The punch took the wind out of me. He ripped my nightdress and spat straight at my chest. He shoved his fingers up…up. It hurts."

As she was speaking Celine had brought her knees up to her chest and was clutching them tight to her. She rocked back and forth. Back and forth. Possessed by her memories. I was terrified for her. My own body was clenched like a tight fist. Celine was not one of my children suffering a sports injury or a broken heart, things I knew reasonably well how to deal with. Celine was in a distraught state like none that I had ever witnessed before. She reminded me of myself as a small help-less child after a beating. I knelt down beside her and with the lightest touch possible stroked her back and arms.

"What can I do, Celine? What should I do?"

Celine shook her head and continued rocking. My heart crumbled for her. I was out of my depth. I was scared for her.

"Celine, you told me you've a good GP, Róisín McCarthy. Re-member you recommended that I went to her about the menopause. She's always been good to you." I spoke quietly.

Celine nodded.

"I'm going to call her for you. Okay? I'll be right back."

I went into the hall and dialled the doctor's number. The recep-tionist answered. I explained that I needed to talk to the doctor about Celine Murphy. The secretary suggested that if it was urgent I should bring her to the Emergency Department. I was in my calm-in-cases-of-emergency mode and I held firm.

"If I could just speak to Dr McCarthy first, please. It's a very diffi-cult situation and bringing Celine into the horror that is our Emer-gency Departments will only make things worse."

"Perhaps you should call an ambulance."

I had to pause and take a deep breath or I might have screamed at that silly woman. Why do some doctors' secretaries see their main role as being to keep patients from seeing or speaking to their doctors? Is it in their job description? I took another deep breath.

"Thank you. I've considered that. Unfortunately, an ambulance will just bring her into the same Emergency Department just perhaps a bit quicker than I would bring her myself. I'm sorry but I really need to speak to the doctor please. And as soon as possible."

"She's with a patient. I'll take your number and she will call you back when she has time."

"Thank you for your help. But could I stay on the line please?"

"You could be waiting a while."

"Okay. Thank you." You stupid cow…I didn't say it out loud.

The tune to 'She'll Be Coming Round the Mountain' came down the line. Hideous, tedious music. Guaranteed not to calm a person down. I don't think anything would have calmed my inner being down at that time.

I looked into the kitchen. Celine was still in her chair, rocking in a slower, more rhythmic movement now. Mumbling to herself. I prayed that the doctor would answer the phone soon.

I paced along the corridor, up through the hall to the front door and back again. To distract myself from the present horror I studied my surroundings. The entire hall, stairs and landing was painted in a warm burnt orange, offset by white dado rails, white doors and door frames and white ceilings with ornate plaster coving. Above the dado rail the walls were hung with paintings large and small. No one style prevailed but all oozed colour. Some were as real and exact as photographs. These left me cold. Others were more expressionist and others again were abstract shapes that were beyond my comprehension but appealed to my eye. There were some painterly portraits, one in particular of a teenage girl. I was drawn to stare at it and was wondering if I saw a resemblance to Celine in it when a strong Cork accent came down the line.

"Dr McCarthy. Is that Celine?"

"Sorry, no. This is her friend, Martha. I saw you once for womanly problems, menopause. But I'm ringing about Celine. She is in a very bad way and I don't know what to do." I felt a lump in my throat and I swallowed hard.

"My receptionist suggested that you call an ambulance."

"She did but please can I tell you the situation first." My voice was taut and my words stilted in an effort to keep from crying. I didn't want to cry. I'd had a lifetime of practice of switching to stiff stilted mode when I might otherwise cry.

"Okay, go on."

I told her about what Joseph Mary Murphy had done to his wife. I tried to contain my anger that that bastard was still out there, walking the streets with a swagger no doubt, free to beat any woman he chose. I told her about Celine's current state.

"It sounds like delayed shock to me."

"Yes. You are probably right. I am afraid that I've no experience of this sort of thing and I don't know what to do." This was my way of pleading with Dr McCarthy, my way of saying to her, please come, I need you, Celine needs you, I don't know what I'm doing…

"I should finish surgery in about an hour or so. Can you stay with Celine until then?"

"Yes. I can."

"Keep her warm and comfortable. Give her warm drinks. Probably best not caffeinated ones. Maybe herbal teas. Okay?"

"Okay. Thanks." Professional help was coming. I was relieved.

When I hung up I saw five missed calls from Zara and eight texts. I was in no frame of mind to deal with her but there were some things that I needed. I called her. First, I apologised that I hadn't called her back then I asked her to bring me down my phone charger, a couple of hot water bottles and some herbal teas.

"Where are you, Mum? We are supposed to go looking today for an outfit for my pre-Junior Cert night. I've sent you loads of texts. You haven't replied to one of them." I had intended on going with her after lunch but once I had seen Celine's damaged face, it hadn't crossed my mind again. Typical teenager, it's always all about her. Anyway, she only wanted me for my credit card. I struggled to keep my cool.

"I'm sorry, Zara. I can't do it today. Something serious came up."

"What came up this time? Your hormones. Again. I suppose."

"Yes. Something like that. Please just bring two hot bottles, charger and the peppermint and chamomile tea to Celine's soon please." I spoke through gritted teeth.

"But Mum what about—"

I hung up.

I checked on Celine again and was relieved to find that she had virtually stopped rocking. I went upstairs to see what state her bedroom was in. There was a chair on its side and I automatically picked it up. Drawers were open in the chest of drawers and items of clothes and jewellery were strewn across the floor. There was blood on the sheets and pillows. A lot of blood. I was about to strip the bed but stopped when I realised that if it was a crime scene, I shouldn't touch it. I felt my blood run cold. My body shivered and I left the room. I closed the door quietly but firmly. I turned and went into the room next door. It was a lovely, homely room with two single beds, both of which looked freshly made up. The sun was shining through the large sash window and the room felt warm. This would be the best room to bring Celine up to.

Zara almost threw the bag of stuff at me when I answered the door with the bell stuck on blaring again. I rammed my elbow hard against it and it stopped.

"Thanks," I said. Zara grunted in response, an I'm-really-pissed-off-with-you grunt.

"Celine should get that bell fixed," she declared as she stamped down the garden path. John, my handyman was walking up against her. His grey hair was lifting off his shoulders in the wind. They nodded at each other.

"Good timing, John," I said, struggling to sound almost cheerful.

"Is this the door you want the locks changed on?"

"Yes. What do you think?"

John inspected the Yale lock and the Chubb. He smelt, as he always did, like an ashtray that had not been emptied in months. I hated the smell but I liked him too much to hold it against him.

"Fairly standard. I'll be back with replacements shortly. They'll have those in O'Rourke's."

"Thanks John. I appreciate it."

John was already down the path. He was a doer, not a talker. No fuss and all done on a diet of John Player Blue cigarettes and cups of tea. *Sure, I'd throw up if I ate anything else,* he told me.

I sighed and went back into the kitchen to put hot water in the bottles and to make some herbal tea.

I went into the second bedroom and put the hot bottles into one of the small comfortable beds and the teas on the bedside locker. Then I gently persuaded a shivering Celine to move upstairs and into bed. Each step she took caused her to wince. I winced with her. It was unbearable. I moved to lift her in my arms. She seemed light enough for me to manage. But she insisted that she could manage by just leaning on me and the bannisters. It was the longest walk up stairs that I have ever experienced.

"I did it," she said with a swollen half-smile when we got to the edge of the bed and she drew breath.

"You did," I said. It was a small victory but felt a major one.

I helped her into bed. She rested her feet on one bottle and hugged the soft, woolly sheep one to her like a childhood teddy. I offered her the choice of chamomile or peppermint tea as she sat up in bed propped on pillows. She pointed at the chamomile which I handed to her. She nursed the mug in one hand and the cuddly hot bottle in the other. She sipped the tea and stared at the pretty quilt. I followed her gaze to a beautiful painted sunrise or sunset. I stared at it trying to decide which would make it more comforting. The sun going down on the horrors that Celine was dealing with or the sun rising with the promise of a new start. In the painting rich sunlight appeared behind dark purple hills, filling the sky with a bleed of red, becoming orange, becoming yellow, all gently suggested in the waters in front of the hills.

I sipped my peppermint tea and took in the other artistic touches in the room. The beds were covered with handmade patchwork quilts that included the many colours in nature. The ceiling lampshade was large and stitched with bold flowers. Behind the bed hung a large painting of an open window and a closed door surrounded by a wall of flowering wisteria, draping itself up and across the painting, leaving no harsh lines of window or door frames, soft wispy green leaves going this way and that, providing a rich backdrop to large teardrops of purple flowers. Like the bold portraits downstairs and the rich sunlight painting, the signature was a 'C' with a long tail which I saw now was wrapped around the letters 'eline'. I toyed with the metaphor behind the closed door and the open window. I was looking for hope for Celine, a way back to her true self.

Dr McCarthy arrived, as promised, within the hour. The doorbell didn't stick because John had fixed it.

I led her upstairs and opened the door on the main bedroom. Some part of me needed to share its horror. She stood one step inside the door and took in the scene. Her face remained fixed in a serious frown but her fingers clenched and opened, clenched and opened.

"Leave it as it is for now. Okay?" She turned and walked out onto the landing, pulling the door behind her quietly, but firmly, just as I had done.

"Now so," she said as she walked into the room where Celine was propped up on pillows, still staring at the painted sunlight.

I went downstairs and headed for the kitchen but decided that the doctor might assume that I had left if she didn't see me. I let myself into the front sitting room and left the door wide open. To distract myself from Celine's horrors I focussed my attention on the room around me. Distraction was my well-practised habitual coping mechanism. It allowed me to avoid facing painful truths.

The room was painted a warm grassy green. A massive painting of the red-and-white Pigeon House towers and the wooden bridge leading to Bull Island hung over the fireplace. The painting was primarily rich shades of blues depicting an expansive sky and water. Sparkles of light hit the water like fairy dust, perhaps reflecting the unseen stars above. I decided that it was a night scene, lit by nature, uncontaminated by manmade light. I looked for a signature and found it, Fitzharris. I was familiar with his work. Patrick and I owned three of his paintings, but they weren't anything like this one. Ours were abstract shapes symbolizing a half-sunken boat, a light house, a rug hanging in a souk. Patrick and I loved our Fitzharris paintings and we marvelled at how we could normally agree on the art that we liked, with one notable exception. Patrick loved William Scott while I was almost indifferent to him. I believed that Patrick was entitled to his odd extravagance given how hard he worked. When, back in the boom times, he had purchased a large Scott, I had given it pride of place in the hall. I had told myself that our small art collection was part of our pension fund. The death of the Celtic Tiger had put paid to that notion when art prices hit the floor and there they had remained long after the post-austerity bounce.

I heard the doctor call my name.

"In here," I replied, thinking that the doctor might prefer to talk to me in the sitting room, rather than the hall where Celine might hear us.

"You were right to call me. An Emergency Department would only have added to Celine's trauma. I have had a long chat with her but I haven't given her anything for the shock. In my opinion there would be no good in that. Apart from paracetamol for the pain, which she can have at four- to six-hour intervals. Try and stretch it out. What she needs most is plenty of tender loving care. She should not be left alone in the house at this stage. I've suggested that she gets you to call her daughter, Karen. She has reluctantly agreed to that."

"Okay. I'll do that…I'm not sure how it will go but I'll give it a shot." I paused, feeling like I had betrayed Celine by giving away that she and her daughter were not close. I changed tack. "She has a sister up North too, I might ring her as well."

"Good. This is going to be a slow process. I've taken photos of her wounds and her bedroom with her permission in case she wants to press charges. These things can wait. My priority is her mental and physical health. I have your number and I will liaise with you. That is what I have agreed with her, although I'm not sure what she is processing. It will be a day at a time for a few weeks and then we will see. If there is any significant or worrying change then I suggest you call an ambulance."

"Thank you. I'll do what you say. I will make sure she is okay," I said with a lot more confidence than I felt.

I walked the doctor to the front door and expressed my sincere gratitude for her help. She said that Celine was lucky to have a friend like me. As I closed the door, I had a faint sense of déjà vu. I had heard those words before about me being a good friend, from another doctor, back when my best friend Trish was ill. Back then I had struggled

76

with the need to support a husband with a business suffering from the full impact of the crash while feeling that I needed to be with my dying friend. I never felt like I got the balance right. This time I didn't know any better how I could possibly be there for Celine and manage to juggle all the balls in the air which included, amongst a long list of other things, being around to try to keep Matt on track to get through his Leaving Cert exams. I was more worked up about his exams than he was. I was forever threatening to stick a torpedo under him. He just shrugged, stuck his face back into his phone and laughed at something or other that one of his friends had shared on snapchat or whatever. I wished they'd share a few exam tips from time to time! Fat chance.

And when Zara wasn't getting worked up about her Junior Cert Exams, she was getting worked up about his Leaving Cert.

"Mum, he's not supposed to be on the Xbox until he's done at least two hours' homework." "Mum, are you letting him go to that eighteenth and he hasn't looked at a book all day?" "Mum, shouldn't he be studying and not watching TV?"

As I stood in Celine's hall I felt overwhelmed. I was in danger of imploding. If I had struggled last time, I was definitely going to struggle this time. I listed the things that were different, that added to the challenge. Unlike Trish, Celine had very few people to rely on; when I was up to my tonsils being there for a dying Trish, while also helping Patrick save his business in the dark days of the post-crash horrors, Mum and Fergal, lovingly known as Gran and Pops, had been in the full of their health and been more than a willing help. Now Mum was waiting for a hip replacement and Fergal was waiting for a cataract operation; Matt needed close monitoring to get him to apply himself, otherwise he had no hope of getting the marks he needed to get his chosen course, and on top of that I was on a promise to bring and collect Fiona from her job teaching on the other side of the city once a week to ease her daily trek and to use it as an opportunity to give her

77

much needed driving lessons. All that and then all the appointments for the aging parents – why can't there be a one-stop, all-in-one-day clinic, for older people's health appointments?

My mind was a mess trying to process all I had to do in a normal week and I was panicking at the thought of adding Celine's needs to that melee. I told my mind to shut up, *pull yourself together, Martha*. I walked slowly back up the stairs to check on Celine.

"Celine, you look a little better," I said, trying to convince myself that she did.

Celine tried a small smile.

"Don't worry we will look after you. Dr McCarthy says you've agreed that I will ring your daughter, Karen."

I could read the uncertainty on Celine's face even through the swelling. "I thought I might try your sister, Jacinta, too. Okay?"

Celine nodded and passed me her not-so-smart phone.

"Thanks. Would you like to give me the code so I can get their numbers please?"

"A.R.T.I.S.T., artist."

"I mean the code, you know the numbers."

"A.R.T.I.S.T."

"Oh, I get it." I punched the numbers matching the letters into her phone and bingo. I gave her a thumbs-up.

Celine smiled a swollen smile.

I went back down to the sitting room and, using my own phone, I called home. I told Zara that they were to help themselves to the left-over dinners from earlier in the week. Patrick wasn't yet home so I asked her to make sure that he got fed when he got in. She said that she was going over to her friend's house to study. "Matt can do it. It's not as if he's stuck to his desk or anything."

I was getting annoyed and I could have let fly at her at any moment. "Can I speak to Matt so please?" It was pointless calling him on his own phone. He wouldn't answer it.

Two grunts from him later and I hoped that he had got the message. We rarely clashed because he either said little or else humoured me with a kind comment or a joke. He regularly showed me amusing videos that his friends had shared, which we would watch together. I'd laugh at them, grateful for the sharing but at the same time thinking that he was distracting me from whatever issue I had raised with him and that he might be better spending the time actually studying.

I sent a text to Patrick filling him in a little on the Celine situation and asking him to keep an eye on whether Matt was actually doing some study.

I think I was subconsciously postponing calling Celine's daughter. How do you tell a daughter whom you have never met that her mother has been badly beaten by her father? I decided that you don't. Certainly not on the phone. I would PBE, Play *Be* Ear, as Patrick's father always said, not knowing that the phrase was play it *by* ear. I doubt that he had a clue where the expression came from. Music didn't feature on his radar.

Karen didn't answer her phone when I called her from her mother's number or from my own. I sent her a text hoping that it hit the right balance between urgency and not causing panic.

Hi Karen, this is a friend and neighbour of your mother's. I need to talk to you as soon as possible as something has happened to her. Just to reassure you that it is not life-threatening. Regards Martha

I edited the text a number of times before I was happy with it. Part of me wanted to say that it is no longer life-threatening in recognition of how serious her father's assault on her mother had been. I was aware that Karen's generation would see my text as coming from some old fogey incapable of using text lingo, but I feared that, in another generation or so, full words and sentences would be no more. Also, with the hardworking Fiona having dyslexia, I thought the last thing needed was proper English having to compete with text speak.

I decided to allow Karen ten minutes to reply before calling Celine's sister but Karen called me on Celine's phone within two minutes of my sending the text to her.

"Hi, this is Karen."

"Hi Karen, this is Martha…"

"You texted me."

"Yes. I did. The doctor suggested that I call you. Something has happened to your mother. She is in shock and she needs all the support she can get."

"What happened? Where is she?"

"She is here. At home. Can you come over?"

"What happened? Is she alright?"

"The doctor thinks that, with the right care and support, she should make a good recovery. I think it may be best if I explained more when you get here. When do you think you can come?" As I spoke, I ran my finger along the mantelpiece and gathered a thick pile of grey dust as I did.

"Did she try and top herself or something stupid like that?"

"No. She did not do anything stupid like that. She's not that sort of person." I was exasperated at Karen's response and as a result I shouted at her.

"Okay. Okay. I'll be there. I can get the DART. I am beside Harmonstown station…I should be there in under an hour. Okay?" Karen spoke in rapid fire.

"Okay. I'll see you then…and…could I ask you to call or text me when you are at the door please so as not to wake your mother."

"I have keys."

"Still, do you mind texting me when you are nearly here please. I'd be grateful."

She snorted at me in response.

I felt about to lose my patience with her and was tempted to tell her that the locks had been changed to keep her brute of a father out. But I bit my lip.

Harmonstown, I thought, that's only a couple of short train stops away. Yet Celine said that Karen rarely had the time to see her. How sad. Children grow up, have their own lives and distance themselves from their parents. I supposed it was going to happen to me too. I hoped not to that extent.

I looked in on Celine. She appeared to be asleep. She remained propped up on the pillows, her swollen face turned upwards in full view as a stark reminder of what her husband had done to her. Her arms gripped the woolly bottle tight to her chest. Its sheep's eyes peered at me, popping out of its head, wondering why I was there. The bottle was at best lukewarm at this stage. I pulled up the covers around her and left the room.

I sent a text to Jacinta similar to the one I had sent to Karen. She called me immediately.

"Hi Martha, it's Jacinta. What's the story with our Celly?"

"Jacinta, there's no easy way to explain…"

"Joe's gone and done something to her, hasn't he? He's a wee bastard. He was a wee bastard in college and he's still a wee bastard. I'll fucking banjax him. I will."

"Oh Jacinta, I'm afraid he has. I want to kill him myself…" My voice was trembling and tears were pushing their way to finally escape. I burst out crying. "Sorry Jacinta, just give me a minute…" I held the phone tight to my chest to mute my sobs. I took three long deep breaths, letting each one out as slowly as I could. Then I went back on the call. "Sorry about that…"

"What's he done this fucking time?"

I paused to compose myself some more. I didn't want to tell her the whole story over the phone.

"He's beaten her horribly. The doctor says that she's in shock."

"The bastard. The fucking wee bastard. How effin' bad is it?"

"It's pretty bad. But the doctor says with plenty of TLC, she should make a good recovery."

"I'll fucking kill him. There're people up here who've dealt with lesser bastards. They'd give him something that would put a stop to his fucking stride. Killin' would be too good for him."

I presumed that she was referring to what had been the IRA and loyalist's preferred punishment for perceived deviants and lesser enemies, a kneecapping: a bullet behind each knee. From where I was sitting, I could see the merit of Joseph Mary Murphy getting a kneecapping or another more severe and fitting treatment that cut straight to his manhood. My faith in the Irish justice system when it came to crimes against women was right there beside my belief in Santa. It was nice to pretend that justice existed in these situations but, in reality, we all knew it didn't.

"Martha, are you there?"

"Sorry Jacinta. Yes. I was just considering the merits of an alternative and more effective justice system when it comes to such bastards but, I know, right now we really should be focusing on getting Celine better."

"Sorry. You're right. How is she?"

"She's resting. She is in deep shock and the doctor says that she will need someone with her at all times for the next couple of weeks."

"Poor Celly, always a sensitive one. Kind to a fault. That's why she was drawn to him you know. She thought he just needed some TLC! It won't be fucking TLC I'll give that bastard…Shit! Here I am ranting on when I should be packing my bag to get down to her."

"Can you come? Thank goodness. She really needs you."

"I'll be there in four hours or so. I just need to sort a few wee things out here. Did someone call Karen or Shane?"

"I did. I called Karen. She's on her way. Eh…to be honest I didn't call Shane. I don't think that he's been in touch with Celine much so I thought that I might leave it to Karen to contact him."

"That bastard Joe is inside wee Shane's head. Always has been. He's pulling his strings."

After I hung up I wondered at the contrast between Celine's measured way of talking and her sister's plain-speak. I had been measured myself in what I had revealed to Jacinta about what Joseph had done to Celine. I hoped that I hadn't said too much by telling her that Shane hadn't been in touch much. I knew from Celine that Shane and she hadn't spoken in the two years since she had taken out the barring order against his father.

The barring order! A new one needed to be applied for. Would Celine's solicitor take instructions from me? Probably not. Perhaps he might with a call from Patrick, as one solicitor to another. I called Patrick in the office. He was naturally very concerned about Celine. He promised to do what he could, including sorting it out himself if necessary. Patrick was always someone you'd call in a crisis, especially a legal crisis.

Chapter 5

After the Dinner Party

Late June 2018

With Isabel and Gavin gone in their separate taxis, Celine busied herself clearing the table and sorting the kitchen. I stood up to help but found myself frozen at the kitchen door listening to Patrick moving around upstairs.

I envisaged him packing his clothes neatly, one item at a time. When he was angry or frustrated, he moved slowly and methodically. I had often tried to replicate this habit but with mixed success. I could do 'calm in time of crisis' most days, as long as it was someone else's crisis. Patrick seemed to do it regardless of how personal the situation was. Another habit he had was silences. That was a habit which I had vowed never to replicate. When there was something bothering him, he let it fester and brew, often allowing it to grow into something more than it might have been. Early in our relationship, his silences had sent me into overdrive and I would yell at him "For God's sake. What's eating you? How'll I ever know if you don't bloody tell me?" It took me a long time to learn that yelling at him only drove him in to a deeper silence; before we married, I had come slowly to the realisation that the answer lay in a period of quiet acceptance on my part, followed by the two of us having a slow meal out. Over a leisurely dinner and a few glasses of wine, I could subtly prise out of him the source of his anguish. It could be his father, work, finances, or anything. I learned to listen quietly, not to question the veracity of his version of what had triggered his bad humour, even when I had my doubts that he was the entirely innocent party that he painted himself to be. I was seldom the source of those bad humours or if I was, perhaps, it was that he did not always tell me. Whatever the cause of his silences, talking lifted him out of it and it united us.

Early in our relationship when something bothered me, I had let it sit too briefly and I would say it out loud and unadorned. It could be something small that might set me off, like Patrick adding a new shirt to the ironing pile, just when I had the ironing board folded and was ready to put the iron away, or that every time I went to lay the table for lunch or dinner the sports or business pages of the newspapers would be spread across it. There were times that I had wanted him to shout back, knowing I deserved it, but he rarely did. Over time, through sheer determination to bring the children up in relative peace, relative to what I had grown up in, I became less explosive and more measured in how I dealt with things. When the children were young and on up into their teens, I had my say but I only yelled at them or at Patrick on rare occasions.

Unfortunately, for all of us, I had reverted to my old full-on yelling form when midlife and lack of hormones threatened my sanity. Flying off the handle for silly reasons, real or imagined, became part of what I was.

"Who left those dirty dishes on the cooker? Who left this mess in the kitchen…in the sitting room…in the bathroom?" were common complaints of mine. There was one time in the not-too-distant past, but before my hormones had hit the fan, I had lifted the lid on a dirty saucepan and a frog jumped out. I yelped. Matt and Fiona laughed. Zara went ballistic at the cruelty to the frog and went scurrying after it. Patrick said nothing and managed to maintain an almost straight face until I actually burst out laughing. Then laughing became something that no longer came easily to me.

"Why is the laundry basket overflowing and nobody thought to put on a wash?"

"How many towels does it take to dry one body and one head of hair?"

I rarely got a response to any of these questions and if I did it was usually a provocative smart one from Matt like "Laundry is women's work" or "who said it was only one body? There may have been more…you never know."

That I had said nothing about Patrick's affair for nearly six months was an unprecedented move for me. I had plodded through those months with the prime purpose of allowing Zara to get through her dreaded Leaving Cert exams without having to face the trauma of Patrick and me splitting up. It had taken every ounce of my emotional strength but I had even worked at being supportive to her. When she studied, I praised her. When she partied, I had bitten my tongue and suggested that she take it easy on the drink and come home earlier than she might have. I had cooked good vegan food that she liked and approved of. I had tried to create a decent atmosphere for her to study in with less bickering and more calm. I succeeded some of the time but I was living in an emotional minefield with all that was going on in my head and in the lives of the people around me. I guess that, to survive this minefield, I had gone into a zombie-like state of emotional shutdown that brought on a sense of an imminent meltdown happening inside me, starting at my core but slowly, despite my best efforts, making its way to my outer being, at which point I expected to implode. But I couldn't implode, not until Zara had done her Leaving Cert and I had held my planned dinner party.

I had concluded Patrick had had an affair because he no longer loved me. He had put up with me for longer than I deserved. It followed that our marriage was over and therefore our beautiful Victorian home would have to be sold. Neither of us would be likely to move into one of the three houses that we had bought-to-let during the Celtic Tiger. They were in the wrong location for us. But with more than twelve years paid on the mortgages, they were at least out of negative equity. They too could be sold.

I had concluded that if we were going to sell our house, it needed a facelift. And whenever the matter of our failed marriage pushed its way to the forefront of my brain, I forced my mind to focus on my home improvement project with the objective being to give the main rooms a thorough but economical makeover, ready to make a positive impression on potential buyers. I had planned it all carefully for minimum disruption. In between times I had supported Celine as she considered her options regarding the serious assault charges against her now ex-husband. With all that she was going through I curtailed my rants and comments to her about my own family situation. For the most part I screamed and cried alone. After all that, the energy that I had left went primarily on keeping the house and, to a lesser extent, the business in order, putting proper meals on the table at allotted times and looking after our ageing parents, Patrick's father in particular.

Throughout those six months before the dinner party, I had determined that it was easier for me to say nothing to my wonderful and supportive friends Máire and her mum, Mrs O'Reilly, and not even to my mum. I used my very busy life as an excuse to avoid Máire and Mrs O'Reilly and I put huge effort into giving nothing away to Mum. She and Fergal were heading off on a long cruise to warmer climates. She had recovered well from the previous year's second hip operation and they were determined to travel while health permitted. They were going to have their every need met, sailing on a four-star cruise in the Caribbean, cheaper than a nursing home and better food and freedom, she said. Then they were stopping off in America to spend time with their sons, my two half-brothers, who were living there with their young families. When Mum spoke about my half-brothers living in America, she added words like "hopefully only temporarily", and she always blessed herself – right hand to the forehead, chest, left shoulder, right shoulder, then hands together prayerfully, willing them to come home and leave that gun-carrying country with its narcissist sociopath president. Having been reared in a Protestant family, I was bemused by the act of her, my own biological mother, blessing herself. She and my half-brothers were born and bred Catholics, or Roman Catholics as we Protestants would say. But religion never came between Mum and me. We valued each other too much for that.

By not telling Mum, I had told myself I was sparing her the problem, sparing her from wondering if she could go on her planned travels when my marriage was falling apart. But maybe that wasn't true. Maybe I didn't want her to try to use her perspective to convince me to rethink my response to the affair. I had doubted that I ever deserved Patrick; that he had put up with me as long as he had was a miracle; that he had had an affair could only mean one thing, he'd had enough. And I couldn't blame him.

As I listened to Patrick packing and moving around upstairs that night, my subconscious mind must have been looking for an excuse to reach out to him. I can think of no other reason why I remembered the dry-cleaning tickets that I had for two of his suits and ties. I took the tickets out of my purse and I walked into the hall as soon as I heard him walking down the stairs.

"You'll need these," I said, holding the tickets out to him.

"What?" He looked perplexed.

"Your dry-cleaning tickets."

"Oh."

Our hands touched and neither of us pulled away. I looked into the pools of his normally clear blue eyes, they looked bloodshot from crying. Patrick never cried. He looked at me, perhaps imploring me to change my mind, perhaps resigned to his departure. Either way, years of unifying love lingered between us. It was not what I had anticipated when I planned the night. My chest and head were filled to bursting with unplanned emotions. If Patrick had reached for me in that moment, I would have struggled to refuse him.

The tickets floated to the ground. He lowered himself to his hunkers and picked them up. His eyes remained locked with mine. I felt overwhelmed with confusion.

"I'm sorry Martha," he said.

"Me too," I said, wanting to say more, wanting to say, stay, don't go...

He took a step towards me, paused and stepped back.

"I'd best go. Seamus is expecting me."

"Okay."

"See you."

He turned. He walked out the door pulling two suitcases behind him and a large bag over his shoulder. His departure took the oxygen from the air. See you, I responded. But the words didn't make it to my lips.

I crumbled to the ground. My head hurt, my heart hurt, the core of my being hurt. Celine knelt beside me, her hand on my back. I sobbed until I retched. I crawled to the downstairs bathroom and threw up with Celine by my side.

This was not how it was supposed to be. I was going to feel relief once I had brought the whole bloody affair out in the open. I was going to knock back a few drinks and look forward to embracing the freedom of single life, unhindered by a wayward, overworked husband.

Celine cleared the rest of the table, leaving a place laid for each of us. I put two plates of dinner in the oven to heat up. She had loaded the dishwasher and wiped down the counters. I rearranged the dishwasher my way; I couldn't help myself. Then I filled our wine glasses. Mine to the brim with Rioja, Celine's with Pellegrino water. Celine said nothing and filled a large glass with water for me. I again offered her wine. She shook her head.

"Not tonight, Martha."

I put our reheated dinners back on the table and we sat down. We were just two friends having dinner together sitting under some emotional dark cloud.

I chewed on a mouthful of food, slowly, until I could swallow it down. I gulped some water.

"A good wee friend of mine told me, more than once, that it is important to eat properly when you are going through a difficult time."

"Sensible friend…I hope she will heed her own advice." I sighed and shook my head thinking advice is easy given but harder to take, especially when your world is falling apart.

"I wouldn't be where I am today without her."

"Me neither," I said.

We clinked glasses but my heart was elsewhere, wondering where it belonged.

Celine offered to stay over that night. I said no, I have to get used to it, this is how it will be. I refused myself a sleeping tablet. Tonight is the first night of the rest of my life, I just need to adjust my programming, change how I feel, learn not to feel sad that my only companion in bed was Saturday's newspaper; I had brought it upstairs with me and spread it out across Patrick's empty side of our big bed. I picked up the cultural section and looked at the pictures. I considered the possibility of Celine and I getting dressed up, 1920s style, and going to the play *The Great Gatsby* which was running in some obscure location in London. But I dismissed it as too depressing a storyline. I looked through the TV guide for the next week but nothing appealed to my current mood. I turned off the light and did my equivalent of counting sheep. I imagined an extended ending for the most recent movie that I had seen, *Good Will Hunting*. I had watched it alone in our sitting room with the stove lit and a glass of wine in my hand. The psychologist's love for his dead wife inspired Will to follow his heart. But I couldn't find a romantic thought in my head to take the story beyond its on-screen ending. I fell asleep anyway.

I got up to go to the bathroom during the night. As I sat on the toilet, I considered that I no longer had to worry about disturbing anyone. I could turn on lights and there was nobody there to care. I wanted someone to care.

I went back to bed and my mind got stuck in a cycle of replay and rewind. I wished that I could rewind back to when I had decided on my plan to say and do nothing until after Zara's Leaving Cert. It was a terrible idea and far too late in the day to be rethinking it, especially after all that I had said and done at the dinner party. Then I thought, as I had so often thought before, of all the years that I had put up with Isabel, the conniving bitch; she'd been a bitch, right back to our days in boarding school. I had enabled her then by never standing up to her. And I did it again as an adult. I never should have let her weasel her way back into my life. But I had and I had kowtowed to her and sucked up to her, like an eejit in need of her approval. How pathetic was that?

If Patrick had stood up at the dinner table that night and said something like, "I made a mistake. I'm sorry. I love Martha. I promised

Martha I would be there for her. I want to be there for her," that might have made all the difference. Then again it might not. We will never know. He slept with Isabel. He had sex with her. A vision of her naked, plump body stretched in some sexual pose on white cotton sheets came to me. I visualised her large, voluptuous, bare breasts and thought of my own modest breasts and I hit my hands against my thighs trying to slap away my feelings of inadequacy. He doesn't love you, Martha. He doesn't want to be with you. He was relieved. I want to be wanted. I need to believe I am loved and wanted. I want to be wanted for being me. I grew up as the unwanted accident in a family dominated by a woman who saw me as no more than her skivvy. Patrick knew what it had taken for me to accept his love. He knew what it had taken to allow myself to love him and to trust him. He had broken that trust. He knew how much that would hurt. He had made choices. I was no longer the one he chose.

I had chosen to bring everything out into the open over dinner because I had wanted to see Isabel squirm, in revenge for all the times that she'd made me squirm. For the years of put-downs, I owed her. I still remember the first time she belittled me for all to see and hear. It had been in accounting class and I had got the answer wrong to a simple question because I couldn't read the blackboard for want of a new pair of glasses. Isabel had refused to let me borrow her glasses for the few minutes it would have taken me to read the board. She had deliberately put them back in her school bag when I asked for them. The teacher waited patiently for me to say the answer. The longer she waited the more I squinted and panicked but the numbers did not come into focus. Eventually, I spurted out some random number that bore no relationship to the correct answer. Isabel burst out laughing. "Well done, Martha, they should have you running Quinnsworth – then the local supermarkets wouldn't have anything to worry about!" The whole class laughed. Isabel smirked and took her glasses back out of her bag and put them on, pushing them back up her nose as if to confirm her superior intelligence. Years of opportunistic put-downs followed. I was an easy target. I had no quick answers; I wore out-of-date hand-me-downs; I walked like a duck; I couldn't see properly until I got new lenses for my government-issued glasses that looked like they came from the Soviet Era; I bumped into things, with or without my glasses; nice teachers liked me – perhaps that was my biggest sin. On and on it went. I was glad to see the back of her when secondary school was over for me. Then somehow her only child, Melanie, and Fiona ended up in the same Montessori and Isabel was back in my life and I was collecting *her* Melanie from school when Isabel's childminder was out sick or whatever. Then Patrick ended up doing business with her, she became a goddess in the banking world and in between using me, she abused me, just as she had before. My clothes were hick, my car was an oversized heap of remodelled metal, the secondary school my children went to was for dope smokers and working-class wasters…the list went on.

"I don't understand why you still let her," Patrick said on one rare occasion that he responded to one of my rants. I didn't know why either, other than I didn't know how not to. The dinner party was my way of saying fuck off out of my life, Isabel, once and for all. She may have had an affair with my husband but I was going to make sure that she didn't manage to also stay married and continue to milk the innocent Gavin.

Isabel. I hate the name. Knock, knock. Who's there? Isabel. Isabel who? Is-a-bel necessary on a bicycle? Isabel necessary in your life? No. Never again.

I fell back asleep with tears and sweat stinging the psoriasis in my scalp and at the side of my eyes. Until menopause I only had scalp psoriasis. Now it was in my eyebrows and the outer corners of my eyes. Something else to add to the list of woes that I had to get used to.

I tossed and turned and sweated the night away. I finally woke after 8 o'clock and I felt spent, as if I had not slept at all. I dragged myself to sit up and take in what was different. There was an empty space on Patrick's bedside locker where his book and alarm clock had been. His side of the bed was perfectly flat and untouched except by the newspapers. There was no sign of life to be seen or heard in the house. A feeling of sorrow hung in the air. I inhaled it. It came with me down the stairs to the kitchen where the garlic aromas of last night's dinner lingered. I was the tragic sole survivor of a catastrophe. I was the perpetrator of the catastrophe. I was lonely. I was alone. Over the previous months, these were the feelings that had been creeping over every part of me, working their way into my soul. Now they were all that was left. It was how it was going to be. Alone. Lonely. Unwanted. Unneeded.

Fiona, Matt and Zara, they will blame me for the disintegration of our marriage. I should have tried harder. I should have gone on HRT, got over my hormone crisis by throwing more artificial hormones at the situation. I should have confronted Patrick about the affair when I found out about it. I should have sought marriage counselling. I could hear them – build a bridge, Mum, that is what you always told us to do. Yeah, but…some bridges are easier to build than others.

A poison had set in me the moment I realised there was an affair. Despite my many distractions, the poison had defined me for the last six months. At first, I had ranted and raged, especially when I was alone; I was catty and sarcastic with everyone in the house; I snapped at the slightest affront. This went on for the first couple months.

Then one time Matt had got up from the table leaving behind his breakfast bowl, mug and coffee pot and I screamed in an ugly, shrill, angry voice, "Matt," at him as he left the kitchen. He came back a couple of minutes later.

"Mum, I was going to the bathroom. I was coming back." He paused making sure that I was listening. "Mum, I'm worried about you. You seem to be losing it with everyone for every little thing these days. It makes the atmosphere in the house very tense. Perhaps you need to think about doing something about it."

Matt could get away with saying things like that to me. I'd have had a full-blown row with any of the others if they had said half of what he said.

I resolved to scream less and feign better humour. That was when I started to enter my emotional zombie phase.

The whole emotional mess had begun when I had unwittingly smelt Isabel's perfume on Patrick a number of times before the end of last year. I had registered it as a familiar smell that conjured up a bad feeling within me. I had not fully processed it until I bumped into her in Aldi. Aldi, of all places. Isabel had me believe that she was more of a Marks and Spencer's person. I have no idea what she said to me or what I said to her as we stood amongst the half-priced Christmas stock. The smell of her wafted into my brain and set off an explosion in my head. It stopped my heart and silenced my tongue. It screamed at me, Isabel is having an affair with my husband. The evil bitch. Isabel, take that cat-that-got-the-cream look off your face before I fucking wipe it off. I had stared at her with deep felt hatred as I thought these thoughts. Then I'd turned and sped away.

With only half my grocery shopping done, I had charged with my trolley to the cash desk, thrown the groceries into my bags and paid. Another customer came after me with my credit card. I hope that I thanked her. I have no memory of driving home. There was no one there. I shoved the groceries into the fridge and cupboards. I stamped my way up to the bedroom and lay down. My heart and head were pounding hard and fast. My skull and chest were not big enough for them.

Isabel and Patrick had had a business relationship during the boom years. She had been Head of Lending in SIB. But SIB was no more. It had long since imploded with a bang due to excessive lending to an over-inflated property market. Why would they be meeting? Back when he used to meet her for business, he used to tell me. Back then, he didn't come home reeking of her perfume.

Yes, we had had some shitty years when the bubble had burst but we had worked together and, overall, I thought that we had weathered them well.

After the crash Patrick had to work harder and harder to keep his business and his clients afloat. Most clients had no money to pay his fees.

"They paid me well during the good times. I will stand by them through the bad," he said. I didn't object to this. I agreed with it, in theory. "Despite their best efforts we must accept that some will still fail but I'll do what I can for them," he added, as if convincing himself as much as me of the need to accept the inevitable failures.

"The cute hoors will survive or better and they won't be prioritising paying their hardworking solicitor his long overdue fees. They'll be swanning around in their big, shiny Mercedes with their children still in private schools and their racehorses still in training. Just you wait and see," I said.

"You're too cynical sometimes, Martha," he had said, putting an arm tightly around me. "But I love you."

Fee income had gone into a downward spiral. We could have just about coped if it wasn't that Patrick, like so many other solicitors, hadn't bought into his clients' belief in the endless nature of the property boom. When the crash hit, we had found ourselves with three houses in negative equity. Keeping all three of these houses paying rent had been a constant struggle. Invariably tenants lost their jobs and couldn't make the payments. It broke our hearts that we couldn't afford to let them stay on at rents they could afford on their unemployment benefit or under some other government scheme. At full rent there was still a cash requirement to meet the mortgages and the inevitable repair and maintenance expenses. It was like pulling hen's teeth to find enough money each month to meet our necessary outgoings. It could have been worse. We had tracker mortgages and the base interest rate was at a record low. It would have been a whole lot worse if we'd breached these mortgages and lost our tracker rate, or worse again if these mortgages had been called in and we couldn't settle the loans. Then we could've lost everything. Patrick's solicitor's practising certificate would be immediately and automatically suspended if he was adjudicated bankrupt.

Paying off the mortgage on our home was the best thing that we had done in the boom years. We had bought the house near the bottom of the market well before the Celtic Tiger let out a roar. Our good timing had been luck, not design. Back when Matt came along nearly four years after Fiona, I had still been doing accounting work for clients from home and we were running out of rooms as I used our third bedroom as an office. I took to pushing the buggy with Matt in it and with Fiona trotting beside me or on the buggy board, around our area in search of a larger house that we could afford and that we could make a home. Eventually, I fell for a neglected, damp-ridden, Victorian house of character. It had been owned by two spinster sisters who had a path worn to mass in the local church. There were miraculous medals pinned to every curtain. The architect declared them ineffective against the dry rot and wet rot. The house would have to be gutted. There were only two bidders willing to even consider it. Ourselves and a builder. That spoke volumes about the state of the place. The bank offered us a twenty-year mortgage, as was normal back then. That was back in the less intense days, when we didn't all sit around at charity balls and dinner parties discussing mortgages, rents, so-called builders and property prices.

We were able to close the deal on a Friday and have honest, decent builders start the following Monday. Five months later we sold our small three-bedroomed, terraced house and moved into the parts of our new house that the builders were no longer occupying. When the builders were having their afternoon tea breaks, Fiona sat with her milky tea and interrogated them all. Did they have wives? How many children did they have? Did they read bedtime stories to their kids? Matt became Bob the Builder and went around hammering everything. In the interest of equality, I got Fiona a hammer too. She hit Matt on the head with it when he put marker on her doll's face. Chaos ruled but it was a happy chaos. How I managed to get any work done in the midst of it all still baffles me. Fiona and Matt were only at childcare or playschool for four hours of the day. Mum was my saviour. That was some twenty years ago; when she was young and healthy and more than willing to help.

"Martha, that is what grandmothers are for. Minding and spoiling the grandchildren. They keep me young and laughing. Fergal, or Pops as they love to call him, loves them too."

"But Mum…"

"I missed watching you grow up. I am determined to enjoy every minute I can get watching my grandchildren grow up."

I was lucky then. My half-brothers were years younger than me and had a lot of living to do before they settled down. There were no other grandchildren then to compete for my stepdad and Mum's loving attention.

Our house cost us all of IR£200,000, including purchase price, renovation and small extension – €254,000 in new money. I remember because I managed it all on a tight budget. Five years later, you could barely buy a one-bedroom shoebox in Dublin for that. Each of the three-bedroom houses that Patrick had bought direct from his builder clients had cost us much more than what our home had cost us. The price of decorating and furnishing them had been similarly exorbitant.

I hated the Celtic Tiger boom years. The fake years. I never wanted a statement four-by-four which all the yummy mummies of Dublin were jamming up the tarmacadamed streets of the city with. I bought a two-year-old, safe and sound, good-as-new, seven-seater car when Zara was eight. It fitted a significant number of Matt's soccer or GAA team and later Zara's basketball team, and it fitted comfortably between the white lines of a normal parking space. Unlike the owners of posh cars like BMWs and Mercedes, I didn't need to park my car in the disabled spot or across yellow lines while I ran into the drycleaners to collect my designer dress for the next charity ball. We avoided most of those balls, going only to those we chose to go to, with good friends and for causes that we cared about.

"Oh Mum, would you not have got a new car, one with this year's registration numbers?" the pre-vegan Zara asked in disgust.

"Why?"

"Because everyone else has a new car. Isabel's one is massive."

"If everyone, including Isabel, wants to waste their money or their bank's money on a new car, then that's their problem. I am not making it mine." I could do arrogant, from my perch on the high moral ground.

How could we stay grounded while fighting our way through the gush brought on by people's latest designer purchases or exotic holidays? We lost the battle. We got sucked in too. Banks and developers flew us on weekends away to golf, the races, a show in London…We were hanging out with people we would previously have crossed the street to avoid. The conversations among the women I was invariably stuck with were on repeat. Builders, decorators, designer clothes,

Gammy Shoes, private schools, Little Johnny's try for the JCTs, Little Johnny taking all sorts of supplements so that he might become Big Johnny. Rugby became the sport of choice to talk about. Good Catholic women reared on a strict diet of GAA and Sunday mass abandoned football and hurling. Religion got sidelined, except when it came to getting baptised to get into the right schools or organising designer communions, over-the-top confirmations and statement weddings. The nouveau riche women and men became rugby aficionados who knew the difference between a forward pass and a backward glance.

Chapter 6

Trish, from boom to bust

2008 – 2011 and beyond

Throughout the gush of the Celtic Tiger, we were pulled back from the false reality of it by Trish, my closest friend. She continuously reminded us that the rising financial tide didn't raise all boats. Trish was the first true Dub I'd ever known. I used to joke that on the days that Dublin played a match she always wore Dublin's blue jersey but when they lost a match, she could be blue for a week. Trish was the best friend I ever had and could ever hope to have. She was a Dub to her roots. For more generations than she cared to count, her family had been from the Liberties, an area in the city centre with loads of heart, less money and no pretensions. Her small family house there was the first place that I felt at home. I loved the chaotic ease of it: always busy; always warm; always welcoming.

Trish had been healthy and well through the boom years. She remained active as a volunteer with the charity Vincent de Paul. She met plenty of people who were left on the bottom, still struggling to make ends meet, struggling to buy the school uniforms and necessary latest editions of the same old school books. These were not luxuries. Schools required proper school uniforms and school uniforms made it slightly more difficult to tell the haves from the have-nots. Old editions of school books had the same information as new editions but on different pages. How could you follow what your teacher was saying if you were on a different page to her? Trish was vociferous in her loathing of the money that was wasted by so-called society women as they kept up with the latest designer gear while others struggled to keep their families fed, clothed and in the 'right' school books. She was known to turn off her wonderful Dublin accent and do a mean mimic of Foxrock Fannies, tottering on their Gammy Shoes, greeting their fellow Foxrock Fannies, fresh out of the designer handbag section of Brown Thomas's.

"O.M.G. it's beautiful. So worth the three-month wait."

"Not to mention the spondulicks, only two and a half grand. It is five hundred more than Melanie paid for hers. But so worth it. I mean look at it. It is at least two shades darker than Melanie's!"

During the Tiger years, these women had so much money that they could afford to wear whatever they liked, but instead they all looked the same with their cake-a-make-up, bleached blonde hair and their own exclusive group's designer uniforms. Their jeans or tracksuits had the same designer names sprawled across their asses. The writing seemed to get bigger each season, or was it their asses expanding to fill their bigger car seats? Trish and I couldn't decide.

When the proverbial shit hit the fan and austerity hit the people, some of these women left their Gammy Shoes in the shoe menders. There were no occasions to wear them to or else they couldn't afford to pay the shoe mender as their owners struggled to live off their husband's reduced salaries, or worse, social welfare. Many of those who had populated charity events were reduced to needing charity. We could have been there with them if the mortgages on those three houses had not been for the low interest rates that held low for all the years of the downturn and well beyond. Even with these favourable interest rates on our investment properties and no mortgage on our home, time and time again we scraped the bottom of every barrel to meet our necessary monthly outgoings.

Then, just when I'd heave a sigh of relief at managing to pay another month's expenses, a tax bill would need to be paid – bi-monthly VAT due for the practice or income tax due on rental income. It killed me that the tax payable on rental income bore no relationship to a landlord's reality. The property expenses that were allowed were minimal and took no regard that, not only had loan interest to be paid, but we had to repay the loan itself too. Cash was king. We would have hit the wall if I had not regularly dipped into a small trust fund that my father had left me.

Patrick and I talked work and lack of money over breakfast and dinner and any other meal or cup of coffee that we had together.

"Do you think Johnny Connolly might be good for a few thousand this month, Patrick?"

"Maybe so. Try Mick Collins too. His forestry money came through this week."

"I'll chase him as well so."

I went back to shovelling spaghetti bolognaise into my mouth in a haste that had become my habit. In between slurps I mumbled, "How is school, folks?"

"I don't think that you will get any money from them…" Matt said.

"Huh? Sorry?"

"Oh, you mean school, school. Silly me. I thought meal times were just for discussing filthy lucre!"

That made me stop my shovelling. Matt had a point. I looked at Patrick and raised my eyebrows at him. He nodded.

"I'm sorry, Matt. I'm really sorry all of you…you're right…" I felt tears of guilt fill my eyes.

"I'm sorry too," Patrick added. "Things are just so difficult at the moment but…"

I gathered myself together. The children didn't need our excuses. "But Matt is right. We shouldn't talk about it at meals times. Please, please tell us how are things at school?"

"Matt scored two goals in the second round of the schools' hockey cup match yesterday. And Mr Brown said that those two goals were worth four as they were against Saint Colm's, a southside private school who are favourites, as always, to win the cup…" Fiona replied.

"We still lost," Matt said, but he smiled.

"I'm sorry we missed it, Matt," Patrick said, putting his hand on Matt's shoulder.

"Tell them, Fiona. Tell them. Or I will," Zara said excitedly.

"You tell them so."

"Fiona got sixth year Pupil of the Year, beating Susan McGrane, no less."

"Wow Fiona. That's fantastic. Well done," I said, feeling proud but horrible that these key events in our children's lives had nearly passed us by.

"And I got Wednesday detention because I was late for Ms Geary's class because Mr Walsh asked me to bring a new first year to sick bay. It's not fair."

"I'm sorry to hear that, Zara."

"It doesn't matter. It's just like free supervised study. I did my homework."

That conversation had been a wake-up call for Patrick and me. Matt did us a favour. For the rest of the recession and beyond, family meals were for non-financial family matters. When I look back on those times now, I realise that I had become obsessive about the business and getting in money to avoid facing other sad changes in my life, changes that I had no control over.

I resented what the recession did to us. I resented the energy it sucked from us. But most of all I resented that at the height of it, Trish, my best friend, died. Trish, who took no nonsense from anyone but would rise a laugh out of the darkest moments, had a relapse of her cancer and, after putting up the fight of her life, died. Every time I said her name I swallowed hard; I had developed a long-established habit of pushing the grief back down into the pit of my being. The good die young. I am convinced that the poison in the mean and miserable acts as a preservative. They live forever or they make others so miserable that it feels that way. Trish was my best friend for twenty-five years. It was too short. We were supposed to grow old together. We had plans. Right up to the day she died we still made plans, as if we were going to live into late old age, happily disorientated to the point where we thought that we were young and beautiful and heading out for a mad night on the town. In between these times of denying reality, we talked about her death, I helped her plan her funeral. She would have pre-recorded the whole thing if she could. I joked that what was killing her was the thought of missing her own funeral. It couldn't happen without her but unfortunately, she had to be dead. My tongue-in-cheek suggested solution was to have a party for her and invite all her closest friends and her family.

"Fair fuck's, Martha. That'd be pure class. We will have a pre-funeral, with a live corpse. You can ask everyone to pretend it is me real funeral and I can play the ghost, listening in on what they might be sayin'."

Poor Trish's husband, Páidí, burst into tears at this suggestion. He had to leave the room while we made plans.

"I'm the one who's bleedin' dying. Wait'll I tell ya he's already goin' for grievance counselling, reiki and whatever yer havin' yerself. Seriously, can't I just have what I want for the next few weeks? I'll be out of his hair soon enough."

"Oh Trish, let me talk to him. It's hard for him too. He adores you. He doesn't want you out of the bit of hair he has left…any more than I do." Trish, in death, had that way of making me feel as if I might laugh or cry, or both, at any minute.

"I know, hun, but humour a dying girl or I might have to actually turn up at me own real funeral."

"Oh Trish. They can't have the funeral without you, you goose."

"Soon-to-be dead goose!"

The pre-funeral was the weirdest party ever. I never ever laughed and cried more in a few hours. Trish was pumped up on steroids and enough morphine to keep her compos mentis but almost pain free. She did suggest that she might attend the party in a coffin and eavesdrop on everyone for a while before she would rise from the dead one last time, as she put it. Death brought out the macabre in her. I wasn't sure if playing the corpse was entirely in jest. When I told her mother, she said that she fully expected her to do such a thing. She had chosen her coffin and I heard that she did make a call to the undertaker asking her if she could use it in advance of the big day. She was to call back to finalise the arrangement but much to the undertaker's mild relief, she hadn't. The undertaker was a carefully chosen woman, Mary Staffon, who always did her best to deliver her clients' wishes. If Trish had persisted with her request, I am sure that Mary would have delivered on it.

Three weeks after the party, Trish died and a few days later we had the funeral proper. The staff salaries were due for payment and there was no cash in the bank. We had already drained the reserves we had built up during the good years. And I couldn't access on short notice what was left in the small trust fund my father had left me. While Trish and I had been imagining our lives after her cancer, knowing that there would be no life for Trish after cancer, the economy had continued bumping slowly along. Property prices were still on the floor. Unoccupied, half-finished housing estates, set beside miserable little small-minded towns, littered the countryside, towns where nobody, other than locals who knew no better, would choose to call home. Businesses were still closing. Banks had failed and been rescued by the government which had been rescued by the ECB and the IMF. Developers across the country couldn't give their housing estates and apartment blocks away. Clients couldn't pay us the fees they owed. We couldn't pay staff.

We had no time to grieve. Patrick and I spent the days after Trish's funeral ringing clients, calling in every bit of cash that they could afford to give us. Chasing fees became part of my daily life. I hated it and I lacked the charm for it. Some of the developers who had jumped up from the country during the boom years wouldn't talk business to me, a woman who spoke complete sentences in proper English. Maybe they were just stalling but when I asked for some small payment on some long overdue bill, they would ask me how're the children or how's the parents keepin'. I hated them for that.

"They would be all the better if I could be at home looking after them instead of spending my time here begging clients for payment of long-overdue fees," I responded to one particularly arrogant client who hadn't paid us a penny off a €25,000 bill in over a year.

"There he is with all his children still in private schools, including two in a private primary school no less, and he won't pay us tuppence," I told Patrick.

"What can we do, Martha, he has it all in separate companies. I know, I helped him set it up."

"And he has ten horses still in training and is still hopping to the races by chauffeur-driven Merc," I added. "Out of common decency alone he could pay us a few grand."

That same man had never taken a call from me again. He rarely answered Patrick's calls either. In all the years of pain for us and most of the rest of the population, he and some of his cohorts continued to live their lives as if the good times still rolled. Nothing had changed for them. Paying debts is only for the little people, who have little debts.

Slowly things changed. The country came out of austerity. House prices in Dublin soared again. Not enough houses were being built. There were too few houses available to buy or rent. Rents soared. We were the lucky ones.

Unbelievably, and against everything I felt might happen, Patrick and I were coming out the other side of the crisis technically solvent. In the bad years, we had been paid full rent on our houses at best ten and a half months of each year. When the economy went back into growth mode, we got paid ridiculously high rents twelve months of the year. If a family was leaving one of our houses, which was rare, then another family would be falling over them to get into it. A different sort of housing crisis had happened. Developers were back building and they couldn't or wouldn't keep up with demand. In the bad old days of the crash, eighty per cent of Patrick's clients had struggled to pay their fees. Now the reverse was true. Eighty per cent of clients could and were paying promptly. Financially speaking, we had weathered the storm.

But it seemed our marriage hadn't.

I had hated the boom times when they were with us. I hated the gush and insincerity of them. I had hated how everyone was so busy doing things that didn't matter. I hated it all even more when it ended. The recession robbed us financially but, more than that, it robbed us of normal conversations as a couple and a family and it robbed me of the time to grieve the loss of my best friend. Everything became about trying to save Patrick's legal practice. I worked all the spare time I could find in the office. I regularly trawled through every business expense item making sure nothing was wasted. I had kept this habit up long after the danger had passed and the business was back in profit and positive cash flow. I had looked closely at all expenses right up to the night of that dinner party.

Six months before that dinner party, as I lay on our bed after meeting Isabel in Aldi, the sickly smell of her perfume still lingering in my nostrils, I remembered a few unexplained monthly payments that had been made from the firm's bank account. They were recorded as being to a vulture fund. They are not called vulture funds for nothing. They strip you clean to the bone and then come back for the flesh of your children. What was its name? It was religious sounding. Vespers. That was it. Patrick had dismissed my enquiries about the payments as mis-postings. He said that they related to the client account. I didn't get involved with the client account. That was Rita the legal secretary's area. I simply reviewed the monthly reconciliations that she prepared. After meeting the perfumed Isabel, I thought about it some more. No such payments had ever appeared on the reconciliations. Somehow these payments were related to her. I just knew it. I decided I would enquire some more.

When I was in the office the following Monday, I again asked Patrick about these payments. He mumbled something about a fellow Mayo-man and friend who needed a dig-out.

"Now that things are looking better for us I'm just chipping in enough to keep the wolves from his door. If he pays nothing the vulture fund will call in the loan and shut him down. You know, Martha, what will happen. He'll go bankrupt and lose everything. I'm just helping him buy time while he sorts things out."

Patrick's story didn't ring true. He was unusually vague but otherwise I couldn't work out why I didn't really believe it. In all my years of working in an accountancy practice, fraud and dishonesty normally seemed to go hand in hand with an affair. I had never concluded what came first. An affair or a fraud. Does getting away with the dishonesty

109

of an affair give one licence to defraud? Or does the expense of an affair drive one towards fraud? Or are people who commit frauds inherently dishonest and therefore more likely to have an affair? I have never worked it out.

Isabel had been a manipulative bitch for as long as I had known her. I would have been surprised if she hadn't had affairs, and I mean plural. She had boasted to me about one previous affair as if it was something else that I should add to a long list of things that she had achieved and I hadn't.

But Patrick was my husband. I didn't think that his dishonesty went beyond embellishing a good story to make it worthy of an attentive audience. I knew him. I loved him. He had earned my trust. We shared the same values. We didn't do affairs.

But it seemed that he did.

From that day in January when I met Isabel in Aldi, Patrick never mentioned that he met up with or heard from Isabel, yet from then until well into March, I saw a steady stream of texts that she sent him. Patrick didn't change his habits. He always put his phone on the high shelf in the kitchen when he came home and he only checked it occasionally. He often left it there, especially if he was watching a match or going upstairs to his office to work on something that required no disturbances. Every so often when he was out of the kitchen, I would check his phone and messages would pop up on the screen. I dropped his phone noisily onto the kitchen tiles the first time that I saw a text from her. I was lucky that I didn't crack the screen that time. Maybe it would have been better if I had.

Hello Sexy, you still on for our rendezvous on Tuesday? Usual place? You bring the wine. I'll bring myself. Xx Issy

Maybe, if I'd confronted him after that first text, things would not have got so out of hand. But in my defence, I would say that I was still slipping in and out of denial, a denial that was harder to sustain with each text that I saw and went out the window when a text like this arrived.

Hi Super stud, that was quite the night after the golf classic. So glad you could come up for a nightcap. 😊 😊 😊 I didn't mean to keep you UP so late! 😊 😊 And to think that you'd already played 18 holes and had as many drinks. Quite the impressive finish, don't you think? Xx Issy

That text came through on a Sunday evening. Patrick had arrived home the night before at six thirty in the morning and gone straight to the spare room, making a considerable amount of noise as he stumbled in the front door and around the house. He had spent until after midday in bed and, when he did get up, he had moved sheepishly and tentatively. I'd said good morning to him when he did appear and he'd rubbed his head in response. We hadn't spoken all afternoon as I'd gone out shopping with Fiona. I'd seen Isabel's text that evening while Patrick was in the bathroom. There it was, clear confirmation, slapping me full on in my face. It was as if Isabel had written it with a deliberation that hoped I would see it. That would be just like her. She was the sort who liked to rub my face in it. I came very close to confronting Patrick there and then and might have if he hadn't gone straight from the bathroom back up to bed in the spare room again. He mumbled something about feeling under the weather. He was feeling under the effing weather! How did he think I felt? I got as far as going halfway up the stairs after him but something held me back. I turned around, went back down the stairs, grabbed my coat and half ran all the way to the seafront. It was a filthy night and the rain whipped icily into my face, lashing my skin with small stinging hailstones. On I walked, pushing against the weather, until I got to the grey stone wall at the bridge. Fuck – my – life, were the words that I spat out as I brought my right foot back and kicked the wall with all the force I could muster. My toes hurt and I felt a strange relief, so I did it again, this time shouting the words into the empty darkness, FUCK – MY – LIFE. I turned and walked all the way back with the wind and rain on my back. I went straight to our bedroom and through gritted teeth and throbbing toes, I contemplated my next move. That night was when the idea of the dinner party first hit me. I was mad at Patrick. I was madder still at Isabel. Neither were going to be let off the hook.

Later that week I saw another text.

P Baby, how are you getting on with your homework? Have you told Martha yet? See you tomorrow. I've taken the liberty of booking room 351 at the Berkeley. Same room as Saturday night. See you there. Xx I

That was the last text that I ever saw from Isabel.

I had thought that I knew Patrick. I thought that he would never betray me. Circumstances had proved me wrong. My knowledge of him was not absolute. He was not who I had thought he was.

I was not who I thought I was. I was not the wife he was going to love until death us do part. The pain in my toes was nothing like the pain in the pit of my stomach. He wanted out. In keeping with his non-confrontational ways, he just hadn't told me. I decided that once Zara's Leaving Cert was over, out is what he would get. After many sleepless nights I decided that my solution to dealing with his affair was to say nothing until Zara had gone on her post-exam boozy holiday, then I would have Isabel and Gavin over for a dinner party and let everyone know the story. Isabel would not be left with the luxury of keeping her secret from Gavin. Everyone would know exactly where they stood.

But the anticipated post-dinner party clarity didn't happen. Afterwards I felt more uncertain than ever. If only Trish had still been alive, everything would have been different.

Chapter 7
A Day in Court

November 2016

There was an image in my head of what Joseph Mary Murphy would look like; it was not a fully formed image, but enough of one to know that he was tall and heavy, poorly shaven with untidy, thinning grey hair and beady eyes that darted everywhere.

An athletic looking, tanned man in a tailored grey suit and a crisp white shirt walked through the main door of the courthouse. His fine leather shoes clipped softly off the white marbled floor as he went past us. His hair was short and milk chocolate brown. He ticked all my boxes of tall, dark and handsome and I turned to Celine, about to say something corny and no doubt dated, like, I wouldn't kick him out of bed for eating crisps! I swallowed my words when I saw the look of terror on her face. Celine had become a shrunken, trembling version of herself.

"That's him," she whispered, her head bowed towards her feet.

"Where?"

She kept her head down, half lifted her right hand and pointed in the man's direction.

"That is Joseph Mary Murphy, the bastard."

"Terrifyingly handsome, the bastard," I said, gobsmacked. The image I had had of him in my head was so far from the man who stood before us.

"Aye, keeps a wee portrait in his attic," Celine said, without looking up, hiding her tiny face under her mop of grey hair. I'd have taken more than a few inches off it for her, if she'd let me, but I knew it was still her screen from the horrors of the world.

"The portrait in the attic is working for him." I sighed.

"Always dyes his hair. Works out regularly at the gym in work. And in preparation for his starring role in court today, he's no doubt off the sauce!"

"Butter wouldn't melt in his mouth," I said, casting my eye again in his direction.

"Aren't I the livin' proof?"

"Reminds me of a bad joke."

"I could do with a joke," Celine said unenthusiastically.

"What do you call a Northsider in a suit?"

"What?"

"The defendant."

Celine forced her face to crack a fraction of a smile.

"Sorry, not funny. In the eyes of the law, he's not even the defendant."

"No, today, he has nothing to defend." Celine bowed her head, sighed and spoke to her feet. "He's just a husband before the courts for a harmless judicial separation and, if I'm lucky, divorce. Today, he doesn't have to deny or defend his deeds and may never have to, unless I play my part in assault charges being brought against him. May God give me strength."

Celine and I had been over that possibility many times. I wanted to see the bastard nailed and, as I stood eyeing him in that courthouse, I wanted it even more now that I had seen his perfect false image. But the rational part of me feared that the pretrial process and the court case might retraumatise Celine and send her to a dark place from where she may never return. Since the day I had found her bruised and bloodied, I had become almost obsessed with reading reports and articles on cases involving sexual assault or rape. The statistics spoke for themselves. Few cases that went to trial ended in conviction or a serious sentence. Worse was that the cases that went to trial were only a small percentage, a drop in the ocean, of the number of rapes and assaults that actually happened.

The more I read the more furious I had become. The odds were stacked against the victims and in favour of the assailants. I wished I was a lawmaker, not a mere accountant. Celine reminded me that it was the accountants that got Al Capone on tax evasion when all else had failed. She said I'd done my bit by helping her prepare her Affidavit of Means and for that she was grateful.

"Pursuing assault charges, Celine, is for another day. First things fir—" I stopped. While talking I had taken a closer look at the said clean-shaven, sparkling white bastard. He had the brass neck to smile at me. His smile set off a multitude of reactions. To receive it made me feel like I was betraying Celine. It made my skin crawl. Worse, it triggered unexpected recognition. "Holy feck," I said, gasping for breath, "that's too bloody weird…I know him…I fecking do. I've met him before."

"He lived down the road from you for the guts of twenty years, Martha. Of course, you know him," Celine said as she repositioned herself so that I was between him and her.

I turned around to face her and looked over her head. The courthouse foyer was filling up with besuited men and women broken into small groups of three or more. The barristers were recognisable by their black suits, white shirts and silly split ties, like the ends of a black ribbon. I felt a tentative buzz in the air, suppressed by a fear that emanated from the many parties waiting to be called, waiting for their turn in one of the many court rooms, waiting to face a judge who may or may not hear what they had to say.

Celine's breathing was unsteady and her hands were trembling. I didn't dare turn around but as I thought of her husband standing close behind me, I shivered. It was as if I could feel his presence.

"Years ago, he gave me his seat in Rosie's pub while Patrick was up at the bar getting me a drink. And after that we chatted in the coffee shop down the road a few times…Celine, the hairs are tingling on the back of my neck. I mean it was him all along. Always in a pure white, perfectly ironed shirt."

"He has ten or more of them. Some he likes more than others. They were all the same to me except when I had to iron them."

"I can't believe it's him."

"You'd better believe it, Martha. Trust me, it's the white-shirted bastard. Those effing shirts. Once I was in bed with double pneumonia, he ran out of ironed white shirts. He dragged out the iron and ironed one himself. He finished getting dressed, stamped around the house and out to his car. The house shook to my bones as he slammed the door. I heard his engine start, I dared to breathe again. But the engine stopped." Celine paused and rubbed the side of her face as if itching to pull at her hair. "He ran up the path, pounded back in the front door, thumped up the stairs and into our room. He grabbed my mobile from the bedside table and threw it from the bedroom straight down the toilet in the ensuite. 'Bullseye!' he chirped and left the room. He cut the landline and went back out the door and off to work."

"Looking clean and smart and white. A pure saint of a bastard!"

"Just you watch him charm the judge off her perch." Celine moved to have another look at him and I looked too. He was talking to a grey-haired man dressed in a dated blue suit, a blue shirt and dark crested tie, none of which looked as if they had seen an iron for years. Beside them was an elegant lady in a black suit, white shirt and a silly tie. They were apparently his solicitor and barrister.

"I'd love to see him try to charm the judge but unfortunately, I'll be stuck out here."

"That effing in-camera rule! He'd sicken you to watch anyway. He'll sicken me, that's for sure."

"Celine, I'll be right outside, right here. Don't worry. The judge can't ignore all those medical reports showing all that he did to you, how he left you incapable of working." I spoke in hope rather than with conviction. The judge might not pay any heed to these things at all, regarding them as irrelevant in the context of a separation settlement.

"Look at him. The peacock. The beatings were blips in his past, he'll say. I've exaggerated them. He doesn't want a separation. He told Karen and Shane last week that he has never given up on us! He came over *that* night to ask me if he could move back home but seemingly, I lost the plot and accidents happen. All he wanted and still wants is *to move back home*! They are both convinced I am the problem, I am the she-devil!" She gulped and her voice went to a near whisper. "And perhaps that is how they will always see things."

I had heard it all from her before just the previous week, I just listened again. I made to hug her but she held up her hands, reminding me not to put my arms around her. She did not want the bastard to see her crying. It would remind him of the control that he had over her.

I knew he had claimed in correspondence between the solicitors that Celine had beaten *him* a few times. He said that he wouldn't press charges. The notion of tiny, delicate Celine beating the towering bastard was so preposterous that I had nearly wanted him to take a case. But the worst of it was that Shane had never phoned Celine since he came to see her that one time, a month after the beating. His father had Shane lapping out of the palm of his hand. Total manipulation and projection, the counsellor said, everything they do to others they accuse others of doing to them. It disarms the abused; it annihilates their sense of who they are; eventually the abused believes they are all that the abuser says they are; that they are nothing. It is the way of abusers, be they men or women: power and control by whatever means possible.

"I know, Celine. I know. But Shane might come around yet. And he is being played by his father."

"Yeah, the same man who will manipulate the judge and all and sundry. Just you wait."

"Maybe not. The solicitor and barrister Patrick got you won't let him away with it. They know the story."

"But the judge doesn't know the real story. What about her?" Celine was working herself into a frenzy. Her voice was getting smaller but more urgent. I was struggling to stay calm and positive myself but I was determined to hold it together.

"The judge could blow either way I'm told. Your barrister will handle that, Celine. He has plenty of experience and knows how to respond. He is optimistic that your situation speaks for itself. And your counsellor's report is pretty explicit too."

"He says I'll have to take the stand. He says to be myself. Say it as it was." She was pulling at small tufts of hair beside her ear. Her voice was shrinking to a whisper. I reached across to her and straightened the small colourful silk scarf around her neck. The bit of colour gave her face a lift and drew the eye away from the grey, faded dress that was far too big for the size of her.

"You can do it, Celine. Remember we agreed, it might do you some good. Prepare you for the next thing." My words sounded hollow as they tried to reach the trembling small woman in front of me.

"Yeah. I know. It's what my counsellor says. It's an opportunity to say it out loud in a safe environment, she says. A trial run before I pursue a sexual assault or rape case against him and have him put away for a long time. I wish. I think if he thought that I would pursue a case he'd have me dead and buried and nobody would ever find my body. But if I don't take a case…"

"I can see the merit of a punishment shooting…or a sharp knife." We were playing a game. We had played it many times before. We started with a possible assault case and then wished a punishment kneecapping on the bastard and then worked our way up to more gruesome and torturous possibilities such as cutting off his manhood and putting it in his mouth so that he might slowly gag on it. We would have his hands cut off too and have everything cauterised with red hot irons, to stem the bleeding enough so he would die slowly and painfully.

"A kneecapping would be too kind for him…"

"I am with you there." I nodded at a man and a woman walking in our direction. Celine had her back to them. "Here are Cathy and Paul, your legal team now," I said, putting my hands on her shoulders and looking into her tiny face. "Slow deep breaths, Celine. You can do it. You are stronger than you think and Patrick says Cathy and Paul are the best. You know they're here for you. You are not alone. I'll be right here too."

"I know. But I still wish you could come into the courtroom with me." She was on the verge of tears and so was I.

"I do too. But rules are rules. Don't let the bastard get to you. Stand up to him. Now's your chance," I said, pushing myself to sound confident but feeling like my voice betrayed the truth of how I felt.

"Martha, I'm scared silly."

"It's okay to be scared. Of course, it is. It'll be over soon. It will. You better go, they're calling you. I'll wait right here, I will, I promise." My heart was in a hurry to get it over. I was scared silly too.

Celine said nothing as we walked to the bus stop afterwards. Or as we took the bus home. She hardly spoke at all until we sat at my kitchen table drinking tea and eating Moroccan orange cake that I had made the day before because it was her favourite and I had needed something to do to take my mind off the case.

"I did it, Martha. It was awful but I said my piece. Before we went into the courtroom Cathy told me to tell the truth but stick to the facts. Go easy on the emotion. The barrister in a case before mine warned her. Another woman, from somewhere remote, her ex-husband had taken her phone and both sets of her car keys and never returned them and had left her stranded unable to use her car. She got very upset trying to explain all the things he had done and why she needed a variation in a previous separation agreement. The judge went on a rant and accused her of wasting court time, she said, there's no time for emotions in my courtroom. She adjourned her case and suggested that she went to a phone shop and the garage in the meantime…"

"They call that justice? That's not justice. That's the judge thinking she's a god," I said, horrified. "That poor other woman, I'm sure I saw her outside the courtroom with her barrister trying to console her."

"I was lucky I was warned. I told her my art and my inheritance had paid for nearly everything. I told her about how the abuse going back years had brought me from being chief breadwinner to not working. Dr McCarthy's evidence supported this. I must have gone into emotional freeze I was so scared of what the judge might say. I didn't cry. I focussed on my hands until they stopped trembling."

"My goodness, Celine, fair play to you. You held it together despite the two bastards you were up against, the judge and…"

"I'm sorry you had to find me that day. You did so much for me. Then and afterwards. I don't think I've ever thanked you enough. I am sorry." As Celine spoke she moved from sitting up straight, to pulling her knees up to her chest, to looking at her hands and then to looking at me in earnest. I nearly cried watching her. I held it in until I couldn't. I dabbed a tissue to my eyes and nose trying to not make a big noisy deal of my tears. I didn't feel entitled to cry.

"Celine dearest, please no more saying sorry. You don't owe me or the rest of the universe an apology because your husband did what he did to you. It's not your fault." More tears ran down my face. I blinked and pretended they weren't there.

"Sorry…I mean okay."

"Okay?" I nodded. The question was as much directed at myself as Celine.

"Dr McCarthy spelt out the litany of evidence of years of abuse that she had witnessed, including my own mental deterioration. I told the judge how I had mentally imploded to the point where I could barely hold a paintbrush and that until recently, I hadn't painted in years. I told her that I had no other income apart from the rent, net of the remaining mortgage, from the other house…I really did. I was careful to say it as it was, as if it happened to someone else. I kept it brief. I didn't show emotion. She would have adjourned the case if I did. I needed our marriage declared over as soon as possible. I wanted that behind me." Celine grew a few inches in the chair as she said that. It lifted me to listen and look at her.

"Celine, I'm so proud of you. Well done." I hugged the skin and bone of her.

"I don't know if it changed anything in the eyes of the judge. But I did it. I said what he did to me. She heard me and the court heard me. The judge said she believed me and that Mr Murphy's counter claims of abuse by me lacked credibility. As an aside, the judge suggested that he take an anger management course. Joseph jumped out of his seat with fury at that suggestion. The judge asked him 'Mr Murphy, am I to take your response to my suggestion as a positive one and that you would jump at doing such a course?' Joseph sat down with his tail between his legs at that!"

"One bully to another." I laughed. "The judge could see right through him. I told you she would."

"But you didn't really believe it. Did you?" Celine said, raising her eyebrow with a hint of devilment.

"No. But I wanted to believe it." We both smiled.

"And I get to keep my home, my art and other stuff. He gets the other house, his music paraphernalia and he is to give me a third of his income until such time as I get my wee pension or start to earn more than €25,000 a year."

"Are you pleased? Will you have enough?"

"I'll have plenty. More than I have had in years. And *I* will be in control of it. Like we said, if I need to do Airbnb or something then I will. And now I have started painting again, anything is possible…"

"You might give classes to me and a few of my friends? We'd love that."

"You never know."

"You might even put some more light into your current paintings."

"I don't know, Martha. You may be wrong there…And I do always put a wee splash of red in each one, a symbol of the blood on his hands and the hands of all the other wife-beating bastards…" She laughed a cold laugh. "Anyways, my old agent looked at them and said that they are the right side of dark for society's current taste and for some of the fashionista's various shades of white and grey tastes. You've got to get with the times, Martha."

We continued making light banter, as if all was well, as if the judge's orders in Celine's favour were all that were needed for her to move on in her life. We didn't mention the assault case that night and while her daughter got a few mentions, neither of us mentioned Shane.

A month after the court case Celine and Karen went up North to Celine's sister, Jacinta, for Christmas. Shane spent the day at his father's brother's house with his wife and family. He rang Celine on Christmas morning and wished her a happy Christmas. He said that he would see her early in the New Year. Celine called me before we sat down for our family Christmas lunch and told me; her voice was trembling with excitement. We both cried. It was the highlight of her day and mine.

Shane never got in touch with Celine in the New Year or after that. Celine wouldn't get in touch with him. She didn't want to upset him. She saw him on the street in town with the bastard, chatting as if they were close, really close.

"Yes," I said, "the sort of friendship where one is terrified to fall out with the other."

She shook her head sadly. "Nobody's even a wee bit scared to fall out with me," she said.

Chapter 8
The Next Day

Late June 2018

Online suggestions on how to end your marriage or minimise the fall-out from an affair had not been for me. As soon as I knew with certainty that Patrick had had a dalliance with Isabel, I had decided that I was going to do things my way. I was going to see them squirm. Over all the months of dinner party planning, I leaned towards dumping all the blame on the conniving bitch and even considered that she had meant for me to see those texts. But I couldn't deny the knowledge that Patrick, an intelligent, capable man, who had promised that he would be there for me always, had chosen to have an affair with her. Not with any woman. That would have been terrible enough. But with Isabel…

Isabel must have trapped him. Cast out her diamond-infested net and pulled him in. No, he had his own mind. He had secretly met up with her. He had exchanged smutty texts with her. In the past he had proven himself to be willing and able to stand up for what he believed in. He never did it loudly but he did it, quietly and firmly. If Patrick took a stand, we all listened, we rarely argued with him. We knew that if he took a stand, he had well-thought-out reasons to do so. This time he had taken a stand. He had 'stood' with Isabel. Some bloody stand. Some loud statement. I had decided to respond with my own clear statement, spelling it out to him and to Isabel, making it harder for them, especially her, to come back from. Hence the dinner party.

The night after the dinner party I sat at the same table, ready to share the same dinner with our eldest daughter, Fiona. The clarity with which I had planned everything was replaced by a screaming, sickening self-doubt. I stared at the blue tablecloth and whispered, "Up Dublin." I found no comfort in the words.

I heard the front door open, then shut with a bang followed by Fiona coming into the hall.

"Hi Mum. Hi Dad," she called as she went up the stairs.

"Dad, are you in your office? Can we go over Daniel's CV now?"

I went to the kitchen door and yelled up at her, "Fiona, Dad's not here."

She started walking back down the stairs. "Is he still at that golf club so? Having another pint to console himself that he bogeyed the last hole or what?"

"No, he's gone." I walked back towards the kitchen. Fiona followed.

"Gone where?"

"He's left the house?"

"I get that, Mum, but do you know where he went? When will he be back?"

"I think he's gone to Seamus's house. He won't be back. Not tonight, not..."

"Why'd he go to Seamus's house for goodness sake, Mum? Did something happen?"

"You could say something happened..."

"For God's sake Mum—"

"Dad had an affair. I asked him to leave. I'm sorry, Fiona." I hadn't been able to work out an easy way to tell her and I felt as if it could hardly have come out worse.

"Dad had an affair!" She laughed, a doubting laugh. "Get real, Mum, that's not likely, is it? I mean…you're talking about Dad, our Dad?" She looked at me to confirm what she was saying. The expression on my face must have made her change tack. "I mean…with whom? When? How would he have time?"

"With Isabel," I said, knowing that would cause added shock.

"Isabel! For feck's sake, Mum. You've said it yourself, she's a stuck-up gush bomb. She's not his type. He wouldn't have an affair with her…Mum, he wouldn't have an affair full stop."

"Well, he did." I had gathered the evidence months ago, I had been thorough in gathering my evidence but still there was the temptation within myself to deny it.

"It doesn't make sense. Are you sure?"

"He smelled of her perfume a number of times. And I saw texts. Gushy texts! Maybe he likes gush. What do I know?" I rubbed my hands over my face. I had always thought that we both hated gush but I must have been wrong on that too.

"Gushy texts? That could just be Isabel being Isabel."

"Okay so. More explicit than gush."

Fiona plonked herself down on the couch and looked up at me imploringly. I sat down on a chair at the kitchen table.

"Hold on a minute. What happened? Did they tell you over dinner? He's not leaving you for her. Oh God. Don't tell me that." Fiona's eyelids were fluttering rapidly up and down. It was a family stress thing. Mine might have been fluttering too but I couldn't see through the tears.

"He wouldn't survive two full days with her," I said with more certainty than I felt. "And I haven't seen texts in months, it might be all over, for all I know." I was trying to convince myself as much as Fiona. Maybe it wasn't all over, maybe he was going to set up home with her. "It was me who brought it up last night," I said sullenly.

"Really Mum! You brought it up over dinner?"

I nodded uncertainly.

"Was that with starters or the main course?" Fiona's voice was getting louder and more exasperated.

"Very funny, Fiona." I was feeling exasperated myself, and hard done by.

"I wasn't trying to be funny. I'm shocked!"

"I'm shocked too, you know!" I looked at Fiona staring at me. She paused with her mouth open. I could see her thinking.

"You've known for months, haven't you? That explains it. Even by your hormonal standards, you've been all over the place, you've put dinners on the table and sat down with us but you've hardly spoken. You've taken refuge in the garden, in your office, in Celine's. You've been physically in the same room as us but mentally elsewhere – I even asked you about it at one stage."

Fiona's words stung me into the reality of things from her perspective. I thought I had been quite calm and together throughout most of it.

"I've been doing my best, Fiona. Imagine what it's been like for me? I had to get Zara through her Leaving Cert exams. I had to…"

"Mum, how long have you known?" Her voice was angry, frustrated…

"Nearly six months," I whispered.

"You've known all that time and you said nothing? Not even to Dad?" She shook her head in disbelief.

"What was I to do?" As I asked the question I could hear how stupid it sounded.

"Talk to him. Ask him why. Go for couples counselling. I don't know. You don't kick him out for just one affair, not after more than twenty years of a good marriage."

I was going to remind her that it was nearly twenty-five years. "What do you mean just one affair?" I asked. "Do you mean I should just suck it up? Forgive him, until the next time? Let's all just play happy families, like in the olden days, when women pretended that their husbands weren't playing offside and they kept up bloody appearances. Hey everyone, everything is fine in this house…nothing to see here. I think we've moved on from that. I hope we have." I was getting annoyed with her at that stage. He was the one who had the affair. I was the one left defending myself.

"Come on now, Mum, it hasn't quite been happy families for a number of years. Trish's death, austerity, no money, your menopause, whatever…" Her voice faded as if she was quietly making a long list under her breath.

"So it's all my fault, is it?" I voiced how I was processing her response.

"That's not what I'm saying. Dad didn't help by working God's hours and then golfing the remaining ones. But *you* should have done something about it. You know, dealt with all the shit in your life. Gone to the doctors. Gone for counselling…"

"Counselling! The current generation's answer to everything…"

"Well, the least you should have done is what you guys used to do. You should have talked about it. You told us it's important to talk. That, you used to say, was what kept your marriage healthy and happy for so long, bumps and all. Did you forget your own advice?"

"But…"

"But what?"

"He slept with Isabel for God's sake! How do you talk about that?" I was raising my voice again. I was refusing to admit to myself that I was losing the argument, not just with Fiona but with myself. I had been wrong. I should have talked to Patrick. Instead, I had set myself up as a pathetic martyr. I was a fool.

128

"Maybe you need to ask yourself why he slept with Isabel, Mum. If he slept with her, I might add – that might be a good place to start."

"You don't…it doesn't matter." I was going to say you don't understand. But why should I expect her to understand. She didn't know the half of it. I had never told her.

"I'm going to my room now, Mum. I need to get my head around this…alone."

I had imagined that Fiona would be the most sympathetic. She is very black and white normally. What is right is right. What is wrong is wrong. I had thought that she saw affairs as wrongs that one doesn't get to come back from. She was right. I should have talked to Patrick about it. But would talking have changed anything?

I ate my dinner alone in silence, spending more time pushing it around my plate than eating it. I left Fiona's dinner covered in the oven.

How was I going to tell Matt? He had said he'd phone around 10 p.m. on Sunday night, tonight. Two hours or more to wait. I stared at the volcano triptych above the couch. I had been living in the pre-eruption cold of the snow-covered mountain. Yesterday the volcano had erupted after the slow build-up of intense pressure. Today I was still feeling its red-hot heat. How would it be when the ash started to settle? Would it settle?

I tidied up after my dinner which took less than fifteen minutes. I'd already spent the day deep cleaning from our bedroom all the way down the stairs to the back door. The oven looked as good as new. Nothing was out of place. Everything felt out of place.

I sat down on the couch and put my recent life back on replay, this time through the tinted lens of the conversation I had just had with Fiona.

It was my fault. I had blown it. I had blown it back when I didn't get sufficient help with the menopause; back when I didn't talk to

Patrick about how it was for me; back when I didn't tell him that I still loved him and wanted him and wanted to want to have sex with him even though my body was saying it didn't; back when I was scared to cuddle up to him for fear that he would want something more than my body was capable of delivering. I had let him down by being scared of letting him down. Of course, I should have talked to him before it all went totally wrong. But I didn't. When he took to working late or being out late with his clients or golfing buddies, I had almost heaved a sigh of relief. It got me off the hook, free to wallow in my tired, sweaty menopause. I had taken it as an opportunity to go to bed alone with no one expecting anything from me.

A bad menopause can go tediously on and on forever. I know a friend who has been sweating for the last twelve years. It's still a problem for her. It can still leave her tired and irritable but who's going to spend twelve years talking about sweats, lack of sleep, aching bones, a floppy, spreading middle? People stop listening or caring very quickly.

In my distorted mind I had decided to call it loud and clear on the affair, in my own time and in my own distinct way. I had told myself that was me taking back control of my life. The affair had become the focus of my anger and frustration. I had wanted to throw it, like a pot of boiling water, right into their faces; I wanted to see Isabel scalded in front of everyone, especially her husband. But Gavin didn't deserve that. I hadn't considered the collateral damage of my actions. I had pretended to myself that I was protecting the kids, yet all I had done was prolong their torture. I hadn't really asked why he had the affair. I hadn't sought my part in it, at least not the part where I might have done something to save the situation.

But then nor had he done anything to save us. An affair was wrong. He knew that. It could only mean curtains. The end. Surely, they all could see that. Fiona should feel sorry for me. Matt too. Maybe sorry is too much to expect. I wasn't asking them to revise their memory of the past. For more than twenty-five years, when you count years before we got married, we had been mostly good as a couple. Then things went wrong. Shit happens…we must move on from it. I must move on from it. How would I cope? How would he cope? Where would he live? How would he eat? It was true. I hadn't always been as fulsome with the truth as I should have been. Maybe that played its part too. I had screwed up.

The phone rang.

"Mum, is it true?" Matt launched straight in but his voice was calm rather than accusatory.

"Matt."

"Is it true that you asked Dad to leave?"

"Yes, Matt. I did. I'm sorry."

"But why, Mum? Really, why?

"Because…I presume Fiona told you."

"She told me what you said. But I don't think it's that simple. Is it, Mum?"

"Nothing is simple," I said, feeling the muddle in my head growing with each question.

"I know you've had your struggles but you've worked through them before. I mean, are you sure you've thought it through this time? Have you talked about it?" Matt's voice remained calm.

"This is different."

"I know it is different. I'm not saying that Dad having an affair was right…but talk to him. Please talk to him. It's more than just the affair you know."

"Just the affair. Just an affair…"

"I'm sorry. I don't mean it like that."

"You can't come back from an affair," I said emphatically before adding in a whisper, "can you?"

"I don't know, Mum. Who says you can't?"

131

"We said."

"But…"

"Patrick promised. We promised."

"But Fiona says that you didn't talk to him about it. Why not? That's not like the you we grew up with. That's not what you always advised us to do. You always told us to confront a problem; speak up, listen and be heard before a problem became a bigger problem."

"I couldn't see the point. There are things that you don't know…"

"So, tell me. Help me understand. What do I not know?"

"Things. It's too long and complicated." And too long left unsaid, I thought.

"I'd like to understand, Mum. I really would."

"You know some. You don't know some more. I can't tell you now. Not tonight anyway."

"I know it hasn't been easy for you and Dad in recent years. What with Trish dying, the crash and your other struggles with your hormones, you not sleeping and all that."

"You're right there. And I should have dealt with it all better. Don't think that I don't know that. Because I do."

"Won't you at least talk to him, Mum?"

I was thinking that the half-formed vague plans I had of building a new life of freedom for myself were pie in the sky. I had thought that I could reinvent myself without the ties of a husband, school-going children or a large house. In the space of twenty-four hours my whole mindset had changed. Reality had hit. Those plans now looked stupid, empty and lonely.

"I don't know, Matt. I really don't know."

"Well maybe you'd better think about it. You know, before it's too late."

Chapter 9

The Aftermath

June 2018

I had thought those six months of knowing but not confronting Patrick would be the toughest times I would ever have to face. During those months, putting on an everything-is-okay front and faking an occasional smile, I thought had become second nature to me. But based on what Fiona said the night after the dinner party, what I thought and the reality were clearly very different.

From my light-bulb moment when I had met and smelt Isabel at Aldi, the notion of Patrick having an affair with her had been lodged foremost in my brain. I wavered between denial and anger especially in the first few months while I had processed the whole thing. I had been on high alert whenever Patrick said something like he was going to be particularly late at work. On too many of those nights, I had made an excuse to ring Gavin and made subtle enquiries as to whether Isabel might be out late too. I had exaggerated business problems that a friend was having to have an excuse to run them by Gavin, who had successfully built a small family business into a multi-million one that stretched the length and breadth of Ireland and beyond. I had sought donations from him for school or other fundraisers. I had always casually asked to speak to Isabel at the end of my conversation with him. Invariably Isabel had been out and not expected in until late or had been staying over with her sister. On those nights, Patrick had arrived home late and tiptoed around our room. Sometimes, just as he had climbed silently into our bed, I'd startled him with a comment.

"Patrick, you must be exhausted. Who's keeping you up so late?"

"Just the usual, Martha," he had said in a yawny voice. "Vulture funds and developers." Big yawn.

"Plenty of vultures out there alright," I had responded, before faking my own yawn.

In hindsight, those months of knowing but pretending not to know were a walk in the park relative to the months after Patrick left. I had feared that he would insist on staying, if only to secure his legal right to a share in the house. I had feared his resistance when I should have feared his silent departure. As I lay in bed alone, I wished that he had hurled some of the blame back at me. I deserved it. I had been an unreasonable bitch for far too long. Why hadn't he challenged me on that? Why would I expect him to? Confrontation, outside of legal matters, was never his thing. It was me who should have initiated a conversation. I wished that he had held up his hands and said I did wrong. Martha, forgive me. Then I wished that he thought that I was worth the effort of working through our shit. Finally, I wished that I would stop wishing and I could just know, know where we actually were as a couple, because perhaps it was not where I had thought we were during those long six months of knowing but saying nothing.

He had left without uttering a single word of accusation in my direction. In the slow, anxious build-up to the dinner party I had been clear on one thing. Our marriage was over. There was no going back. Patrick had chosen to have an affair with Isabel. He had been with her – with her, physically with her. Touching her. I would not allow myself to think of the physical side of what might have happened; I would not, could not think about him gorging on her large breasts, her naked voluptuous body, his lean one. When such thoughts or visions threatened, I distracted myself with visions of her Oompa Loompa tan with its silly tidelines running under her chin and across her back. What I did dwell on was the time and energy he had spent texting her, not me; she had sent him texts, texts that were coochy-woochy, innuendo-laden gush. He must have liked them. He must have encouraged them.

Where did that leave me now? It left me alone in bed. Alone in the house. Alone.

After the dinner party, I had anticipated I would feel released from having had my life on hold and feel ready to embrace a new life. There was no feeling of release or relief. There was only a sense of drowning in confusion. I remembered the look he gave me that night when I walked into our bedroom in the turquoise dress, the dress I had chosen because I knew that he would love it. I remembered him sitting on our bed watching my every move. I could torture myself with the memory of my own sexual desire pulling me towards him and his reciprocal sexual energy, all left to dangle wasted in mid-sentence; an energy and desire I had thought was dead for both of us but was all the time maybe below the surface, deep rooted in years of a love laced with shared experiences; happy, sad, good and bad. We had known them all. Our shared secrets had created the magical magnetism of those moments, a magnetism that I should not have denied then or ever. But I had denied it that night. I had left the bedroom at speed. For what? For some stupid fear that the evening of the big reveal that I had planned would become unravelled. Yes, I had had my say that night but I found myself ill-prepared for the after-feelings. I was both tortured and, at times, buoyed by the memory of that same sexual and emotional magnetism that hung between us in the hall as I handed Patrick the dry-cleaning tickets before he walked out the door.

I rolled back the clock and I realised that it wasn't that I had stopped looking at his phone for those texts. It was that after a few

135

months, there had been no texts. Maybe they got clever. Maybe not. Maybe it had been over before it had really begun. I slowly realised that from the moment I smelt her perfume at Aldi to the moment she walked into our house for the dinner party I had not smelt so much as a whiff of her scent, not from Patrick, not anywhere.

I realised something else; I had found it harder to avoid Patrick in the preceding months, he had been around more, there had been heated family discussions around the dinner table about Trump, Syria, the abortion referendum…Fiona loved a good rant and there was nothing like her perception of the nastiness and undemocratic behaviour of the anti-abortionists to get her going.

"If they are so fecking pro-life then what are they doing for the homeless single mothers? I bet it's the same people complaining about that homeless shelter opening around the corner as are out canvassing to keep abortion out of Ireland."

"Now, Fiona, we don't know that…" Patrick said.

"Come on, Dad, you know what those holy Joes and Josephines are like. Not in my backyard when it comes to the homeless or when it comes to abortion. If they had their way, they'd send the homeless to the UK just as we do with women who need an abortion."

"But do women *need* abortions or is it just that they *want* them?" Matt interrupted.

I bit my lip. He was looking for a rise out of Fiona and she rarely let him down.

"For God's sake, Matt. Ask yourself if some girl you spent the night with got pregnant, would she *need* an abortion or just *want* one?"

"She might *want* one but I am not convinced that she would *need* one. And where does that leave me? Like, I'd be the father, have you considered that?" Matt was deadpan.

"Okay Matt, good luck with that. I hope you enjoy early fatherhood…how about if Mum got pregnant? Would she *need* an abortion for her sanity and for fear of how she might, at her age, look after a child who in all likelihood might have special needs?"

She was on her feet pointing at me, *in my old age*, I wished she wouldn't rub it in. Is it okay for their generation to be ageist but PC about everything else? Anyway, I was thinking that I would definitely *need* an abortion. Rearing children requires energy. Rearing a child with special needs requires extra energy and they might need you forever. But who says that the child would have special needs? We don't know that. I know of other so-called *geriatric mothers* who were an embarrassment to their existing teenage children but who had perfectly healthy babies. Then I had thought that I'd have to be ovulating or having sex to actually be at risk of getting pregnant. Fiona, Matt and Zara had looked at me, all their faces agog at the suggestion that I could get pregnant, at my age! Patrick was looking at his hands, his right hand twirling his wedding ring on his left hand. His legs were crossed and the upper leg was jigging, as it so often did. A response from me was expected.

"Well, in the unlikely event that I was to get pregnant, given my age and all that, I think in all honesty…" I looked from Matt to Fiona to Zara and they were all waiting to hear what I had to say, a rare event and one to be savoured. I glanced at Patrick, he too was staring at me. "In truth, and I have considered this, I think I might *need* an abortion." I rushed to explain. "I really don't think I could manage a healthy baby right now, never mind a child with special needs, anyone can see that it would be a bad idea…" I spoke from the heart. I was struggling to have the energy to do what was needed to keep going as it was. How could one safely throw a baby into my fragile mix?

"You'd kill a baby, Mum. How could you? You'd take a defenceless life." Zara was aghast.

"Well not willingly, Zara. It's not that simple. But then I would not willingly get pregnant now and I wouldn't willingly rear a baby at this stage of my life…" She was totally shocked. Her mother, who got upset when she stood on a snail or slug, would have an abortion! "I'm sorry, pet, but I'm too old to have a baby. It wouldn't be fair for me to bring a baby into my life right now." I had been thinking as I listed all the obvious reasons not to have a baby at this time in my life that I was not stating one big reason: that my marriage was falling apart and me with it – who would want to bring a baby into that?

Zara was speechless. She sniffed loudly and tears made their way to the corner of her eyes and slowly ran down her under-nourished face. I felt awful. I was pro-choice but not fully pro-abortion. I would hate to have to make the choice. I didn't know if I could ever recover from another pregnancy leading to a baby any more or less than I could recover from an actual abortion.

Patrick put his hand on Zara's shoulder. "Hey Zara, it's not a real possibility. Mum is unlikely to get pregnant. Don't upset yourself, pet, especially not over things that, in all likelihood, will never happen."

"Zara, all I'm saying is that if a woman, any woman, gets pregnant they should have the right to choose. I'm not wishing abortion on anyone. It's about choice," Fiona said putting her hand on Zara's other shoulder.

"But what about the poor babies?" Zara sniffed.

"We have to think of the women too, Zara," Patrick added gently.

"It's all about the women, there we go again. It's a wonder we men are even allowed to vote," Matt said with fake indignation.

"Don't get me started on male vs female voting rights and representation…" Fiona said, jumping on the opportunity to change the subject, for which I was very grateful.

While we both regarded abortion as a serious and challenging topic, Patrick and I had laughed together afterwards at our children's different opinions and personalities and at how Matt never missed a chance to get a rise out of the girls. They nearly always fell for it. We had reminisced about our own youth and how black and white topics like abortion had been for us back then; with maturity and wanted pregnancies, these issues had become a lot more grey. I realised that I had, without thinking, parked my sarcasm and narkiness for that entire evening.

Matt was in Canada when Patrick left the night of the dinner party and after that Fiona and Zara were increasingly elsewhere other than home. Fiona had collected Zara from the airport after her post-leaving holiday and taken her for a coffee to fill her in on the situation. Zara went straight to her room when she came home. I called "hello" and received no reply. I got a text a few minutes later from her.

I'm not talking to you. I'll talk to you when I'm ready. I've a lot to process first.

She didn't talk to me for days; she came down and collected her meals and ate in her room; she went out to her friends; she went around the house with headphones on her ears; she avoided eye contact with me; she left a room if I came into it. I had expected this from her and I tried to be as normal as possible but inside I was in bits. I had a headache; my stomach was in spasm; I couldn't sleep; every time I said "Zara" when I was in sight of her, her hand would go up and the open palm would face me, she was a policewoman telling me to STOP. On the fifth day I got another text.

I need money to top up my phone please. I'll pay you back when I start work.

She must have spent all her monthly allowance that was supposed to cover her phone and have run out of money after her trip. I considered ignoring the text. I let it sit unopened for an hour. It begged me for attention from my untouched phone until another two notifications bounced it off the screen. Eventually I texted back.

I'll give it to you over dinner at 7. Xx Mum

139

Dinner with her was strained initially but once I got her talking about the cities she had visited and how clean or dirty each one was, what the vegan food was like…she couldn't help herself. Almost normal challenging relations were resumed but she continued to be not at home more than ever.

I was left alone with plenty of time to reflect on the preceding years and, in particular, the first six months of that year. I realised that in those months when life was on hold, Patrick and I had actually had the occasional other good conversations too, not just the one about our family's opinions on abortion. But about family matters: careers, personalities, ageing parents…I remembered that there had been occasions when we had talked and my smiles had been real, not fake. But in between these conversations my anger surfaced and there continued to be times when I came close to exploding. I tried to save the explosions for when I was free to scream alone. I got so carried away one time at the screaming experiment that I expected the glass in the windows to shatter. I hoped the neighbours didn't hear. I took my pent-up anger and frustration out on the vacuum cleaner and the mop. If they could talk 'fuck' 'bitch' and 'bastard' would have come naturally to them; the paintwork on the skirting boards and corners of the kitchen cupboards still bear the scars of my fury.

With hindsight, all the signs were that it had been a short affair, that it had ended long before the dinner party. But before the dinner party, I had missed these signs and had launched myself headfirst into the abyss of ending our marriage as the logical next step after an affair. In the uninterrupted, uncluttered light of being completely alone everything looked different.

I found myself asking what if the affair wasn't an ending? What if that was a principle that I had set in another time when everything was different for Patrick and me? We had had a shitty few years. What if an affair was what we needed for a new and necessary beginning? An article appeared in the weekend supplement of *The Irish Times* that added weight to this thought. It was written by a counsellor who worked with couples recovering from and even rejuvenating their relationships after an affair. I wasn't ready for counselling. Or I was way beyond counselling. I didn't know which.

I took the train out to the other side of the city to walk the pier and watch the yachts at Dun Laoghaire. I thought the change of scenery might give me a fresh perspective. On the train I watched a young couple. She had her back to me. Her hair was cut sharp and short up the back of her neck. I had changed my hair to short and sharp since Patrick had left. I had worn it that way before we were married. The young man was sitting sideways beside the young woman, with his back to the window so he could look at her easily and admire her. She was laughing and chatting with a guy sitting opposite her. He was gay, I reckoned, given his foppish hair style, bright clothes, jeans with cuts in all the right places, earrings and, in particular, his amplified hand gestures. Of course, he might just have been flamboyant. Her boyfriend's arm stretched across her shoulder reaching so that his fingers gently tickled the back of her neck. His admiring eyes were fixed on her. She turned towards him occasionally to include him in the conversation. His response was a smile spread the width and breadth of his face. Her face was alight with a look of happy, carefree love. I bore witness to the joy and assurance of requited love singing between them. I recognised it because Patrick and I had been there.

But he had had an affair. I had no choice but to end it. Maybe that is what he wanted. Maybe the affair was his declaration to me that he wanted out of our marriage. He had an affair with Isabel for God's sake. Who was I fooling? It was like spelling it out big and bold. MARTHA, OUR MARRIAGE IS OVER. GOODBYE.

I went around in circles. I met myself coming back. I bumped into things. I always bumped into things. I took it to a new level. Twenty years of driving in and out of our gateway and not a scratch on any car that I drove through it. First, I took the rear side light off, despite the parking sensor screaming at me to stop. Then I scraped the whole length of the side of the car. Time to get rid of my much loved ancient seven-seater. My friendly not-so-young mechanic and car dealer found me a second-hand Golf, mint condition and bright red. Just right for the new me. He knew the story. He'd known Patrick for years. Bad news travels fast, gathering legs as it does. I was glad I'd checked the car websites before I agreed the price. He was definitely looking to cream it by an extra few hundred. And the tyres on it were heading for replacement. What is it about some car dealers? Do they think that once the colour and look is right that we women will take a car at any price?

Six weeks after the dinner party, Zara got her Leaving Cert results. She got her second choice. She and her friends don't discuss points. It's all about the choices. Environmental Science and Technology at DCU. A pretty good choice I'd say. But it wasn't Trinity College where all her friends were going. Well, where two of her sort-of friends were going. Her best friend was going to the National College of Art and Design. Her other close friend got a place in Galway doing what she wanted, marine science. And most of the gang were actually going to DCU. You wouldn't think it by Zara's reaction.

"You should have been stricter with me, Mum. Why did you let me out to every party? To all those eighteenths, for God's sake."

"I didn't *let* you out to them. You didn't tell me about the half of them. You told me you were staying at Ellie's to study. More fool me, I believed you. I only found out after…" I stopped. She only told me after I 'kicked Dad out over just an affair'. Her comment went something like, "You're hysterical, Mum, you think you know stuff, you're sick."

Then she'd cackled and said, "All the time you thought I was studying at Ellie's, I was off at all those eighteenths that you wouldn't have let me go to…ha ha!"

Those comments had hurt as did so many of her comments.

"I didn't know, did I?" I replied in my defence.

"Well you let me go to Ellie's…"

"Well you lied to me? And you chose to drink your head off at each party. If I remember rightly, I grounded you for a month at one stage…" I was damned if I was going to take the blame for all her devious socialising.

"Well why didn't you make me give up hockey? Why didn't you do more accounting exam papers with me?"

"Because, as you kept telling me, you were over eighteen since last October and not going to do what I say or even asked." I considered reminding her that I had offered to do exam papers with her regularly but I had been rejected more times than I had been accepted. I drew a deep breath and added, "Maybe DCU won't be so bad. You might actually like it. It looks like a good practical course. It's well recognised, you know when it comes to getting a job." She burst out crying. If Mum says it's good, then it must be shit!

"You're sick, Mum. You're stuck in the dark ages and destined to stay there." She paused then and added, "Alone!"

That last word hit my already painful spot. She walked out of the kitchen and stomped up the stairs. She could be such a self-centred wagon. It was all about her. I had tried so hard with her. But everything was my fault. It was a few weeks later that I found out that the guy that she had fallen for while at French college the previous summer had got a place in BESS in Trinity. It seemed it wasn't her course that was the problem after all.

She went to DCU a month after her results and promptly joined Friends of the Earth and declared us all Destroyers of the Planet. She stopped waxing her legs. I was banned from buying cling film, plastic sandwich and freezer bags, wipes of all kinds, plastic cotton buds, normal toothbrushes, anything with micro beads…the list grew longer every week. I fully agreed with the logic of most of it. I had never agreed with wipes and I reused plastic bags and hated cling film. I'd seen the images of the dead whales their innards strangled and suffocated by plastic, the turtles with their shells distorted into obscure shapes by plastic beer holders. But I thought that a bamboo toothbrush was a step too far. When Zara bought me one as a present, I didn't dare not use it. I was surprised that I liked it.

But still I was forever in trouble. She would walk into the kitchen as I was unpacking the groceries.

"How could you buy that, Mum. Look at it. It's got palm oil in it."

"Zara, maybe it is sustainable palm oil. Maybe it's not from the Amazon rainforest."

"What makes you say that? If it was sustainable palm oil, Mum, it would say that it was sustainable palm oil. And those oven chips. Oven chips should have only two ingredients: potatoes and vegetable oil. These ones have nearly ten."

"How would I know to be looking at chip ingredients? I just thought chips were chips."

"Mum, I keep telling you READ THE INGREDIENTS. There are three different types of sugars in these ones and a tonne of salt."

"No wonder they taste so good."

"Mum!"

"Zara, give me a break." And let me eat steak…not because I particularly want to but just to say feck off, Zara…

"Does everything you buy have to come covered in plastic? God even the organic vegetables are covered in plastic. You should buy them in the market on Saturdays. So much plastic. I can't bear it."

"Well Zara, I can't bear that every time I go to the market with you, I come home broke. Nine euro for a small tin of organic deodorant! Three fifty to get a tiny jar of cinnamon refilled. I can't afford to save the planet at those prices."

"But can you afford not to save the planet? Anyway, the Glasnevin market is better value for vegetables than where you go. I'm going to buy Dad's groceries there from now on. Then at least one household will be doing its bit for the future generations."

"Good luck with that. He's a self-confessed, fully committed carnivore."

"You're wrong there. I cook him vegan meals when I visit and he always says they're very tasty. I might go and live with *him*. He needs some TLC, after all *you* did to him. Tonight, I'm making him good hearty Miso soup. He loves that."

I found myself more than half-hoping that she would go and live with her father. Nothing I did was ever good enough for her. But I didn't think that Patrick would ever agree to going vegetarian, never mind vegan. A meal wasn't a meal to him unless it involved a piece of an animal or at least fish. I don't think Zara knew that Fiona brought food over to Patrick whenever she was going over to him. Fiona had told me that he had become an obsessive runner and was losing weight as rapidly as he ran. I imagined the ounces falling off him onto the pavement. She was worried about him. My response was to always cook plenty of extra stew, shepherd's pie, curry, bolognese or whatever else I was cooking so she could bring some over with her. She told me that she had persuaded him to go and talk to someone and that I might try it too. I said I'd consider it. But I wasn't convinced. I had my own inner conversations and my friends to talk to. I was pretty sure that Patrick wasn't sharing much personal information with his friends.

Celine kept me walking. I thought it did both of us good. But I was measured with what I told her. My problems seemed small relative what she had been through. She warned me not to drink alone. She had been there and done that. I did it in style a month after the dinner party, on the day that was the twenty-fifth anniversary of the day that Patrick and I got engaged, as opposed to our wedding anniversary which still lay well ahead of me. I took out one of Patrick's favourite wines and drank the whole bottle from one of our large John Rocha cut glasses that we had been given as a wedding present. I resisted the temptation to smash a few of them on the tiled kitchen floor. The tragedy of drinking alone on such a date was overwhelming. I cried the whole evening, drowning in my sorrows and in a good bottle of red wine followed by a large brandy and port to settle my stomach; I told myself the brandy was a digestif to help me digest the misery of the occasion. It was a bad idea. I didn't attempt to repeat the experience.

Celine only recently had the occasional glass of wine with me. She kept no drink in her own house for fear of temptation. I didn't go that far but I promised myself that I would not drink alone. It would be the slippery slope. But there were evenings when I was so lonely and empty that I came very close to breaking my resolve. I need to get out more, I told myself. I need to get out. I need to sign up to something new. Something short term in case I had to go back to work. I settled on volunteering as a paired reader. I'd meet new people on the training course and the weekly session would be a positive commitment. I applied for the next course which wasn't scheduled until late January, a few months away. I had just missed the start of the previous course. Sod's Law.

The black rings around my eyes grew darker. My face grew whiter. My enthusiasm for doing things waned.

Friends, including Máire whom I'd known and been close to for years, called or texted me trying to persuade me to go for a walk, play a game of tennis, meet for a coffee…anything to get me to out and about. I turned them all down with whatever lame excuse that came to me, too much work to do being the most frequent one. I avoided Máire rather than face telling her about Patrick's affair and my response to it. I had told her we were selling our house and between that and looking after our ageing parents, I had not a minute of spare time. She was understanding as always. She had known about our financial troubles and I deliberately led her to believe that selling our house was all part of sorting our finances out. "As long as you're okay, Martha, don't worry, we will catch up when things settle down. In the meantime, if there is anything I can do, please tell me, promise..." "Of course, Máire. I will. Give my love to your family and I'll be in touch," was a typical exchange between us. Regardless of what Máire thought or felt about by brush-offs, she would always be too non-confrontational to challenge me.

My dreams took me off into new dimensions. All of them dark. I was trapped in a labyrinth of ancient tunnels. I was in a state of panic. I arrived at a small open space. Patrick was there. I experienced a moment of relief. We were together. I looked at him. I looked at me. I saw that we were two damaged old people stretched to our limits, tied to two separate plinths. I freed myself through prolonged and fierce determination, repeated thrashing about with a madness-induced strength that gave me power that I knew I was not safe with. I freed Patrick. My relief was fleeting. His plinth split. The ground opened up under him. His large athletic body tumbled and bounced down stone steps, long arms and legs in all directions as he went. He landed on a floor of flat hard stones. As he landed he uncurled and his arms and legs stretched straight out to their full length as if nailed to a cross. His face looked up at me and begged the question, what have you done, Martha?

Each dark dream woke me up and brought on a hot sweat. Sweat oozed from the pores in my scalp irritating my psoriasis. It filled every crease and crevice in my body. I would throw off the bed clothes, dry myself with whatever T-shirt I was wearing. Then put on a clean one. More often than not I slept in Patrick's T-shirts. When Fiona commented, I responded that they were a better length and quality for absorbing the sweat than my own. Zara told me clearly and loudly that they were not mine to wear and that she would wash them all and bring them over to her father. She had a point. I hid them from her and didn't wear them for a while. Then I took them out from hiding one at a time and after wearing them, I washed and dried them when she was not around.

Chapter 10

Mum Returns

Early September 2018

Mum and my much-loved stepdad came home from their four-month trip to the Americas. They had relished a six-week cruise and then spent two and a half months staying near or with my two half-brothers who had settled, in Mum's words hopefully only temporarily, in Massachusetts. I collected them from the airport early one morning of the week before Zara started college. Mum and I had spoken on WhatsApp at least once a week during her time away, strained and awkward conversations where I encouraged her to talk about her travels and experiences and, if she pushed me to talk, I spouted on about the children. My communications with her had been unusually poor since that post-Christmas bumping into Isabel and I had insisted it was just hormones compounded by other things, like Celine or Zara's trials and tribulations. It wasn't until mid-August, two weeks before their return date, when they were staying with my elder half-brother John, that I finally decided I couldn't hold off telling Mum any longer. She deserved time to process it before her return and I needed her to have recovered, at least a bit, from being frustrated with me for not telling her sooner.

I had gone up to my bedroom and sat on the bed with my feet outstretched, primed for a long and challenging phone call. I contemplated a large painting that hung where it had always hung, above the unused, black cast-iron fireplace opposite the end of our bed. Previously my eyes had been drawn to the crumbling remains of the castle at the Rock of Dunamase, sitting determinedly against a dark threatening sky, the castle's days of glory long passed yet its majestic position assured it was not diminished. Now I considered the unseen claps of thunder, lightning and heavy rain that would have appeared in a later scene if the artist had but waited.

I swallowed hard, knowing it was time. I knew Mum would be at home in John's house because he and I had arranged it when I called him to fill him in on my current situation and to warn him that I would be telling Mum that day. John didn't know what to say and repeated "Oh" and "Oh dear, I don't know what to say." Luckily, we were interrupted by his three-year old daughter, Aisling.

When I rang to speak to Mum, Aisling picked up the phone and said in her child-playing-the-adult voice, "Hello, are you Auntie Martha?"

In the pause before I answered the question, I overheard murmurings in the background.

"Shush," Aisling said in a stern grown-up version of her three-year-old voice. "I'm trying to talk to Auntie Martha."

"Hello Aisling," I said. "Nana tells me that you're a great girl and you've made some lovely colourful paintings for her."

"I didn't paint them. I drew them, with markers, silly." She giggled. "I'll be four soon. I use markers."

"Oh, I'm sorry. Markers so. Well I look forward to seeing your drawings because Nana says they are really lovely."

"Daddy says that you want to speak to Nana so I have to go now. Bye."

"Isn't she wonderful?" came Mum's voice down the line.

"She really is, Mum. I can't believe she is nearly four already." It seemed like no time and yet forever since they had brought her home to Ireland as a young baby.

"She'd talk the hind legs off a donkey." I heard the smile in Mum's voice and I hated to spoil it for her but if I kept making small talk the opportunity would pass.

"There is something I need to tell you, Mum."

"What is it, Martha?" Her voice switched to anxious.

"There is no easy way to tell you but I've messed up."

"It can't be that bad. What is it? Tell me, pet."

"Patrick and I, we've…well, he's moved out." The lump in my throat was too big to swallow and I almost gagged before a strange crying sound, more like a keening, escaped.

"Martha, oh dear, Martha, what happened?"

"He had an affair. I found out. And I asked him to leave."

"Patrick had an affair? When? But he adores you. He wouldn't do that."

"Well, he did. Maybe I drove him to it. I know I've been a cold, nasty bitch for the last few years. But there's more to it, Mum. I know there is. I just don't know what."

"But he wouldn't…I mean lots of women go through tough times, but…"

"Yeah, I know, but I took it to another level, didn't I? Even you tried to persuade me to do something about it. Fecking hormones. I hate them." I was sniffing loudly at that stage.

"Oh, dear goodness, Martha. It's not your fault, darling. It's not. I need to come home. I should be there for you. Don't worry, pet, I'll get John to change my flights."

"Mum, trust me, there's no need to come home early. Honestly. I'm dealing with it. I am."

"Of course you are but I should be there for you."

"You will be there for me, I know you will but I can wait another couple of weeks."

"But…"

"You see, Mum, please don't be hurt but, I knew that as soon as I told you, you'd want to come home, it's been nearly three months since Patrick left."

"Three months and you didn't see fit to tell me. Three long months and I've been off enjoying myself and I should have been at home with you. Oh Martha. Martha!"

"I didn't want to ruin your trip. You'll be home in two short weeks, Mum, you will. And I'll be glad. I will be very glad then."

"I want to be there for you now." Mum's voice was thick with tears.

"I know that and just knowing that helps. And if you come home, I'll feel terrible because I'd be depriving John and his family of time with you. And I'll have you long after your trip is over."

John told me later that night in a WhatsApp text that, as expected, Mum came straight off the phone and asked him to change her flights, she wanted to come home immediately. John and the high cost of a flight change worked on persuading Mum to stay on as planned and make the most of her time with John, his wife and Aisling. I think it was Aisling who clinched the deal when she took to cuddling up on her nana's knee and playing with the chunky bright-coloured hand-made jewellery which Nana promised to teach her how to make herself, when she was older.

Mum rang me every single day for the remaining two weeks of her trip. These conversations brought home to me that I was in a muddle of denial and grief. But even on those calls I could feel Mum get inside my head, supporting me, understanding me; she said things like, I know how hard it must be; it must feel so lonely, it must feel as if nobody else could possibly understand what it is like for you; but all is not lost Martha, I'll help you work it out. Her words came from her own heart-breaking experience and reached from her heart to mine, and with each conversation I started to feel a little more loved and a bit more compassionate towards myself.

Mum would never dream of saying it, or even thinking it, but I knew that the scale of what I was experiencing in emotional turmoil relative to what she had been through was like losing one's kitchen in a fire versus watching one's entire house and home disappear in red-hot flames. Some fifty-four years previously, no compassion had been shown to her when she and my father, a married man, had fallen in love and she became pregnant with me. But, he was trapped in a marriage to a woman he realised he had never liked, in an Ireland governed by a uncompassionate church and state, both of which worked on the assumption that for a single woman to get pregnant, no man had to have committed any sin. The burden had been significantly Mum's.

My problems by contrast were largely of my own making. I should have and could have done more to save my marriage. I had put my hormonal demons in the driving seat. I had let a good man go. I had failed to communicate. I had failed to talk. Mum knew trust and love had been slow to come to me, that I had for a long time denied myself the possibility of them, that I had resisted and doubted. But Patrick had broken through and for twenty odd years of our marriage and before marriage, I had trusted him and had enjoyed the certainty of his love.

When Mum and I hugged at the airport, the tears in her eyes said my heart is breaking for you and the tightness of her hug said, I am there for you. I needed that. And she was there for me and for Fiona and Zara too and for Matt in his absence. A little bit of the dark cloud shifted from over our house when she arrived back. Occasionally I even felt a less judgmental and more supportive attitude emanating from Zara. Those moments lifted me; it had been years since anyone bought

153

me flowers but she bought me a lovely posy of colour from her first week's pay at a new local vegetarian café; a week later I felt chuffed when she treated me to coffee and a treat at the same café, and introduced me, with a smile, to her manager and other co-workers, as a fellow crusader on the road to saving the planet! I decided that it must have helped that I chose to wear some colourful vintage-style clothes that I had bought in a charity shop.

All the years that I had known Mum, she would not interfere in family matters unless specifically asked and then only reluctantly, if at all. But I felt the shift in her and was glad of it. Within two weeks of her return, as we sat on the couch in our kitchen-cum-living room, she took a conspicuous deep breath and raised the issue of counselling.

"Martha, I've been thinking." She paused and slowly and neatly folded a piece of paper in her hands until it was so small it could fold no more. It was as if she was waiting for the response that our family normally gave her when she opened a conversation with, "I've been thinking." The prompt response was usually, "Granny's been thinking, quick, man the guns, get out your diaries, prepare for the unexpected…" When Granny had been thinking it was usually that she had concocted a plan for an outing to Tayto Park, to a beach, to a play or even, one time, to Rome. This time it was just the two of us alone on the couch and I said nothing.

"Martha, it might be time for you to bite the bullet, to go for counselling. You've nothing to lose this time, pet."

She had suggested it gently before, many years ago, but I had refused. She opened out the piece of paper that she had been folding and written, in her own clear hand, were the names, addresses and telephone numbers of three well-recommended counsellors. She had, she explained, done her research among her wide group of friends.

Her face opened long and wide with surprise when I took the piece of paper and said, "Thank you, Mum. I've been thinking the same. I will ring them tomorrow." I bent across and kissed her on the cheek with gratitude. She took my hands in hers and held them on her lap.

"Actually, I was planning to ask you today if you could get some counsellor suggestions for me. Fiona tells me she persuaded Patrick to go and see someone. If he can do it, I can certainly do it." I laughed at the thought of Patrick going to see someone. He was of the opinion that too many people reinvented themselves as victims as soon as they went to a counsellor.

"So Fiona told me." Mum smiled.

"Yeah, I've been trying to imagine a counsellor succeeding in dragging personal stuff out of Patrick. It's not something that comes naturally to him."

"Oh, they have their means, you know." Mum laughed.

"I can just see him facing her with his fingers clasped and his thumbs twirling, his legs crossed with his right leg on top, jigging up and down." I imagined that he no longer wore his wedding ring and so he wouldn't be twirling it. I still wore my *everything ring* as I always had since the day of our wedding, on the third finger of my left hand. I pretended that I would have to get it cut off but I knew that with soap and water I could remove it myself. "He will look at the counsellor but his mouth will be shut and his eyes open as if he is waiting for her – or him – to speak." As I spoke, I moved my hands and legs as I imagined Patrick would and I jigged my top leg. Mum brought her hand over to rest on the knee of my leg. I remembered all the times that I had rested my hand on Patrick's knee to guide his leg to stationary.

"I suspect that the right counsellor will get through to Patrick. Just as he told me once that you'd a great knack of breaking through to him…"

"He did? I didn't know he'd told you that! I did, I suppose," I said, remembering with sadness that it was a knack I had forgotten to employ in recent years. "I used to insist that we went out for dinner, I'd talk about this and that, mainly the kids or his father or whatever and along the way I'd ask him his opinions or thoughts and before he knew it, he would be telling me stuff…it worked for us for years." It had worked, that much was true, I thought. "I wonder, why did I stop?"

"Life got in the way, Martha. You did your best. You always did."

"But did I? Did I really?"

"You did and you still do. Fiona tells me that you make extra meals all the time so she can bring Patrick over plenty of good food to fatten him up."

"Yes. I do. But I'm still worried about him. Despite all the shepherd's pies, Thai green curries and Irish stews, Fiona says he is still losing weight."

"If he loses any more weight, you'll hardly see him sideways! He says he's in training. And he's not playing any golf at the moment, says he can't hit a ball out of his way."

"Mum, did Fiona tell you all that?" She hadn't told me about the golf, but I was not surprised.

Mum looked at me a moment and lifted her empty coffee mug to her lips, then put it back down on the coffee table with more care than was required.

"I've a confession to make," she said. "I went to see Patrick last week…"

"You did? How was he? How did he look? Is he really thin?"

"You're not mad at me?"

"No, Mum, I'm not mad at you." Her hands were back resting on her lap and I put mine on top of them. I could feel them tremor. "Were you really scared I'd be mad at you? I don't think I've ever been mad at you."

"Nor me you." She gave a loving smirk. "Maybe not knowing each other for twenty-six years has its advantages!"

"Maybe it does. Twenty-five less years of the usual mother-daughter baggage."

"Other baggage though." Her tone saddened.

"Yes. Other baggage." I sighed, acknowledging that I finally accepted that I had been carrying *other* baggage for too long. I was coming to the realisation that the longer I carried that baggage without stopping to put it down, the heavier it had become.

"And about Patrick…" Mum interrupted my thoughts.

"Yes. About Patrick." I was all ears.

"He blames himself entirely. He betrayed you. He says he let you down at the deepest level and you never deserved that. He seems to believe that you are better off without him."

I raised an eyebrow of disbelief at her and she acknowledged it with a slight nod.

"There's more. There is something he alluded to that he said goes back ten years ago, just before the crash. He said he did something you specifically asked him not to do. Before you say it, yes, I know Patrick can be given to exaggeration and sometimes self-serving embellishment, but I believe him when he says that some big mistake of his kicked off his litany of mistakes. I think more than anything else he is racked with guilt."

I looked at her for inspiration as to what she was talking about. I scratched my eyebrows. "I can't think of anything he did then. Surely I'd have known, that would have been around the same time we found out that Trish was dying,"

"He said you don't know what it is and he didn't tell me. All he really said was that it wouldn't have been such a big mistake if he had only told you about it, right at the start."

"What could it have been? Why didn't he tell me? Was it another affair?" I was getting agitated.

"No. Definitely not an affair because he said it was something you asked him not to do. But he did it and quickly realised his mistake. Seemingly, he was about to tell you just when Trish told you her cancer was back and it was serious. There was no way he could tell you then about what a monumental mistake he had made."

"Poor Trish. Those were up there with the worst times of our lives. Remember, she and I researched everything and we decided she should try a vegan detox diet but she didn't stick with it because everyone else around her said it wouldn't work. They persuaded her to try chemo again, even though the doctor wasn't promising it would change the prognosis, and it was all useless and awful. Every bit of it." A vision of a bald, sickly white Trish sitting up in bed making funeral plans came to mind. "There was no one like Trish. We were going to grow old and contrary together and happily drive everyone mad." I gave a little laugh at how out of sync with the reality of her early death our big and happy plans had been.

"I know, pet. I know."

"She died just as the recession hit us like a tornado. And the very day after her funeral Patrick and I spent ringing clients trying to get in enough money to pay the monthly salaries. Imagine that I didn't even get to honour her with the grieving time that she deserved. Our lives became hijacked by the need to get in enough money to survive. It was all so fecking tragically wrong."

"I could never forget. And in all that time I never saw you cry. I saw tears trying to escape but you fought them back and got on with it. Patrick rang me a few times about you back then; he was very worried, he could see your pain, he tried bringing it up with you but he told me you would freeze and say that you had to get the accounts sorted. I tried too. But neither he nor I could get you to talk about Trish. You never got a chance to grieve her, Martha."

"No, and she deserved better. There was no time. Life, shitty life, got in the way." I didn't fight back tears as I spoke. I let them run down my face as I thought of my wonderful, funny, caring friend.

"Martha, don't be so hard on yourself, please pet. Patrick and you were both struggling. You were working all the hours just to make ends meet, bringing Patrick's Dad and the kids to where they needed to go, feeding them all, keeping the house, there was no end to it for you. And I was waiting for my first hip operation so I was of limited help."

"Trish and Páidí were our best friends, the four of us had more fun and sorrows together in the nearly twenty plus years we knew each other than many friends have in a lifetime. I loved her."

"I loved her too, Martha. It would have been impossible not to. But she was your best friend. Patrick and I both cried too when we talked about her last week." Mum patted tears from her eyes with her soft hankie and sobbed gently.

I moved nearer to her on the couch and we brought our arms around each other's waists and pulled ourselves into one self, our heads rested against each other, and together we produced a gentle chorus of sniffing while a river of tears ran between us. Patrick cried last week, I thought, I don't think I ever saw him cry in the nearly thirty years I knew him, not even when his adoring Mum died. Patrick cried. Was it for Trish or was it more than that? Was it for us?

Neither Mum nor I heard Zara come through the kitchen door as we sat locked in our cocoon. The first we knew of her arrival was when she clattered the dishwasher open on the other side of the island unit. Mum and I jumped and Zara laughed, a laugh that said she got a fright too.

"Sorry about that, Gran," she said with a grin. "Would you like some of my extra special super greens smoothie to get you over the fright? You can have some too, Mum."

Chapter 11

Matt Returns

Late September 2018

A couple of weeks after my conversation with Mum, I was back at the airport collecting Matt. As he walked through the arrivals door, he was every bit a more solidly built version of his father when we first met, the same dark curly hair but more untidy, the narrow face and strong chin and those big blue eyes, framed with thick eyelashes. He hugged me in a way that said I care about you but I don't know what to do with you. We made small talk until we got home.

"I'm sorry, Matt," I said as I sat down beside him on the same couch as Mum and I had sat on and cried our communal cry.

"Yeah. I know. But I don't want to talk about it right now if that's all right with you. I just need a breather to get on Irish time. Okay?"

"Sure," I said, feeling there goes another child who thinks it's all my fault. "I understand. Tell me about Canada so."

"I like it…a lot."

"Oh. What do you like a lot about it?"

"It's clean. It's honest. The people. The outdoor life. It was good for me."

"Right up your street so." I smiled.

"Certainly is."

I paused before I asked the next question, a little bit of me dreading the answer. When Matt said that he liked the people I knew that it meant that he liked one particular person. For the best part of the four months that he had been there he had been swept away in his first ever serious relationship, an athletic Canadian whom he had met at the sports centre where he worked.

"Have you plans to go back?"

"Maybe."

"Dare I ask might we get to meet Sophie anytime soon?"

"To be honest, Mum, if things were different, she might have come over here this Christmas but…with things the way they are, I don't think that will work. Do you?"

"I don't know, Matt. I don't know." This wasn't the Matt I'd been expecting or hoping for. This Matt was annoyed and, I suspected, lovesick.

"So, Mum how are things?"

"How are things?" I repeated.

"Yes, how are things between you and Dad?"

"Messy. Complicated. Upsetting. Confusing…"

"And what are you doing about it? Fiona said that if you clean the house one more time she is going to leave home. So, what are you going to do other than clean the house?"

This was the other side of Matt. Not one we always saw. Matt, like Patrick, normally placated me, not confront me head on. But every so often he wasn't like Patrick. He challenged a situation when it needed to be challenged. I admired him for that but I didn't always enjoy being at the receiving end of it. Nonetheless, I have to acknowledge that over the years, Matt and I had had some deep, open and hard-hitting conversations and I loved his capacity for honesty with compassion.

"Yes, Fiona told me a few weeks ago that I needed to stop cleaning. I agree with her. I hate housework. That hasn't changed one bit. I've agreed that we will share it out more between those living here. Mum reckons I was doing it because the house was the only thing I felt I could control."

Matt made a sideways gesture with his head which either poopooed the notion of sharing the housework or my excuse for all the cleaning I'd been doing.

"Anyway, we agreed that we'd sit down last night and talk about things, the three of us, Fiona, Zara and me. It was a long conversation. I told them things about my family story that I should have told all of you years ago."

Zara was furious with me when I told her my side of the story. She told me that I had lived a lie by not telling the truth. I should have seen that coming. By her measure, I had pretended to be open and honest and all the time I had been keeping a big bloody secret. It wasn't just my story. It was Mum's story as well and therefore as Mum was her Gran, it was Zara's story too, as far as Zara was concerned. She cried when she heard how Gran had been treated when she was pregnant. I felt it was all my fault. Fiona had cried too but said very little, though she had made some reassuring nods and had hugged me before she went to bed. I had tried to suppress my crying while I spoke. I had thought telling them would bring us all closer. I had been wrong. At the end of the night, I felt drained and isolated, as if every sentence from my lips had widened the gap between us. But still I was determined to tell Matt myself, probably because I wanted him to hear it directly from me and not relayed by Zara with the added bitter spice of her renewed resentment towards me.

"That sounds ominous, Mum. Are you going to tell me so? Or should I wait and hear the more dramatic and embellished version from the others?" As he spoke, he sat with his right leg jigging gently, crossed on top of his left leg. He was so like his father it was scary.

"No doubt you'll hear their version later tonight or soon anyway and no doubt there will be drama. But I would prefer to tell you myself first. That is why I suggested in my last text to you that we have dinner together tonight. Is that okay?"

"It can be." I could feel that Matt was not going to make it easy for me in his current mood.

"Thank you, Matt. Early dinner here so. Zara and Fiona are making dinner for Patrick tonight at his place." I paused because those words still didn't sound right. "And I gather you three siblings are meeting in town afterwards."

"So I've been told by she-who-must-be-obeyed."

"Fiona or Zara?" Either was possible.

"Fiona."

"Hah. I thought it might be Zara because she sure likes to lay down the law with me. You're lucky she lets me cook meat at all, especially beef."

Matt laughed. "Don't worry. I've seen her Snapchat and Instagram. Those beef cows are what's putting holes in the ozone layer. All that methane."

"Scientifically speaking she has a point. Have you seen how much water it takes to produce a pound of steak, never mind the gasses? However, tonight, I will cook you a slab of thirty-day aged Irish Angus sirloin steak with some extra hot horseradish sauce, spicy wedges, mushrooms, onions and broccoli. As you ordered." I could hear the girls comment, "Oh, the apple of Mum's eye is home, all hail Matt." It didn't seem to register with them that when they came home from even something like their post-Leaving Cert holiday, I cooked each of them their favourite meal.

"Perfect Mum. Still my favourite." He gave me a kiss on the cheek before he got up from the couch and disappeared upstairs. Just like his father, the way to his heart was through his belly.

I laid the table with care, nice new colourful mats and some late roses from the garden. I had given the Dublin blue tablecloth to charity. I was feeling nervous. The counsellor had warned me that each child would respond differently and that I could not assume to predict who would respond which way.

I offered Matt a beer with his dinner but he said that he'd join me in having a glass of red wine instead. That was a first. That must be what having a serious girlfriend can do to a guy, I supposed. I passed no remarks.

"Matt. How do I begin? First, let me admit straight out that, while I have always preached openness and honesty, I have not always practised it as fully as I should have. I know I have been guilty of being, at best, vague about my childhood."

"Hmm. I think vague might be an understatement, Mum." Matt raised an eyebrow.

"Fair enough. And I am sorry. Don't hold back." Why did I say that? It sounded chippy. "Anyway, maybe before I start, tell me what you think you know." I had made some wrong assumptions on that score the previous night.

"That you grew up in Sligo. You loved the sea and sailing but still you were unhappy as a child. You've never said that actually. But we know. Your dad died quite young, and a woman whom you call Heather, on the few occasions that you *do* mention her, reared you. Obviously, she was not your real mother."

I nodded. I'd often thought thank God that bitch wasn't my real mother.

"Gran, whom you call Gran when you are talking about her but Mum when you are talking to her, is your real mother. You didn't meet her until your late twenties but you've explained very little about that and we all assume you were adopted!"

He paused before continuing and I mumbled, "Sorry."

"Gran adores you and us and spoils us. But Zara is her favourite. We think it's because Zara's most like you."

"Zara most like me! Do you think so?" I was surprised Matt thought so, although the thought had threatened to cross my mind and Mum had hinted at it.

"Of course. That is why you clash. You care about the same things!"

I sighed and rubbed my face with both hands. "That's true. Maybe," I said, reluctantly letting the thought sink in.

"Gran is always telling Zara that she looks like you and acts like you too. Zara isn't too fond of being told that!"

"What teenager would want to be told that they are like their some-times off-the-rails mother?"

"Exactly!" He touched my had gently. "Only joking – Zara adores Gran too so it's no biggy. Gran tells us that she treasures watching us grow up. She says that it is her small consolation for what she missed with you...but the whats and whys of that whole situation have never been explained. We have learned that asking gets us nowhere."

"I know. I was wrong. It should never have been that way. I did what I thought was best for me and for Gran – Mum. I thought that by not talking about the past, I was letting go of it...it seems I have a lot to learn. I've been going to counselling for the last couple of weeks and I'm trying to do better, starting last night with the girls. I told them a lot and I am not sure they took it too well...but I want to tell you the full story too."

"Wow. Fair play. Counselling. That's good. But you don't need to tell me everything, you know. I don't need to know all the gories."

"Oh, okay, I think." I was feeling wary, thinking of the previous night's conversation when Zara had cut me short and told me that she didn't need to hear much more. It was all in the ancient past and shouldn't I be getting over it like, at this stage. She loved her relationship with Gran. *So, to be honest, Mum,* she said, *I don't want to hear anything that might take from that.* On the one hand Zara was angry with me for not telling her before and on the other hand she only wanted an edited version. One that wouldn't spoil anything for her. The previous night I was suppressing tears before I had really begun. And as I started to tell Matt, my tear ducts were already primed and I could feel tears looming large in the corner of each of my eyes.

Chapter 12
A Conversation About the Past

Late September 2018

When I remember the conversation that night with Matt, I can't be sure how much I told him straight out versus how much I remembered as I spoke to him but did not say out loud. I know I tried to make up for all I had not said before. I remember that I pushed a mushroom around my plate, circling my small steak, marking my territory. I remember that every so often he interrupted me with a few kind words for which I felt very grateful.

"It's okay, Mum."

I took a tissue from my pocket and wiped my eyes. I blew my nose quietly, reminding myself that I was not alone. When I had the house to myself, which was most of my waking hours, blowing my nose like a trumpet had become one of the things that I allowed myself to do with impunity. There were other liberties to be enjoyed too free from the fear of comment. For example, I imagined that I could have had a giggle with Trish about the pleasures of the 3 Fs of Feeling Free to Fart – knowing there was no man nor child around to comment – but with no Trish, there was no giggle. Such silly conversations can only be had with best friends. I missed her for the big stuff and the small. Celine was now the friend I spent most time with, but she hadn't Trish's outspoken ways or her bawdy sense of humour and I didn't confide all my inner most secrets so totally to her either. She didn't demand that of me the way Trish had.

"It's okay, Mum," Matt repeated

"Sorry. I am a bit of a wreck these days. I have been for some time really. I know that."

Matt squeezed my hand but said nothing.

"I really thought that I had put my past behind me. I had a husband who loved me and whom I loved and we had a good family. Why would I go delving into my horrible past? But the past made me who I am. Heather reared me but she was not a mother to me. When I was twelve, she told me to call her Heather. It was many years later before I found out why…I wanted to forget her…" I paused as I pictured a woman with thin pursed lips and a tight face framed by the short, fixed curls of permed hair; hair dyed too dark for the years that were well-told in her deep wrinkles. She was diminutive in size but large and hard in the feelings she induced in me. Thinking of her sent a ghostly chill through me. Matt's hand still held mine and his grip tightened. His eyes reached out to comfort me.

"I'm learning that the attachment you have with your mother, or in my case mother figure, in the form of Heather-the-Horrible, has a knock-on effect on the attachment you have with your spouse or your own kids. I am starting to understand that growing up believing that Heather hated me has played its part in my relationship with Patrick, and with you guys. I had convinced myself I was the better for my upbringing. That it had informed me and made me better equipped to be a good wife and mother myself." As I spoke, I realised that it sounded like a bizarre thing to believe, particularly given the childhood I had experienced. Since my first visit to the counsellor, I had read some interesting articles on attachment theory. I would have wanted to have given our children *secure attachment* and I now feared I had failed in that regard.

Matt said nothing for a moment. I would have liked him to say something then. I wanted him to say that I was a good mother. Finally, he spoke.

"Mum, we are all lucky to have you. All of us, Dad included. If anything, you have been too good to us and as a result we often take you for granted."

"Thank you, Matt, but I know I've not been my best at times in the last few years. But I'm working on it."

"You have had plenty of challenges and we could have been more supportive. Being away has helped me realise that."

His comments of support touched me and new tears fell. I appreciated his empathy and I could relate to the fresh realisations he referred to, getting away from family when I was young certainly had given me new and different perspectives.

"Matt, thank you. And just so you know, Gran knows I'm talking to you guys. She's glad that I am. It's very much her story too. I know she thinks that I should have told you all sooner. She did suggest it in the past. But I chose not to…she is a good woman, my mum, your gran, the best."

"I know, Mum. I know."

"Sorry, of course you do, pet. I should get on with telling you."

He shrugged encouragingly.

"I was the youngest of the four children in the house I grew up in. I thought I was the unwanted accident whose destination it was to be the family skivvy. I arrived six years after the previous child. From the day she first saw me, Heather told me I was useless and ugly. She set the standard. My three siblings followed. I was their punchbag. School was somewhere I escaped to. It was my salvation…especially boarding school. I guess you'd say it was where I started to discover my true self and to build some self-esteem, especially when I met Mrs Connolly there. She was my House Mistress and Careers Counsellor and, as you know, she became so much more to me."

"I do remember her, Mum. She was lovely."

"She is. Every ounce of her. Her dementia has got worse these last few years. When I go to see her these days, sometimes she asks me why I'm not wearing my uniform. Bless her. Without her I might have spent my whole life feeling like an unwanted dog waiting for the next kick."

Matt cast a disbelieving eye at me, as if to say I was being over-dramatic.

"She was my saviour, Matt. She was the first person I ever spoke to about the beatings and abuse at home."

Matt flinched, then nodded slowly and cut himself a bite of steak. He put it in his mouth and chewed it methodically as if it required it. I had never lifted a finger to them and neither had Patrick. The notion of receiving a slap from us would have horrified any of them. They'd have been on to Childline in minutes. I paused and got up to refill the water jug.

"Mrs Connolly helped me see that I didn't deserve the abuse. That it wasn't normal and it wasn't right. Heather broke all her wooden spoons on me. Then she got my father to saw the handles down to a straight line and sand them smooth." I could see them in my mind's eye in the big utensils jar on the worktop of the kitchen where I grew up, a constant reminder of the damage they could do, a constant threat of pain.

I picked up a wooden spoon out of the utensil pot beside my spotless clean hob and brought it over to the table. I held each end of it in my fists and moved as if to bend or break it. There was no give. Matt took the spoon and did the same. He shook his head and put down the spoon.

"Shit Mum. I'm sorry. She must have been one very sick woman."

171

"I know. It wasn't until I was an adult I realised what force it took to break those spoons. The bruises took weeks to disappear. They would start off with just a little bit of colour. Then go to purple, then gradually fade to yellow…" Matt's face was an expression of horror. He brought his hand up to his mouth. I wasn't sure what he was thinking. I needed reassurance. "Sorry. TMI."

He swallowed hard. "It's okay. Tell me as much as you want to."

My mind went back to a typical beating. First, she would find something wrong with something I had cooked or cleaned. She would yell at me about how useless I was. Then, fool that I was, I would protest, in all honesty, that it was one of my siblings who had burned the food I had made or dirtied the table I had left clean. To speak such truths amounted to answering back. A mortal sin in her books – if we Protestants had mortal sins. She would reach for a wooden spoon. She would yank out a chair and make me lift my skirt or dress, pull down my pants and bend over. I remember the strength of the venom with which she hit me with the spoon across my bare bottom. Sometimes, I fell forward with the force. That earned me extra venom. The physical pain was not the issue. It always passed. It was the humiliation and the knowledge I was hated that got to me. That hurt was always with me. I believed I deserved to be hated. That I failed to understand why I was hated was my problem too. I was glad the bruises were where no one could see them. As long as they weren't visible, I could pretend that I was worth liking, that I was like the other girls in my class. I didn't tell Matt much of this. It would definitely have been too much information.

"What about your father, Mum? Surely he tried to stop her?"

"I have wondered at that. Did he speak to her about it when I was not around? He was quietly kind to me when he was at home, but he was rarely there. Funny she never beat me in front of him. She was clever that way. Mrs Connolly suggested I try to talk to him about it but I couldn't work out how or when. He was at work, or golf, or rugby…strange, he was captain of the local golf club too. Like Patrick I mean. I think he loved me in his own inadequate way and for the most part denied or turned a blind eye to what was happening. Or, maybe, he thought if he interfered more, she would treat me worse…who knows? He was rarely there to see how she treated me, I will never know how much he knew or didn't know but I don't remember her ever beating me in front of him.

"I remember it was the height of The Troubles. There came a time when the house landline would ring every night, a number of times in the middle of the night. It went on for months. Dad put a tape recorder by the phone and used to tape the conversations – actually they weren't really conversations. I used to sneak a listen to the recordings before he gave them to the Gardaí, Dad rarely uttered a word in response to the cackling couple's rants! We were Protestants and by some distorted ignorance, this man and this woman, who claimed to be members of the IRA, decided that this meant we were Unionists and that, in their books, made us fair game for the IRA. They called my Dad a fucking West Brit, a fucking Unionist, said it was time Brits like him got out of The Bank of Ireland and give it over to its rightful owners, the People of Ireland. They needed more than a history lesson. They demanded change or else…or else his fucking beloved children wouldn't make it home from school one day. We know where you live; we know the route they walk to and from school. We know…they laughed, big dirty laughs, evil laughs. For months Dad left us all to school on his way into work. Heather, whom I still called Mother at that stage, was supposed to collect us after school. She collected the others but never me. I would have had to walk home every day except that Máire's mother, Mrs O'Reilly who lived a few doors from us, used to look out for me and give me a lift – and here I am, I lived to tell the tale." I smiled, perhaps proud to be alive.

"Feck it, Mum, Heather was evil."

"I know she was, and do you know what else? A huge part of me wanted the IRA to kidnap me or even kill me. That would teach her, I thought!" I laughed at how, through my child's logic, I had played out the scenarios, how they would teach Heather. I hadn't considered what it would teach me.

"Did your dad not know that you would have walked home from school all the time if it wasn't for Máire's mother? Did you never tell him?" Matt's eyes were opening wider and his face was getting longer with each horror I revealed.

"I can't explain why, but it never ever dawned on me to tell him way back then in the cruelty of my youth…I think I thought I deserved it…He died a few years after I finished school. Who knows, I just might have told him when I got older and maybe wiser. But he died. And after that I was up in Dublin with no good reason to go home so I seldom did. But shit happens. Three years after he died, she had a stroke and from then on, I went home one weekend every month, cleaned the house and stocked her freezer with dinners. The dinners the carers cooked were never good enough for her."

"You did all that for her, even though she had treated you so…so horribly…" Matt's grip on my hand tightened again. The diamond on my *everything ring* pierced the skin on the finger next to it. It hurt but not so much that I considered asking him to let go.

"Oh Matt, I've asked myself many times why did I do all that for her. I think I was still hoping for her to love me, to give me some approval, say I was the good one. The so-called sisters and brother I grew up with were never around then. They were too busy with their careers, their precious children and their fancy cars. I hoped that she would change and see me as the caring child I was trying to be. See that I was better than them. I think I hung on in there in the hope of a miracle! But never a word of thanks did I get. Just put-downs and abuse. I did sometimes warn her that if she kept it up, I would stop coming...I don't think she believed me. Who knows the hold she had on me?" Who can ever understand the hold an abuser has on the abused? Maybe that was why I could identify with Celine and all she had put up with.

As I spoke Matt's wide eyes remained firmly fixed on my face. He had eased his grip but he squeezed my hand momentarily tighter with every new revelation.

"What did Dad make of her? What did he say about you doing all that for a woman who treated you so horribly?"

"Your dad never met her. I never brought him back with me to Sligo. I told him the story bit by bit. He was there for me but he passed no remarks. Just as your grandad always told him, PNR: Pass No Remark."

"Yeh. Grandad still says that." Matt laughed and I laughed too.

"Well passing no remarks can come back to bite you! Your dad and I went to Zimbabwe for a holiday. A friend of his from college was working there. It gave me a taste for Africa. A few months later I saw an advertisement looking for a volunteer accountant for an Irish charity in Sudan and I applied for it. I didn't discuss it with a soul other than to mention it briefly to Patrick. I guess I thought I wouldn't get it. And true to form, your dad passed no remark. It was two years later before I found out that he got a shock when I left and he was miserable for a long time after. That's Patrick for you."

Matt nodded, probably remembering some incidences between him and Patrick where he wished his dad had spoken up. "Don't I know!" he said.

"So, I went off to Sudan and left my miserable siblings to look after Heather-the-Horrible. They were all flabbergasted, each and every one of them." I smiled as I remembered their reactions, the letters they had sent me demanding my return.

"The siblings you're talking about are your adoptive mother's children? The ones you haven't seen for years?"

"It's more complicated than that…"

"Gee, Mum, how much more complicated can it be?"

"It's a long story…"

Matt gave an exaggerated yawn, waving his hand to his mouth. "One of those stories…I do hope I can last the distance." He shook his head.

"I'll keep it as short as I can so…"

"I'm only messing, Mum. Take as long as you need."

"As you know I spent the best part of a year working in Sudan. It had its challenges and its moments. At first, I wrote long and informative letters to Patrick, sending them home with returning expats as the Sudanese postal system wasn't the best. All communication was difficult. Phone calls were rare. There were no mobiles and no internet back then. Anywhere. Not just in Sudan. And the landlines there only worked on a rare good day. Patrick wasn't the best letter writer. The few letters that he sent told me about the great gigs that he was going to. It was one good gig after another."

"Some things don't change so!" Matt laughed warmly.

"Be careful. There can be a pair of you in it at times!" I was thinking about how much time the two of them spent talking football and how long it had taken Matt to tell me about Sophie, but I knew part of the delay was a reflection of the depth of his feeling for her.

"Ah Mum, I'm not that bad!"

"Indeed! But anyway, I became convinced that he had moved on to new and fresh pastures. I decided that he wasn't writing to me because he had found someone else and in one of the few telephone calls that I managed to make to him, I broke it off."

I stopped as I said those words. A sweat broke out on my forehead and down my chest, trickling down between my breasts. The realisation struck me. I had been wrong back then. Twenty odd years ago. Patrick hadn't fallen for anyone else. He had been back in Ireland building a career for himself, planning to be ready for me to come home and marry him. He just hadn't communicated any of that to me. Back then I had filled the gaps with my own distorted suppositions. There was some phrase Patrick used to use, something about known facts and unknown facts. It was a warning not to come to conclusions with only half the facts. As I sat there talking to Matt, I was still certain Patrick had an affair with Isabel and I had played my menopausal part leading to that affair, but I wondered if that may not be the whole story, there could be something missing, something he had not communicated to me, an unknown fact – such as that mistake he had alluded to with Mum.

I picked up my glass and swirled the ruby red wine around in it. I watched it settle, leaving its translucent wine-red legs running down the inside of the glass. Strong legs indicate good quality wine, they say. But is that true? Or is that only part of the story?

"Sorry Patrick."

"Mum!"

"Sorry I meant Matt…Where was I?"

"Sudan."

"Yes… I finished there and I wasn't ready to come home and go back to Heather duties. Anyway, I had messed up with your dad. I'd no reason to go home so I decided to try Kenya. I got a well-paid consultancy job there through the office here. After Sudan, believe me, Kenya was a working holiday. I lived the expat life and more. I made new friends from far and wide, including Kenyan friends. Safaris, the coast or other trips nearly every weekend. I had fun and I rarely took time to think of home, except for the likes of Trish and a few other good friends, that is." I felt upbeat remembering Kenya and my tone reflected the sense of escape and freedom I had felt.

"Then Heather died and my siblings didn't see fit to tell me." I sighed a can-you-believe-that sort of sigh and Matt nodded in response.

"A solicitor got in touch with the office back home where I was still on an extended career break. He spoke to Trish and told her Heather was dead and he needed to communicate with me. Trish rang me in the office in Kenya. When she told me, I felt nothing. Confused maybe. But not relief or sorrow. If anything, I felt empty, as if I became aware of a void within me, a space where mother–daughter love should have been. A space I thought would always be empty. Maybe it will take it a while to hit you, Martha, and you and I will celebrate, Trish said, maybe in time you will feel free of that thundering bitch. Trish never minced her words! I loved that woman."

"Trish who died some years back, Fiona's Godmother?"

"Yes. She was the best. She was my friend from our first day at work."

"She and Páidí used to spoil us rotten whenever you and Dad went off on some of your weekends or when they took us on days out to give you guys some free time or whatever. We all loved her." Matt smiled at his own good memories.

"Me too, Matt. Me too…we haven't seen Páidí properly in a few years, not since he and his new wife, Ann-Marie, had their second baby." Páidí was building a new and happy life for himself. I didn't hold that against him but I was sure that Patrick missed his friendship.

I was crying again. I was thinking if Trish hadn't died that we wouldn't be in this mess. Trish was my no-nonsense rock. Dead or alive I should have talked the whole thing through with her. We knew each other well enough. She and Páidí knew us both well. Once Trish had got over thinking of Patrick as nothing but a boring solicitor, she saw him as a decent, fun-loving man who adored me, her best friend. We had never looked back. The four of us were best friends until death us did part; her tragic, early death.

"As Trish told me to do in her phone call, I rang the solicitor. He had a letter for me from my father. He was to give it to me when Heather died. I was in Kenya. I was escaping all that family stuff. I was curious but not so curious that I wanted to go home. I was living the life. Trish wasn't feeling the best. She was desperately trying to get pregnant. She thought that the drugs weren't agreeing with her. I didn't want to go bothering her or Páidí. One night, alone in my apartment in Nairobi, I took a notion. I picked up the phone and rang Patrick. I didn't know how much it would cost me. And I couldn't get him to ring me back because I didn't know my own telephone number. I remember being scared that some woman would answer his phone. But he did. We had one of those giddy flirty exchanges. It was very strange. We had never done that before." I felt myself smile at the memory, the sort of smile that starts with a flutter in your chest.

"TMI, Mum. TMI."

"Sorry. I know." I laughed. "But it is such a good memory! Anyway, he had swapped his Volvo for an Alfa Romeo which he had promptly crashed on a bad bend in Donegal. No serious damage done, he said. Just a bruised ego. I laughed and suggested that unless his driving improved that he might want to switch back to something safer."

I loved remembering that flirty conversation with Patrick but I don't know how much of it I told Matt...maybe I gave him a censored version of Patrick's and my African romantic interlude but I certainly played out the whole thing in my mind...

'Maybe I will switch to something safer,' Patrick said. 'But not until I'm old and wed.'

I got a fright when he said that. 'Have you got plans on that front?' I asked, dreading the answer.

'Are you asking?' he said.

I remember that I paused. 'Not at the moment I'm afraid. I've tried it and long-distance love isn't for me.'

There was a silence. 'Me neither to be honest. So, you're not coming home soon?'

'No plans. Heather died and I've got a legal situation.'

'Oh? I'm sorry, Martha. I don't know what to say really. How are you about it?'

'Not sorry. Not sure. Numb. Mourning what I never had. I don't know. She is dead a month or two now I gather. I only found out last week. Trish rang me.'

'Let me guess. She's left you a fortune as compensation for all the years of grief?'

"Matt, I remember your Dad saying that because that conversation was one of the few times that Patrick actually commented on how she had treated me."

Matt nodded knowingly in response.

"'God no,' I said to your dad. 'Nothing like that. Seemingly my father left a letter to be given to me when she died. As I said to Trish, I can't bring myself to say may she rest in peace. I have to stop myself from saying, may she rot in hell.' Your Dad laughed. 'Fair enough, Martha,' he said. 'She gave you hell on earth.' She certainly did, Matt, do you know what Trish always called her? Cruella Deville!" I said, laughing at how appropriate the title seemed.

"They had Cruella way back in your day?" Matt asked with a gentle twinkle in his eye.

"There've been Cruellas for forever, I'm sure," I said, hitting him playfully with the back of my hand on his upper arm. "Anyway, moving on with the story…I explained to your dad that, with Cruella dead, there was now some letter for me from my father that the solicitor thought that I should come home to get rather than have him stick it in the post. The problem was that I didn't want to go home. But I did want to know what the letter said."

"And?"

"And I asked your dad, as a solicitor, to solve the problem for me. He was wary at first. He said that there may be conditions under which it could be released. It could contain sensitive information. Information that my father, or the solicitor for that matter, might have thought it inappropriate for me to read alone in the wilds of Kenya. I don't know the legalities of it all.

"'I'm a grown woman. Can't I decide that for myself?' I said."

"I could not think of anything that might be in the letter that I would want to hear sitting in a solicitor's office back in Sligo that I wouldn't prefer to hear in the wilds of Kenya, as your dad had put it."

At this point I remember Matt nodded and smiled as if to acknowledge that he understood the part both our personalities played in the scenario.

"Patrick suggested I get a signed and witnessed note to him with a friend of mine going home to Ireland from Kenya for a three-week holiday. The note was to say that my father's letter and any relevant related information could be released to him. Then he could maybe get my father's letter to me with the same friend when he was returning to Kenya. I promised Patrick I would stay in touch with him to ensure that he could keep me posted. It wasn't quite communication by pigeon in Africa back then but relative to nowadays it might as well have been! Within two weeks Patrick was able to tell me the letter had been released to him and he was giving it to a work colleague to deliver to me two days later. He told me his colleague was having a holiday in Kenya and was spending the first night at the Stanley Hotel where I was to meet him." I smiled, remembering all this and how convoluted it now all seemed.

"I asked if the colleague would be travelling alone and if I should invite him for dinner somewhere. I hoped that Patrick would say no. Once I had the letter, I knew I'd want to run off somewhere alone and digest its contents.

"'That's a lovely idea,' Patrick said. 'He loves good food and can be adventurous. Choose somewhere different to what we might get here.' I was sorry I had asked. This was a typical response from your dad, you know, thinking of the other guy!"

"Well, it was better than you having to go home to Ireland to get the letter." I wasn't so lost in my memories not to note that Matt was quick to defend his father.

"It was. I took him at his word and chose an Ethiopian Restaurant where you sat on the floor at low tables and the traditional food was served by beautiful staff in vibrant African costumes. They wore tall, twisted fabric head pieces adding further height to their natural elegance. I always wanted to try wearing a whole African outfit like that but you need to wear it walking tall and straight, the same way they carry urns filled with water on their heads. I don't think I have what it takes though; they make it look so easy. Don't they?"

Matt smiled. "They sure do. It's as if they are glued on. They don't spill a drop and there is no sense of the weight of them. It sounds like an interesting restaurant to take someone you don't know to."

"Well, yes and I was a bit uncomfortable that, as part of the experience, diners were expected to participate in at least one dance. As I walked from my apartment to the Stanley Hotel that evening, I thought I might have taken Patrick a bit literally when he suggested I choose somewhere different. His colleague might find the whole experience a bit intimate! But it was too late to change my mind.

"My eyes blurred when I walked from the bright sunshine into the dark lobby of the hotel, with its mahogany floors and heavy furnishings. I walked straight up to reception to ask for the person whose name your dad had given me.

"As I waited for the receptionist, I turned sideways to look at the people sitting in the lobby, wondering if I could pick out Paddy, the Irishman, I was to meet. I spotted a Paddy-the-Irishman all right! Patrick sat looking up at me from a low seat in the lobby!"

I paused as I remembered his face pale against his dark shadow beard, he looked white but gorgeous. Even his hairy white long legs declaring themselves from under his khaki shorts looked good. A small backpack rested on his knee. He looked at me, more tanned than he would ever have known me, a sort of dusty dirty brown. I stood there in my batik-dyed T-shirt and blue voluminous trousers, tied at the waist and ankles. My hair was tied in a loose bun, to keep it out of my face but still allow some air to circulate. His face was asking, is that you, Martha? And I was thinking is that really you Patrick or have I had too much sun? I smiled quizzically, lifted my hand to shoulder height and waved tentatively at him. This memory was so vivid that I paused to savour it. It was a moment of magic that cannot be explained. It was a moment of perfect equilibrium, the moment I knew I loved Patrick and he loved me. That he had surprised me by coming all the way to Kenya, without any certainty of the reception I would give him, was an unequivocal statement of love. I was blown inside out. I was laughing and crying at the same time. A smile spread across the width of his face as he stood up out of the seat and his backpack fell to the floor. He didn't bend down to retrieve it. He just stood watching me as I made my way over to him.

Matt didn't interrupt my thoughts. He just sat watching me expectantly, his elbows on the table and his head resting on his hands. He waited for me to resume.

"It had been nearly two years since we'd seen each other. I'd forgotten how tall he was until we hugged. When you hugged me today, Matt, that memory came back to me." When Patrick had hugged me that time I was filled with the feeling of belonging. I wanted that feeling back. It was lonely and painful without it. I felt like I didn't know the woman in my story anymore. I didn't know the man in the story either. But that was for another day.

"Patrick offered me the letter there in the hotel lobby. He said that we could skip dinner and go and look at the letter in my place. I said it could wait and he should see a bit of my Africa. We went out to that Ethiopian night of dinner and dancing." I remembered that it had been as if we hadn't been apart. It was better than that.

"I read the letter when we came home that night. Patrick sat patiently and silently beside me as I digested its contents. It was the strangest letter to receive – coming from beyond my father's grave – telling me I was not the person I had believed myself to be, which wasn't all bad…once I'd come to terms with it! The letter told me for the first time that Heather was not my mother and Mum, whom I had never heard of before, was my mother."

"And you were well and truly a fully fledged adult by then!" Matt gasped.

"I certainly was. And I can't begin to tell you how confusing it was. It forced me to look long and hard at my childhood memories. They felt as if someone had taken them and rewritten them without ever consulting me about it. It was bloody hard to process."

Matt was looking at me in sympathetic anticipation. I felt his kindness towards me and I was relieved. I hadn't felt that level of kindness when I had told Fiona and Zara the story the previous night. Fiona had said little other than that's tough Mum and that it would take her a while to get her head around it all. Zara had told me that I had no right to withhold the story from them all for so long, I, who had always

184

encouraged them to be open and honest, had withheld such funda-
mental facts that ran to the core of her very being, *her* being!

I poured Matt and myself each another glass of wine before I continued.

"It's nice, the wine. Good rich, dry flavour and a nice long finish,"
he said.

"Gosh Matt, you've become quite the connoisseur in the last few
months, haven't you? I'm impressed. Your dad and I used to say that
wine is one of life's great pleasures." I sighed. "I guess we could have
done better at keeping an eye on those simple pleasures."

Matt whirled the wine around in his glass and studied its movement. I considered him wise to avoid responding to my comment, although I would have liked to know his thoughts. I resumed my story.

"As I said, Gran knows I am telling you all this. She says she is
happy to talk to any of you about it if you wish. You will be sensitive
to her, I know that. However hard it all was on me, it was harder for
her. What I am about to tell you came from the letter and from various
conversations with Gran.

"My father said in the letter that he married Heather back before
he knew what love was. He worked in the bank where her father was
the manager. They dated and it was assumed they would get married.
Three children later and years of ticking along in low-key married misery, my mum, your gran, came to work in the bank. Mum says it was
love at first sight for both of them. She's a complete romantic still.
Look at her and Fergal." I laughed, thinking of them. They cuddled
together on the couch. They nearly always held hands when they went
out walking, the exception being when they had been happy to make
room between them for their young grandchildren.

"Don't I know! I used to find it embarrassing..."

"Imagine her as a young woman. She was fifteen years younger than my father's forty years but she says that they connected intellectually first as they read similar historical books and had other shared interests. The passion followed. No denying the passion end of it! Mum got pregnant. Which was horrendous in those days. This was twenty years before the Kerry babies' case so that will tell you where Holy Catholic Ireland was at. My father had the crazy notion that they should leave the country. He'd get a UK domicile, divorce Heather and marry Mum. No divorce in Ireland back then. Mum was beside herself but was more realistic and said that would leave them both outcasts and jobless. He would have no way of supporting his existing family, never mind a new one. My father then said that he would apply for a transfer within the bank and they could set up home in Dublin where no one would know them. It sounds like love made my father blind to the reality of the times that were in it. And him a *bank manager*…bank managers had to be seen to be pure back then. They were up there with priests and school teachers. It was all about appearances!"

"Plus ça change," Matt said.

"Indeed! Anyway, my lovesick father told Heather his plan. I think her response sent him hurling into the harsh reality of the situation. Her father was, by that stage, regional manager and of course still senior to my father. Once she told him the story, her father could and would ensure that any transfer for my father within the bank would be blocked. Heather was adamant that there was only one solution, Mum should go to a mother and baby home and put the baby up for adoption. Then Dad and Heather could go back to presenting their happy family image to the rest of their little universe. Mum flat out refused. Dad was torn. By all accounts it was a horrible emotional mess."

"It sounds awful. All of the options were bad for Gran."

"Yes. My father and Mum were both distraught. Mum said that he hated Heather at that stage and he was ready to leave her and set up home with her. Mum said that he couldn't. It just wouldn't work; they would both be jobless and homeless and then where would that leave the child? Heather came up with a plan B. She would, through her father, but without declaring the details, arrange for Mum to get a transfer within the bank to Dublin. Mum would get to keep her job, despite being single and pregnant. Heather would feign pregnancy and temporarily move to Dublin before the time that the baby was due and then she would take the baby, me, home as her own. Heather presented it to Dad as her making a huge sacrifice. Mum could see no other option so she agreed to the plan, consoling herself that I would be in a so-called 'good home' and I would be with my father."

"It sounds pretty extreme, as options go."

"It does now but back then there were few alternatives. Does it shock you? I mean, what I'm telling you."

"It does and it doesn't, I guess. The beatings, yes, they are shocking. The other is kind of in keeping with what Fiona pieced together. When we were younger, she spent a lot of time surmising. Zara tried asking Gran about it but Gran said that it was for you to tell, not her and that you would tell us when you were ready."

"It took me longer to be ready than she expected I suspect! The next bit probably goes beyond Fiona's surmising. Against every string of her heart, Gran signed the adoption papers and Heather came to collect me. Heather took one look at me lying in the nun's arms and said, 'My God, she's ugly'. I grew up with Heather always telling me how ugly I was. Once, I mumbled under my breath you should take a look in the mirror; it was nearly the end of me!"

"How could anyone call a baby ugly? How horrible!" Matt visibly shuddered.

"Mum said that she jumped out of bed, shoved Heather to one side and tried to grab me back from the nun. The nun held onto me and left the room, telling Heather to follow her. Mum was screaming, 'She's not ugly. She is beautiful.' Another nun appeared and restrained Mum. That was the last she saw of me until many months after that letter when I made contact with her. The first thing she said when we met was, 'You are still beautiful.'" I remembered the tears in her eyes and her arms reaching out to me as she spoke. I went willingly into her arms, which was very strange for me. I wasn't affectionate back then. I think it must have been because I recognised her tears as tears of certain love. My eyes were wet with the memory.

"I've heard her say it to you many times."

"It always makes me smile."

"And you are still beautiful, Mum, you really are."

I toyed with my wine glass again, rolling the stem of it between my finger and thumb, staring at the dregs of the red wine in it.

"Thanks Matt. I wish I felt it. I have never told Gran much about how Heather treated me but, in her heart, I think she knows. I know she is always trying to make up for those lost years – I suppose I am too."

"Oh Mum, I had no idea. Poor Gran. Poor you," Matt said, standing up and pulling me up into a tight hug. I cried into his big chest, memories of my upbringing mingling with memories of being hugged by the man I had lost, followed by thoughts of my wonderful Mum and son.

Mum had been hurt and upset with me for letting her go off on a cruise and not telling her all that was going on for me. But I didn't tell Matt that. She was there for me now. Mum said that counselling had helped her and that she was sorry that she hadn't got me to go sooner, back when I first got in contact with her. It wasn't her fault that I hadn't. It was mine. Trish had told me to go then too. I'd gone to counselling before I ever went to Sudan, back when I was trying to process my relationship with Heather. But I thought that in my two years away, I had it all worked out. And back then, after I came back from Kenya, I had not only Mum but Patrick, Trish and Mrs Connolly too and I felt loved, really loved.

As Matt hugged me, I looked up at his face and I saw his father as a young man. Involuntary sobbing took possession of me and as I tried to suppress it, hiccups moved in to take its place. Matt released me from the hug and handed me a glass of water which I drank in gulps from the wrong side of the glass while bending forward. Eventually my hiccups stopped.

"It was my dad who taught me that one as a cure for hiccups! He could be a good laugh whenever I got him on his own, which was sadly rare. For as long as I remember, he was a drinker and rarely spent time at home. He said in his letter that he was racked with guilt but, to his shame, he couldn't ever bring himself to do anything about it; he acknowledged that Heather treated me badly and in particular that I had been treated like a skivvy. He said he should have done something but he was weak and no match for her. Poor excuses, he admitted. I felt angry with him for years but Mum talked me through that anger. She put it in the context of the times that were in it and his alcoholism. The two things that he did do for me were to insist that I went to boarding school and, unbeknownst to Heather, to set up a trust fund. It was for me to use as I wished but he hoped that one day I might use it to go to university, as I had always wished."

"You told us you just didn't see the point in university back when you were young and that's why you didn't go."

"It was another lie, Matt. I'm sorry. I didn't want to remind myself of the truth. Heather wouldn't let me go." I shook my head, disgusted with my own lies. "One untruth or lie leads to another. And now...see

189

how when I reveal one truth, it leads to having to reveal another, and another…"

"You can still go to university, Mum. What's stopping you? Follow your heart. Like you tell us all to. You always said you didn't want to be an accountant."

"I said that I fell into it by a series of incidents and accidents. That is true. But, as a mother and a wife accountancy has served me well."

"But still…have you still got some of your trust fund money?"

"Your father didn't want me to touch it even for our wedding or when we were struggling to pay the bills. He called it my running away to university money. I didn't want to use it at first because I called it blood money."

"And?"

"I had to use it. We needed it when the Celtic Tiger hit the fan and when its guts got strewn across our lives. We could not have survived without it. I never told Patrick. He was always adamant that money was mine alone, for fulfilling some personal dream. It seemed simple to me; you guys were and are my dream. How else would I spend it? My dream was that you would all go to university and I held some back for that. Even when we were scraping the cents together to pay to put food on the table, I held onto that dream. I suppose some people might call it living my life through my children."

"I don't think we'd accuse you of that. You've always encouraged us to live our own lives not the lives we think others want us to live. You could still live the life you wanted, you could."

"Maybe. It was no miracle that the money stretched so far even after the markets collapsed. That was thanks to Trish. She told me, as only Trish would, to convert it to cash before the fecking bottom fell out of the effin' markets. Well she said *fucking* markets, of course! I rarely dared not to take her advice! It wasn't worth the penance. She'd have been insufferable."

"Good old Trish."

"God, I miss her. I had it invested in bank and other so-called safe shares, known as 'widows and orphans' shares. If I had left it in those it would have been worthless. After we started coming out of the recession, I put the cash left back into shares. So, between that and the stock market performing well there is a bit of money there still."

"You might still go to college? Why not? I hope you will, Mum. I do." Matt was distinctly excited at the thought.

"Thanks Matt. I really appreciate your support."

"But, and it is a big but, can I ask what about you and Dad? What do you see happening on that front now?"

"I don't know, Matt. I wish I knew."

There was a long silent pause. Then he spoke.

"What do you think Trish would tell you to do?"

I said nothing. I tipped the last of the red wine from the bottle into our two glasses. I considered knocking it back in one long gulp. I brought my glass to my mouth. Celine's words of warning stopped me. "Whatever you do, Martha, don't get drunk with your kids. Not now anyway. Trust me you'll regret it." Celine had made that mistake once in an attempt to dull the pain. Shane and Karen and the bastard never let her forget it. He could drink himself all the way to violent and obnoxious at least once every week but after the one time that Celine drank until she slurred with affection towards her beloved children, she got labelled the family lush.

I put down my glass and looked at my watch.

"Where did the time go? You'd better get going if you plan to meet the others for a drink."

I got up from the table and picked up our plates.

"Think about what Trish would have said, Mum. Won't you?" Matt said, planting a soft kiss on my cheek.

I knew what Trish would tell me to do but, without her, I didn't know if I had what it would take to face the inevitable emotional roller-coaster ride, a ride that I knew had a possibility of ending with a severe vertical drop. But how much worse might that be relative to where I was currently suspended in torturous uncertainty?

After all those long months of avoiding my dear friend Máire, that night, with the house entirely to myself, I picked up the phone to her. I burst into floods of tears as soon as I started to tell her my story. She started to insist on coming straight over but we settled on meeting for a morning walk the next day. Her family had been neighbours when I was growing up. Her mother had been my guardian angel when I was a child, always looking out for me as and when she could. And then thirty years ago, when I lived in Sudan, Máire's and my paths had crossed and we had become and remained close friends. Máire was always a tremendous listener and just talking to her about my break-up with Patrick and all the fallout helped me process it. And the beauty of talking to Máire was that we had known each other so long and so well that some things needed no explanation. Our walk rolled into a long lunch. As I made my way home, I was emotionally drained but strangely lighter. I admonished myself for not calling her sooner.

Chapter 13

Getting Legal

Mid-October 2018

After Patrick sorted out the legalities of getting my father's letter from beyond the grave all the way to me in Kenya, I had taken to jokingly referring to him as 'my solicitor and lover'. After we got married, I told him he had been promoted to being 'my solicitor and husband'.

Sandra MacDonald, my new solicitor, left a voicemail for me two weeks after Matt's return. There was no 'and...' when I referred to her. The title felt cold and official, although she was one of the good ones with a firm, no-nonsense but sensitive touch.

I had called her the week after that dreaded night of the dinner. I told her the planned 'party' had happened but that I had yet to digest the consequences. I would be in touch. A month later she called me to ask me if I wanted to talk further to her. I let her call go to voicemail and sent her a text in reply saying,

Thanks for call, I'll ring you soon, no need to call until you hear from me, regards Martha.

This time her voicemail was more assertive. "I have received some correspondence from Patrick, including his Affidavit of Means, and I think it is important that you arrange to call in to see me."

This was not what I had expected. I assumed that Patrick wouldn't send in any legal papers until he received a formal request from Sandra. I wasn't ready for him to take the initiative. I wasn't ready to push forward towards Affidavits of Means and what that meant. I hung up the phone and cried. There was no one there to hear me. Patrick wasn't hanging about. He was going straight for a separation; it must have been what he wanted all along. Mum reminded me of her conversation with him. She didn't believe that he necessarily wanted a separation, she thought that he believed that it was what was best for me, whatever that meant. We still didn't know what big mistake he had made ten years ago and Mum had suggested that I should ask him straight out. I was working up to that when I got Sandra's voicemail suggesting that I call in to meet her.

A week later, she made maybe three minutes of small talk and then put a glass of water, Patrick's Affidavit of Means and his covering letter, written on his own practice's headed note paper, down on her office desk in front of me.

"Take your time and read through that," she said.

The subject heading on the letter felt weird and unsettling.

Re: Your client: Martha O'Sullivan

Our client: Patrick O'Sullivan

Affidavit of Means of Patrick O'Sullivan and related matters

I had taken his name when we married. I was proud to become his wife and I was keen to lose any apparent attachment to my so-called family whom I had been reared with, if you could call it rearing. I had briefly considered adopting my mum's name but at that stage it was early days in our relationship.

Please find attached my sworn Affidavit of Means and the Title Deeds to 54 Battery Road and The Georgian House, Ormond Quay.

Please note the following.

The deeds for 54 Battery Road are mortgage free and solely in the name of Martha O'Sullivan in accordance with the transfer of ownership executed on 30 April 2008.

The loan currently held by Vespers Ltd. is in respect of my interest in an apartment block in Ballydermot. The current balance of this loan is €1,080,100. The loan deed was executed, and remains, solely in my name. The apartment block is currently incomplete and has little or no value.

The 3 properties at Oulton Estate and mortgages thereon remain in our joint names. These were recently valued at the amounts shown and the balance due on the mortgages are as at today's date.

The Georgian House at Ormond Quay is currently the Offices of Patrick O'Sullivan & Co. and of Brideshead Insurance Brokers. The property is mortgage free and is solely in the name of Martha O'Sullivan in accordance with the transfer of ownership executed on 30 April 2008.

The pension fund is stated at current value and remains in our joint names.

Please note that I consider the art and other contents of 54 Battery Road to belong solely to Martha to dispose of or otherwise in accordance with her free will.

I was baffled when I read item no. 1. This was the first time that I had heard anything about Patrick putting the deeds of our house, our home, into my sole name. And he had done it while Trish and I were busy pretending that she wasn't about to die. Why would he do that? The house had always been in our joint names. It was our family home of course it was in our joint name.

Item no. 2 was the answer to *that* question. It was undoubtedly the big mistake that he had referred to when talking to Mum. My reaction was, "For fuck's sake, Patrick," which I said out loud. Sandra cleared her throat in acknowledgement. I had briefed her on what I believed to be all our assets and liabilities. She said Item no. 2 had surprised her too.

"Feck him anyway. I told him to stay away from Joey. I told him not to touch those apartments with a forty-foot barge pole. They are in Ballydermot, for goodness sake. It's a dump of a village in the middle of a bog. His friend Joey was behind the whole thing, a cute hoor to top cute hoors. Instead of paying the legal fees, I know that he offered Patrick a stake in the development and that meant Patrick guaranteeing part of the bank loan." I let out an exasperated near scream of a sigh. "Patrick, what have you done?"

My mind went into overdrive as my accountant's brain struggled to function against the background noise of my feelings. I had failed. As his accountant and wife. Patrick must have invested in the apartments just before the market went belly up. He must have had no means of ring-fencing the debt and on realising that the deal was unlikely to come good he had moved our house into my sole name to keep it out of reach of the lenders. I knew that the lender had originally been SIB but it was clearly now Vespers the vultures. The payments I had found going through Patrick's accounts marked as re Vespers had been related to this nightmare. I had failed to convince him not to invest. I had failed to be the wife to whom he felt he could have confessed his mistake.

"In all the years, more than ten long years, he never told me about that fecking investment. What does that say about us? We used to…we used to be straight with each other, warts and all…"

I looked at the words and numbers on the page through blurry eyes. Effing Celtic Tiger, fucking cancer killing the best friend I ever had, the fucking menopause, and now this. My head was overflowing, tears were spilling down my face. I bowed my head down on to my arms folded on the desk and I sniffed loudly. A box of tissues appeared in the corner of my eye and, without lifting my head, I took two and then another two.

"Sorry," I said.

"It's okay. You're not the first person to cry in my office and you won't be the last."

I told myself to stop. In front of Sandra wasn't the place to cry. I tried to swallow my tears and gave myself hiccups which was just typical of me. If Sandra wasn't comfortable with crying, she wasn't going to appreciate a tears and hiccups combination.

She pushed the glass of water in my direction and I drank it down in three straight gulps. I sat back in the office chair and resumed reading the letter.

Item no. 4 was as big a surprise to me as item no. 1, but I could see that the transfer of the offices at The Georgian House to my name was consistent with Patrick's effort to protect our assets from Vespers. Like our home, Patrick's offices had always been in our joint names. We had bought the building pre-Celtic Tiger at a knock-down price and in a state that wiser people would have knocked down. In our naivety we had underestimated the cost of refurbishment of such an old building and had been forced to do it piecemeal when cash flow had permitted. While the building looked beautiful in the finish, unless there was a re-visitation from the Celtic Tiger, we were never going to recoup what we had spent on it. But it was debt free and it was now mine to do what I might with it. What was he at?

Through the fog in my brain there appeared a glimmer of new understanding. Patrick had made a monumental financial mistake. Patrick was going to tell me about it all those years ago but couldn't because Trish was dying. So, he made all the right legal moves to save our assets by moving them all over to my name. He might go down but he would not bring me with him.

"This is not what I expected. This is not it at all." I sniffed.

"Me neither. Strange in some ways. Well-thought-out in others. It appears that he has done or is proposing to do everything to protect your assets and make sure that you are looked after. And of course, he is putting himself at the real risk of going bust and therefore, worse still, of losing his right to practise as a solicitor."

Sandra verbalised what I was thinking. As she spoke, I looked down at my legs, my right leg crossed over my left, my right leg vibrating endlessly. I was doing a ladylike version of that Patrick thing. I stopped myself by putting both feet flat on the floor. I used to put my hand on his knee to stop him. I used to say, "Tell me about it, Patrick," and after that we might talk.

The letter continued with some further minor clarifications and concluded with a suggested division of assets and liabilities on separation. In summary, Patrick proposed that I retain full ownership of the house to live in or sell as I was free to determine for myself. He also proposed that I retain ownership of the offices which would be rented, in accordance with the long-standing, but previously ignored, lease, in part to Patrick O'Sullivan & Co. for the foreseeable future, the rent to be set at market value (we had never previously properly applied rent between ourselves and Patrick's business, save in so far as it made tax sense to do so), and in addition, the basement to remain rented to Brideshead Insurance Brokers who had been renting it for twenty years and were unlikely to be going anywhere anytime soon. In addition to my earning all the rent on the building, Patrick proposed that if his net earnings exceeded the rent earned on the property then he would pay me fifty percent of the difference. Furthermore, he proposed that all costs associated with our children that would normally be borne by us as their parents, would be shared equally between us.

Everything was reasonable to a fault. The more I read the more unsettled I became. Patrick was no fool but it was clear that he had left himself heavily exposed to Vespers and in protecting our assets he was protecting me. Still, I knew that he was going beyond that by making sure that I would be looked after both immediately and in the long term.

My head and heart were working overtime and not entirely together as I tried to process that letter. I couldn't decide what led Patrick to his proposals. Were they driven by guilt? Guilt that he had, against my express wishes, lost over one million euro of our money through a disastrous investment that I had specifically asked him not to make? Guilt that he had had an affair, however short, with Isabel? Or was it that he knew that Vespers the vultures were looking for full repayment of the loan and he felt that, if he didn't leave as many of our assets as possible in my name and as few as possible in his, they would seek every drop of the debt possible and leave us with little more than our home? *If* they left us our home. Could I dare to think that some of his apparent generosity was because he still loved me?

"I don't see any evidence of Isabel's fingers on this letter at all," I said, as much to myself as to Sandra.

"Nor evidence of any other woman lurking in the background!" Sandra smiled.

"No. What do you make of it?"

"In my opinion, it's the proposal of a decent, legally savvy man who wants to see his wife looked after. I'm not saying that it's watertight legally, should Vespers decide to pursue you."

I nodded and rubbed my hands up and down my thighs as if trying to warm myself. "He is a decent man. I know he is." Somewhere in my hormonal haze, I had forgotten just how decent. Spending more time alone thinking, combined with the recent addition of weekly counselling was clearing some of the haze. I was finding myself remembering more and more of all the good things that we had had and also the hardships that we had got through together.

"I suspect that all those diamonds you told me he kept giving you were part of the same plan," Sandra said in quiet tone.

I pondered her comment and was surprised that I could appreciate the veracity of it.

"Of course!" I said with almost delight in my voice. "And there was me thinking for the last few years that he was assuming I wanted to be walking around wearing bling the value of a small mortgage, in blatant competition to the Crown Jewels-on-heels herself!"

"If I may express a personal opinion, Martha?" Sandra asked tentatively.

"Go on…" I was expecting her to tell me it was time for me to forget about Isabel. I was readying myself for the build a bridge and get over it talk.

"I speak as a friend and as someone who has encountered Patrick professionally and personally over the years. And my gut, and that is all that I can say it is, is that the tone, the wording and his proposals in this letter all seem to say one thing: he cares about you. I don't usually give such personal opinions…"

I looked at Sandra and I wanted to hug her but there was a desk between us and it would have been awkward. I had misjudged her humanity. I looked down at the diamond and sapphire ring on my left hand. I hadn't wanted an engagement ring. Just one ring on the day for when we said 'I do'. I always called it 'my everything ring'. Of all the diamond jewellery I now owned it was the least valuable, but it was all I ever wanted or needed.

"Thank you, Sandra. I needed to hear that. I'm so confused…in every sense, I'm confused."

"Of course you are. You should take that copy of the letter and Affidavit away with you and let it all sink in, then come back to me and we can talk some more."

"It may take time. But perhaps things are not as bad as they have seemed. Perhaps…" I was thinking of the financial situation when I said that. I could see possible ways to ease the situation. I needed to look at the figures and talk to some people. I was moving into accountant mode. In accountant mode I could find clarity. Accountant mode saved me from dwelling on the whisper of hope that was coming to life inside me, a wee bud of a thought that we could possibly rescue our marriage. That hope could only have some hope of flourishing if Patrick and I were to talk. We needed to meet. The state of our finances seemed like a good place to start a conversation. Meeting and talking was what Trish would have ordered us to do. She would have locked us in a room together and we would not have been released until she was satisfied that we had flogged our differences to death. And that would have been after she had given us both a good metaphorical kick up the ass for being such fools in the first place.

Chapter 14

Examining Patrick's Affidavit of Means

Mid- to late October 2018

In a past life, I sometimes managed to maintain a certain amount of reason by doing my personal problem-solving on paper or, when it came to figures, on a computer. I reduced personal problems to a list of bullet point thoughts, pros and cons of different reactions, consequences of doing something, consequences of not; it was a tactic that I hadn't used enough in recent years and, in particular, I hadn't used when planning the closing dinner scene of our marriage. I could hear Trish's voice warning me not to make that mistake again.

"Patrick's letter brings a new perspective to your marriage and its downfall. Use that knowledge, you fecking eejit you. Start with what you know, focus on the finances, the rest will follow."

I knew the bones of the Ballydermot deal from the time that Patrick had tried to sell the notion of our investing in it to me: initially other investors would have put up an amount of cash to buy into the development; Patrick would have put up no cash but would instead have been paid no legal fees in lieu of putting up cash; Joey would have put up the site but no cash and would own the lion's share of the development; the construction of the apartments would have been financed by bank loans, guaranteed jointly and severally by the individual investors, including Patrick. All wonderfully straightforward in its perceived execution: site, planning permission, finance, build, sell at a profit. They got as far as build and then, having outlived and outperformed all reasonable expectations, the Celtic Tiger died and it would have become clear that there would be no selling the apartments; bank loans would have fallen due; investors' loan guarantees would have been called in; pressure on investors to honour the guarantees and pay up would have mounted with the transfer of the loans to Vespers. But where would anyone have accessed cash in those straightened times? If it was a nightmare for Patrick, it was a nightmare for others too. Of all the developments dreamt up during the Celtic Tiger this had to be one of the most ridiculous. A five-story apartment block on the corner of a main road in a one-horse eyesore of a village, a village in a hole in a bog, that was near nowhere and on the road to nowhere. All the beautiful places in Mayo and Patrick had to invest in Ballydermot.

"Martha, you're showing your anti-midlands bias there. Ballydermot's not that effing bad. The odd good thing came from there. Your husband, for example. He's a bit of an alright – most of the time! Now think, use those brains, what would you tell a client to do next?"

I laughed as I dreamt up Trish's comments to cheer myself on. I deliberately censored them of the generous sprinkling of the F-word they would have contained.

I'd make a to-do list for myself, like the one that I had made for Celine, starting with an up-to-date list of assets and liabilities in my name. This would mean valuing our house, now my house, the office building, now mine, the diamond jewellery that I never wanted, our paintings, now mine. I needed to take clear possession of everything and keep them away from the claws of Vespers.

I set up a spreadsheet with assets and liabilities under three headings: Patrick's assets and liabilities in his sole name; my assets and liabilities in my sole name; assets and liabilities in our joint names. My focus was on significant assets that may be at risk of being of interest to the vulture fund rather than a comprehensive list for the purpose of an Affidavit of Means.

Patrick's main asset was his legal practice but he hadn't included a value for it in his Affidavit. I understood the challenges involved in valuing an owner-managed business such as his. Patrick was the main man, the source of most of the clients, the significant primary ongoing contact for over half of them; he was the man the clients loved. If Patrick went bust and lost his practising cert then the business could quickly become worth little or nothing.

The original plan had been that two of the six solicitors he employed would build their own client relationships and would buy into the practice and become equity partners. It had been anticipated that Brendan Costelloe, who had been with Patrick since the booming nineties, would already be an equity partner but Brendan had bought a statement house at the top of the market and was still servicing a large mortgage. He had four teenage children, all in private schools. His capacity to borrow to buy into the practice was currently close to zero.

'The problem with Brendan,' Trish would have said, 'was that he became too big for his wellington boots when he moved up from the country and all the way to Dublin 4, of all places.'

'And bought himself a 4x4 Land Rover that was too clean and shiny to be taken down the country roads, for fear of the mud or scratches such boreens might inflict on it,' I would have added.

Patrick's Affidavit of Means, with the business valued at nil, showed him as having liabilities greater than assets of some €600,000; he was technically insolvent and if he was insolvent then there was an argument to value the business at close to nil. If he wasn't insolvent then the business had a value and it would be safe to say that the going concern value of the business well exceeded €600,000. The problem then became one of Patrick being able to pay his debts as they fell due; technically, the over one million he was being pursued for on the loan for the Ballydermot development was already overdue.

A buy-in merger with another practice could solve the problem. We had previously ruled this out as Patrick was committed to maintaining our shared professional ethos: diligence, honesty, transparency and caring. This ethos we feared would be diluted in a merger. The self-inflicted joke was on us: diligence, honesty, transparency and caring – where had these been in our marriage in recent years? We had both scorned them and in doing so had set ourselves up to fail – unless…unless what? Unless we worked together and reminded ourselves of all that we had been and all that we had stood for. And maybe all that we could be?

I surprised myself that I was seriously considering the possibility that we who had strayed so far from each other might find a way back. It seemed presumptuous on my part given what a self-indulgent menopausal demon I had been and given that Patrick's behaviour had consistently pointed towards a desire to end our marriage. But, after twenty-five mainly good years, I knew that what we had was worth trying to save. Also, Patrick, like Sandra and many other solicitors, would be quick to tell you that the first bit of advice they gave most clients asking them to do the legals for a separation or divorce, was to ask themselves if they had done everything that they could to save their marriage. Many people lived to seriously regret not doing more, especially women, who in hindsight often decided that an imperfect man was better than none. It was time to dust myself off and rise up to my reputation for resilience. It was the one good thing that my tough childhood had given me. Feck it. If we could not recover as a couple, we could at least both recover financially. No good could come from not working on this together. We could both get over the current financial hurdle. If I walked away with all the assets and left Patrick to struggle, I would not forgive myself. The children would not forgive me. I was ready to build a bridge and see what might be on the other side.

My plan of action started with valuing my assets. Valuations for the buildings would be straightforward enough. I only had to tell auctioneers I was thinking of selling and valuations would be forthcoming. The paintings were more complicated. I made a list of the eight paintings likely to be worth over three thousand. I invited two art auctioneers to view them and give me estimated selling values net of costs so I could decide which to sell. Then I rang the jeweller, the creator of my unwanted bling.

"Hi John, you don't know me but I'm Martha O'Sullivan. My husband, Patrick, bought me various pieces of diamond jewellery from you over the years." I got stuck for a few seconds at that part. I decided that if I said I needed to sell them then word might get out that we were insolvent. I settled on telling a version of the truth that we had broken up and so I thought I might like to sell my jewellery, if I got the right price.

"Oh, I'm sorry to hear that. Such a nice man, always a gentleman to deal with." Listening to him go on about the wonderful Patrick, I could imagine him concluding that if I had split up from such a *nice* man, then I must be the problem, the bitch. He wasn't called Saint Patrick for nothing. Who ever heard of Saint Martha?

"Let me see," John said. "I have a list of the pieces here in my files. I'll have a look and call you back with some figures." The tone of his response had turned to all business while I tried to cover up the tears in my voice. I decided that, when I did come to sell the pieces, I would get a second quote elsewhere and I mentioned this to him to ensure his best price. His total figure came in at what I knew was a fraction of what Patrick had paid for it.

I had two separate auctioneers value our house and two commercial property auctioneers said that they would have buyers on their books ready and willing to buy the office building on Ormond Quay. Our pension fund had been recently valued so I had that figure to hand.

Adam's and Whyte's each valued our eight most valuable paintings and gave me an estimated figure net of costs. I offered them each four to sell as soon as their next art sales came up, which as it happened was soon. I considered the possibility that if Vespers became aware of the art, they might challenge my sole ownership of it. To stake my claim I decided to hand them over to the auctioneers immediately. I said an emotional goodbye to each one as I took them off the wall. I would even miss Patrick's favourite painting, the Patrick Scott with its bold shapes. It had grown on me. Despite the note in Patrick's legal letter declaring that all the art now belonged to me, I didn't feel the Scott was mine to sell, but it was too valuable to justify keeping it.

Three of the paintings for selling, including the Scott, were large and cumbersome. The day after I took them off the walls I arranged for a courier to collect and deliver them to the auctioneers. The following morning I woke up to a large empty wall space above the fireplace in our bedroom. I felt the stab of loneliness as I sat up in the half empty bed. Through the house seven more empty spaces greeted me, screws in walls crying out to be occupied. I had been too hasty moving the paintings out before I had considered the gaps their absence would leave me to live with.

As I stood in the hall, remonstrating with myself and wondering what painting elsewhere in the house might sit comfortably above the hall table, I was jolted out of my thoughts by a ring of the doorbell. I expected it to be the courier. I opened the door to be greeted by a large colourful oil painting with two short, thin legs below it.

"It's a walking easel!" I laughed, recognising the legs and the painting. It was a massive colourful, loosely painted seascape with white waves crashing against a lonely sea stack. I loved the resilience of the sea stack in the face of the adversity of nature's elements. I wanted to be that sea stack.

"Delivery for Martha," said Celine's voice from behind the painting.

"Wow, for me. I love it. You know I love it." I lifted it out of Celine's arms and she turned and walked back down the path.

"Leave that in the hall and come with me," she said over her shoulder.

I followed her to her car parked a few houses down the road. She lifted another massive painting from the hatchback and handed it to me.

"You don't know this one. It's from my early days. I did a series of free-spirited women and I've dug some of them out. I've hung one up in my own house where that seascape was."

"It is stunning. So full of life. I want to bottle it. Thank you. Thank you." I couldn't have chosen better myself; it was truly fabulous. To look at it was uplifting in itself. A woman of unknown age, in a short red dress, was running down a steep grassy hill, arms outstretched, ready to defy gravity and soar like a bird up into the open sky. Her heavy walking boots were not going to hold her back. I knew where I would hang it. What better image could I have to get me up out of bed in the morning.

In all Celine brought me six paintings that day and I loved each one of them. She really knew me. One painting was the one that had hung opposite the bed that I had put her in that awful day when I had gone to her house for lunch. We had talked about the painting since. It was a sunrise painted from a happy memory of an early morning trek in Bali. "Back in my free-spirited days," she said.

I hung it on the wall at the top of the first flight of stairs so it could be appreciated from the hall and as you walked up the stairs. We stood back and admired it with Celine standing on the bottom step and me standing on the hall floor behind her, still a few inches taller than her, despite the step.

"I wish you a bright new dawn, Martha, with or without Patrick, whichever is meant to be."

I hugged her to me, her back to my chest, both of us still looking at the painting, basking in its orange glow. Tears of gratitude welled up and streamed down my face. I made no effort to hide them. I felt no need to. Celine and I had shared every emotion over the years of our friendship, every one except lust, that is. We had both agreed over a bottle or two of wine that, despite everything, when it came to sex, it was men or nothing, maybe even preferably nothing. Sober, I wasn't so convinced that nothing was preferable; I wasn't so sure that I would totally rule out a relationship with the right woman. I'd often thought that I could veer towards being bisexual if I wasn't so programmed not to allow myself to be. I just had a preference for men.

Celine refused all offers of payment for the paintings but agreed to allow me to take us both on a trip to Bali in the not-too-distant future. "We need to re-find the free spirits within us," I said. We drank to that and to every other good idea we had over the course of dinner that night in a local restaurant. We did a good but incomplete job of drowning out the little voice in my head that kept reminding me that the day was technically my twenty-fifth wedding anniversary. Fiona and Zara had gone over to Patrick's to cook dinner for him knowing that I had arranged to go out. I had planned it deliberately, rather than relying on them to be there for me and being disappointed when they weren't. Celine and I tottered, in mutual support, up our road after a leisurely dinner, praising each other for our delightful friendship, loud enough for all the neighbours to hear. We were both in great spirits as we tottered. But, when I looked at my large empty bed, I was filled with mixed emotions: I was grateful that I could fall into it without worrying that I would disturb a soul; no one would slag me for being drunk; no one would enquire if I'd a good night; on this, our twenty fifth wedding anniversary, no one would pull me into their arms and tell me they loved me; no one would make love to me even though an important part of me felt ready for that possibility – Dr McCarthy had prescribed me with vaginal suppositories which seemed to be success-fully treating my painful vaginal atrophy – yes, I thought, some phys-ical intimacy would be lovely. I fell asleep crying.

The next morning when the alarm went off, I regretted our ex-cesses. I had a meeting with Barry, an old friend and colleague. I looked at the free-spirited woman in the painting and I thought, this wouldn't happen to you, you probably only drink water and juices. I should try that. Then I lay back down feeling anything but energised. I sipped the Dioralyte and soluble Solpadeine that I had left on my bedside locker the previous night and put my head back on the pillow, closed my eyes for ten more minutes and hoped and prayed that the worst would pass soon.

After a long shower, nausea still threatened but I decided to risk tea and porridge. As I made my way down to the kitchen, I found my vision unreliable. I misjudged the last step and landed hard on my ass. The pain reverberated around my body and settled primarily in my coccyx and temples. As I sat on the floor there was a slow dawning through the fog of my brain that I had forgotten to take out my con-tact lenses the night before and had put my glasses on over them, hence my blurred vision. I turned to walk up the stairs and the early morning light lit up the painting of the Bali sunrise. My blurred vision added a welcome mystical dimension. I was in Bali and the sun was rising, the day was promising good things. I saluted Celine's powerful image, stronger than Solpadeine, I thought, and longer lasting.

Barry and I had been work colleagues years ago and while I had been off making babies and looking after a small number of my own clients, he had been making insolvency his speciality; long before it was even a service that was expected to have widespread demand. He had found his niche. I joked that he was one of the few professionals who was less busy during the Celtic Tiger and that this had allowed him to take up stamp collecting, something that would soon be a declining pastime. He was not amused. He probably hadn't much time for pastimes with all the protracted fallout from the post-Tiger austerity but, in fairness to him, he agreed to meet me promptly. We had passed business each other's way many times over the years so we had good shared history. I called and briefed him on our finances and current separation. He didn't need the gories on the latter. He said nothing, as was his style, but I suspected that the Dublin rumour machine had already given him some version of events.

After the call, I had emailed a full schedule of our assets and liabilities together with detailed notes for each line item. He had them on the screen in front of him when we sat down at his desk to discuss possibilities.

"I see you haven't lost your touch, Martha. Meticulous attention to the relevant details without losing sight of the endgame." He smiled warmly at me.

"You might not say that if you had to live with me," I said, only half laughing.

He dismissed my comment with a slight upturn of his head and eyebrows. "To business so," he said. There was no nonsense to Barry. I liked that about him. I realised that people like Sandra and Barry were my kind of people. When there was business to be done, they kept small talk small.

"Allow me to recap: Patrick landed himself, solely, i.e., not jointly, with a debt of just over a million on an asset that may reasonably be considered worthless. Realising, fairly promptly, the possible error of his investment, he strategically decided to ringfence your valuable assets by securing them in your capable hands, thus leaving the debt in his and the significant assets in yours. "

"In a nutshell, yes."

"Based on the information which you sent me and the information which I received from Patrick via your solicitor, in my opinion and your solicitor's, it is unlikely that Vespers would succeed in challenging these transfers, should they seek to do so. Agreed?"

"Agreed," I said.

"Right. So, Vespers have bought a mixed bag of loans from the SIB portfolio and until they push for payment of each, they do not know the details of each debtor's current financial position. I understand that Patrick is already in communication with them and has made the occasional ad hoc payment."

"I'm not sure that he has actually paid them anything or if he has just paid someone to talk to them and I've no idea what has been said."

"Can we find that out?"

"I can ask him," I said, feeling aware that I was verbalising a commitment I had as yet only made to myself, that I would communicate directly with Patrick. I swallowed hard.

"Regardless, they are likely to be aware that there is no merit in pushing for full repayment. They are vultures not fools." Barry paused and gave a laugh at his own little joke. I laughed too as he expected me to. He continued. "There are many solicitors in similar or worse positions to Patrick. If the vultures push too hard the solicitors get declared insolvent, they can't practise, they have no assets and little income, everyone loses. Right?"

"Right," I said, reminding myself that it always took me a while to tune into Barry's way of talking. I wasn't always sure if his questions were rhetorical or if he actually expected me to answer them.

"So, we negotiate a settlement. I give them the facts on his assets and liabilities. I tell them that Patrick is separated. I suggest an amount that he might just manage to raise from other sources, not you. His father for example?"

I shuddered. "Not going to happen. No way. Fiona, our daughter, tells me that Patrick now has power of attorney for his father who was just a couple of months ago diagnosed with dementia. Patrick won't touch his father's money until the time comes and he inherits it…I wouldn't be surprised if he had himself written out of his father's will, leaving everything directly to the children. Bottom line, any settlement money will have to come from me."

As promised, I had taken Patrick's father to the doctor on the Monday after the dinner party. I had been too wrapped up in my own troubles to be fully aware of his increased signs of confusion and frustration. Fortunately, Dr Lucy had read the signs and had referred him to a geriatrician, to whom Fiona and I had duly brought him two weeks later. The geriatrician diagnosed early stage dementia and suggested home help and more support from family: he would need someone to visit him at least twice a day and also regular organised contact in the evening; then a follow-up review with the geriatrician a few months later. This had not been what I wanted to hear given where we as a family were at and that Patrick was the only member of his family living in Ireland. In my misery, I had silently screamed at the thought of trying to organise carers and a roster, a job that I assumed would fall to me despite our changed family circumstances. I still felt horribly guilty about my selfish response, not least because the very next day, a Saturday, Patrick had found Grandad on the floor with a broken hip and elbow. The trauma accelerated his dementia. He had gone straight from hospital to a nursing home. Poor old Grandad. Whenever I visited him, I had no trouble pretending to him about things at home because he didn't always remember that Patrick and I were ever married in the first place!

"Martha, are you listening?" Barry was not impressed.

"Sorry Barry, my mind went elsewhere…could you repeat from when you mentioned Grandad, I mean Patrick's father. Sorry." I gave a half-smile, feeling like a pupil who had been caught talking in class.

"As I was saying, Patrick has to offer Vespers something. We don't need to tell them where the money might come from. But you do not want to look complicit or willing and able to pay more…"

"I wasn't complicit. I didn't know about the bloody loan until two weeks ago. I didn't know about the assets being in my name either." I knew that I sounded like a petulant child but I couldn't help myself. I got angry every time I thought about Joey, the cute hoor of a so-called friend of Patrick's who had talked him into his stupid deal. That fecking deal, I knew, had played a part in pushing our marriage down the slippery slope.

"I know that but they don't. We just have to keep our heads," Barry said with measured patience.

"If I ever bump into that Joey, I won't be keeping my head."

"Martha, that is unlikely to happen." Barry's voice was unusually soft.

"Oh?" I felt uneasy, something bad was coming next.

"Joey's body was found in the local river two months ago. The family farm was lost in that hare-brained development."

I was too stunned to speak. I felt my face redden and my eyes fill with tears. I had been only thinking of our financial and family mess. We could recover from the financial mess and, however bad our family situation was, nobody had died. "Oh Barry, that is awful…I mean he was a total pain in the ass…but shit. His poor wife and kids…wow." The finality of it hit me. For Joey and his family there was no going back.

"Yes. Very sad."

"Puts our wee problems into perspective, doesn't it?"

Barry nodded.

Chapter 15

Meeting Up

Early November 2018

I was making progress with my counsellor. Once I had my first appointment scheduled I had started making random notes on my phone of things that bothered me about myself, about my life, about people in my life, about how things had turned out.

I brought these with me to our first session. From the haze of these thoughts, the feeling emerged that I had spent my whole life trying to do the right thing, trying to please or look out for others and the more I tried, the more wrong I often felt I got things. I considered that the answer might be to stop trying; get out of other people's lives; leave them to their own and each other ways; spare them my meddling. In the first session, the counsellor got me to turn some of those thoughts on their head and see some of what I had successfully done for others, Patrick and the children in particular. I was glad that the counsellor was older than me and that she had children. If she had been younger than me, I might have doubted her ability to understand me. She was glamorous in an understated way, a warm way. She talked about compassion: how important it was for me to have self-compassion, to respect and appreciate myself, to realise that I too had needs and rights; how compassion without boundaries can be a damaging thing, bad for the person who is receiving the compassion and for the person giving it, the giver can become the enabler of the very behaviour they find uncomfortable. We are more likely to be enablers the kinder we are as people and the more we care about others and what they think of us. I immediately started thinking of some of the many times in my life that I had been an enabler, starting with enabling the woman who reared and abused me, more recently with Patrick, Isabel and with Zara.

I felt exhausted but lighter after the first session. Despite my negative initial conclusion of continuously trying and failing, writing down and processing my thoughts felt like the start of my healing and acceptance. From that first session, putting my thoughts and worries on the modern equivalent of paper became a weekly task prescribed to me by my counsellor. I recorded them in the notes section of my iPhone and, before I met with the counsellor each week, I would import them from my phone to my computer. Once imported onto a big screen I would read through, reorder and expand on them. This whole exercise brought me to the realisation that growing up as an unloved, unwanted child had played a huge part in making me into the insecure person that I was, despite appearances to the contrary. During the third session with the counsellor, she commented on how forgiving of others I was, always willing to make excuses for their bad behaviour, always willing to move on…

I thought about it for a few minutes, then I replied.

"Perhaps I am or perhaps it is a sort of denial. When I think about things like how Heather treated me or Patrick having an affair with Isabel, there is a part of me that believes that what people do to me is my fault. I am in some way to blame." Heather had been good at telling me all the things that I did wrong and how I drove her to beating me. It was my fault for being born! "I suppose forgiving others sooner rather than later was in a sense me forgiving myself for some perceived wrong I had committed. And in another sense, I think I understand that circumstances drive people to extremes. Heather, for example – apart from her father, I'm not sure that anyone else had ever truly shown love for her, certainly not her own children, the half-siblings of mine whom I hadn't seen or heard of for years. They'd left me, who was not her child, to do everything for her for as long as I was around. Her mother had died when Heather was in her twenties and from what I'd gathered, had been a cold fish and tough disciplinarian. Heather had no friends, unless you counted her fellow gossips and begrudgers at church on Sunday. Between them, they ate the alter in search of faith in something or something which might have faith in them. My father had rejected her and she had forced him to stay. I imagine that deep down, she hated herself and I got the brunt of that self-hatred; the alternative would have been to admit to herself that she was so unloved. I, on the other hand, have felt and enjoyed love…Patrick, my mum, our children, my friends…"

"You certainly have, Martha. Love, support and much more. But Patrick, you seem ready to forgive him? Aren't you angry with him?"

"I was, believe me. But I burnt a lot of it up before the dinner party." I smiled, wondering if she would think me naïve. Her face was impassive. I wondered if counsellors practise an 'I'm listening but I'm not judging' expression in front of the mirror. I spoke slowly. I had had plenty of time during the months of emotional turmoil to form my thoughts. "I think Patrick comes from a good place. I don't think he set out to hurt me. I think life contrived against us. Knowing what I now know from Mum, from the children, from his legal letter, and knowing what I know of him for the past more than twenty-five years, I have this feeling that he is hurting as much as me. Hurting, because he knows he hurt me. Mum thinks so too. I don't feel I need to punish him for cheating because I imagine that he is punishing himself. Perhaps you think I am naïve. He did have an affair. I know that. But there is this feeling…" I put my hand up to my heart. "I won't know for sure until I meet him."

"I don't think you are naïve." She smiled and I believed her sincerity. I could see it in her eyes. "I think you are incredibly self-aware and wise. Your upbringing could have made you bitter but instead you seem to have harnessed strength and wisdom from it. If your gut tells you to meet him, then you should meet him."

My goodness those words, they meant so much to me. When I heard them, I sat up straight. I was no longer a lost cause.

I was learning about myself. How could I have expected others, my husband and my children especially, to have understood me when I had barely understood myself? I was realising that to know myself, I needed to examine my past and how it had formed me. I felt I was on the road to greater clarity and to move along that road, I knew I needed to meet my husband. The thought of it filled me with nervous excitement, which was both good and bad.

It is easy to dole out advice to others. Clichéd catch phrases come to mind: *Don't sweat the small stuff. If it's for you, it won't go by you. It will all work out in the end.* I can both dole out and ignore all these platitudes. I spent hours at my desk drafting a simple text to Patrick and still more hours, lying awake in bed, mentally redrafting it. Throughout it all a voice was telling me, this is ridiculous, Martha, spending hours drafting one short text to your husband of twenty-five years. Get a fecking grip.

I settled on the following:

Hi Patrick, thank you for the recent correspondence which you sent to Sandra. I have met up with Barry to discuss the financial situation. You may remember that he is an insolvency expert and he, therefore, has experience dealing with Vespers and other vulture funds. I would like to share his thoughts with you if you are happy to meet up with me. Early most evenings are good for me.

I found myself spending another hour trying to decide how to sign it off. I set myself the deadline of hitting send by lunchtime, regardless of any uncertainties. I quickly ruled out 'love'. It had taken me months of alone time and some tough counselling sessions to be able to admit that, despite everything, I still loved him. But I hadn't signed anything 'love' since my January Eureka moment, meeting Isabel in Aldi now some ten months plus earlier. If I put 'love' at the end of the text it would be weird, especially as I hadn't seen, spoken to, or texted him directly since asking him to leave our home four and a half months earlier. All our communications had been via intermediaries, my solicitor or the children. By 2 p.m. I decided on 'Xx Martha'.

I spent the rest of the day checking my phone. My biggest fear was my old demon, rejection, a fear imprinted on my brain from early childhood. I expected something like, 'Sorry Martha, probably best at this stage if we converse through your solicitor.' Nervous flutters made their way around my stomach settling into a stabbing pain in the pit of it. I tried restricting myself to looking at my phone every fifteen minutes or only if it pinged. I rarely lasted.

During the course of the afternoon my phone rang and I jumped. Patrick wouldn't ring, I said to myself. It was Gavin. I let the phone ring out until it eventually went to voicemail. He said that he was just touching base with me, hoping I was doing okay. He and Isabel were separating. He'd had enough. Would I like to meet up for dinner some time so we could wallow in our joint misery? I felt sorry for him. It couldn't be easy. I had brought everything to a head for him whether he had wanted it or not. I didn't have the emotional energy to ring him back so I sent him a text instead.

Hi Gavin, thank you for your kind message. I am going to be honest with you. I am emotionally drained at the moment and need to stay focussed. I'm afraid that currently, I simply don't have the energy to meet up. I'm sorry. I hope you are holding up ok. I'm sorry for my part in it all. Xx Martha

I got a text straight back from him.

Hi Martha, please don't be sorry. You did me a favour. Trust me, I fully understand you being emotionally drained. Take care. Xx Gavin

I was relieved to receive his text. I promptly sent him a reply.

Take care too Gavin. xx

By evening there was still no word from Patrick and I struggled to chop the vegetables for a stir fry. Tears were streaming down my face when Fiona came into the kitchen. I gulped hard to suppress a sob and blamed the strong onions. Fiona said nothing although she knew or ought to have known that, with contact lenses, cutting onions never affected me.

Back in the height of austerity, when plenty of work but lack of money had dominated our lives 24/7 and the kids had reprimanded us for it, I had introduced a rule: no phones at the table. They had to be put aside and on silent. That night I was the victim of my own rule. I struggled to sit still at the table and engage in the conversation because I was focused on availing of the first opportunity to look at my phone. Relief came when Zara prodded me in the elbow and I spilled my glass of water all over my lap. She got my attention but not the way she wanted it.

"Isn't it true, Mum, that there is a plastic rubbish Island many times the size of Ireland a few miles off the coast of Florida? Fiona doesn't believe me and she's *supposed* to be a teacher."

"Zara, you just drenched me!" I stood up from the table and shook some water off my lap, glad of the excuse to grab the kitchen towel which was hanging near where my phone was lying on the worktop.

"Sorry. Yeah. But isn't it true about the rubbish Island off Florida?"

"Probably. Sure. Maybe even bigger." I grabbed my phone and slipped it into my pocket, spotting a notification of a message from Patrick on it. "I just need to change…"

"See, I told you…"

"Zara, defending the environment begins at home and I do more than—" Fiona said.

"Just going to the loo and changing," I said, hanging up the towel.

"Is it just me or is Mum acting even more weird than usual?"

I didn't wait to hear Fiona's reply. I went upstairs to the en suite and sat on the toilet. My hands trembled and sweated as I looked at the phone and it took three attempts for it to recognise my thumbprint and let me see the whole text.

Hi Martha, sorry for late reply. I was at a meeting that ran way over. I agree that it would be a good idea to meet up. I can meet you most evenings except Tuesdays somewhere in town from 5:30 onwards. Where had you in mind? Xx Patrick

I had already decided on somewhere quiet, where we had never been before, no history and a limited chance of bumping into people we knew. I had come across a restaurant on the southside called The Not So Peaceful Swans, set on a canal bank where swans often drifted past, fought with each other or threatened passing dogs or occasionally people. This was all according to TripAdvisor, where it got five-star reviews. It had some small rooms upstairs with windows overlooking the canal, ideal for quiet conversation. I rang them from my perch on the toilet and checked availability for a discreet table upstairs. They offered me the coming Thursday or the Wednesday or Thursday of the following week. I sent these suggestions to Patrick. Within five minutes I received a reply.

6 p.m. this Thursday perfect for me. Xx Patrick

My heart leapt into my throat. My hand went up to my mouth. Tears welled up in my eyes. I felt as if I was going on a first date with the man of my dreams. But I didn't know if it was going to be the start of a new relationship or the absolute end of an old and damaged one. Keep an open mind, Martha. He chose the earliest possible date. Either way, you will know by Friday. What was I thinking? I was meeting him to discuss finances not to see if we could ever be 'an item' again. There would need to be a lot of bridges crossed before that thought could seriously be on the agenda.

I arrived deliberately early to allow me to sit and wait for Patrick and avoid having to walk into a room watching him watching me. I followed the maître d' up the noisy wooden stairs to a room painted in muted tones of grey. The colour was everywhere, the walls, the window frames, the doors, the serviettes. I craved some warm, brighter colours. I sat and looked out the window at the slow-moving, empty water of the canal. People walked purposely along its bank, hurrying home from a hard day's work. A couple in their twenties held hands and chatted enthusiastically, looking more at each other than the way ahead. The simple pleasure of holding hands…my hands felt hot and clammy. I wrapped them around my glass of iced water and lifted its smooth cold surface to each cheek. Was this how Patrick had felt when he had sat waiting for me in the lobby of The Stanley Hotel in Nairobi twenty-seven years ago? Nervous, anxious, uncertain of whether I would greet him with love or near indifference?

The memory of that evening brought me back to the person I was then, a young woman whose heart had soared at seeing that a good man had loved her enough to follow her to the quirkiness of Africa. There had been the certainty of love in that moment and the happy recollection of it must have beamed itself across my face just as I saw that same man pause beside the maître d' who gestured in my direction. I saw Patrick share the moment. I felt that he too was back in the lobby of Nairobi. His smile said so. He swallowed hard, I saw his Adam's apple leap. It seemed more pronounced. He swallowed again.

He was checking back into the reality of us meeting in a strange unknown restaurant. He brought me with him back to that reality. I too swallowed hard as he walked towards me.

"Martha." As he said my name I tingled. It had been a long time since I'd heard it like that. I used to draw comparisons with how he said 'Martha' and 'Mayo' with similar affection and encouragement. I had teased him about whether it was his Mayo County team or me he would scream loudest for.

"Patrick," I replied, standing up to greet him, because that is what seemed natural to do. My handbag fell to the floor. His hands came to rest on my shoulders and his lips glanced off mine, then changed flightpath and landed on my left cheek, lingering long enough to light a fuse that sparked its way through my body, awakening erogenous zones that I had thought were long dead and buried. It was so long since I had experienced such pure natural pleasure that it felt foreign to me, a strange little *oh* sound come out of my lips. My hand failed to smother a girlie giggle that followed. I could have skipped dinner and conversation and taken my body's spontaneous combustion to the next level. Patrick slowly closed and opened his eyes but, true to form, he passed no remarks. I could see him struggling to reset himself to a more appropriate setting but smiling as he did so. I was silently giggling all over. He bent down, picked up my handbag and handed it to me, allowing his index finger to run over the back of my hand as he did so. My breath shortened with his touch. Another ping of sexual energy tingled through my veins, lighting more warm fires of pleasure along its path. On the outside I was standing still as a statue. On the inside blood was racing around my body. I looked into his eyes, drunk on sensuality, momentarily capable of running out of the restaurant, fecking caution out of the way and letting passion lead us to places we had been before.

The maître d' coughed politely as he led four other customers past us to their table. I became aware of two pairs of eyes looking at us from a table near ours. The moment of near unbridled passion had passed but it had left its mark. My body sat back down on the hard chair at the table, Patrick sat down opposite me. Had he felt what I had felt? Was that a flashback, a moment created by a passionate shared memory or was it a feeling in the now?

We looked at each other. He was as fit and lean as the man I had married, too lean for his age. His face was no longer quite big enough for his skin and there were wrinkles on his forehead and jawline that I'd never noticed before. Crow's feet had made their marks on the edge of his temples. He needed a bit of fattening up. His salt-and-pepper hair was more salt than pepper. He had aged and I couldn't be sure when that had happened. But he was handsome and definitely sexy. He was the man I had married.

"I've gone back running," he offered, as if reading my thoughts on his weight loss.

"A lot..."

"Too much, maybe?"

"You look a bit thin perhaps. But good." I nodded in approval.

"You look well, Martha. Your hair is different. It suits you."

He'd said my name again, in that way that cheered me on.

"Do you think so? I'm still getting used to how short it is." I put my hand up to the back of my bare neck and smiled to myself remembering all the times over the years when I had changed my hair style quite dramatically and he hadn't noticed. There had even been the time when I had gone from a straight shoulder-length bob to a short-with-curls style and all he had noticed was the smell of the perming lotion.

"It's very sophisticated and chic on you," he added with a teasing smile, knowing that neither would be characteristics I aspired to.

"Sophisticated and chic, that's the new me," I said, admitting to myself that I needed a bit of reinvention. I returned his smile.

His hand reached across the table and squeezed mine. It felt natural. I looked at his hand on top of my hand and wondered if it was the gesture of a friend or a lover. I knew which I wanted it to be.

"How have you been?" I asked as he withdrew his hand.

"Fine. The running helps."

"I've gone back to tennis. It's good for me. There isn't much time for thinking in a tennis match. You've got to be in the moment, in between having some laughs." Elaine, a true friend, had called me when she hadn't seen me for a while. She'd heard the rumours but she wasn't looking for gossip, she was ringing to see how I was. A month or so previously we had met for coffee which rolled into lunch and before I knew it she had persuaded me to play tennis – her previous partner had moved on to playing golf. She said that she wanted to play doubles with me because she knew that I took tennis with the same level of seriousness as she did, we would play as well as we could and we would have some fun.

"And I heard from a delighted Zara that Celine got a dog, some sort of Labrador cross-breed who lives more than half the time in our...sorry, your house."

"Yes. Chuckie, from the *Rugrats* according to Celine. But IRA *Tiocfaigh* according to Matt; full name *Tiocfaigh ár lá*."

"Our day will come, brilliant." Patrick laughed.

"You never know...I never thought the day would come and I'd as good as have a dog. He needs lots of walking and I'm as besotted as the rest of them. All the years I said no to a dog...I was scared of all the chewing but this guy is over two and well-trained. The owner had to downsize and couldn't keep him." I was doing what I often did when I was nervous, talking too fast and too much.

226

"Sounds like a good deal. And Celine herself, how's she keeping? I often think of her."

"She is doing well really. The solicitor and barrister you got for her have been fantastic. But…"

"But?"

"I keep thinking that I see the bastard."

"Do you mean near the house? Within the two-kilometre Safety Order zone? Surely not."

"I'm not sure. I never see his face. But it looks like him. It feels like him." I felt myself shiver as I did when I thought I saw him.

"It would be a good idea to say it to the guards. Just in case. Has Celine seen him?"

"She hasn't said and I don't want to worry her unnecessarily."

"Still. Better safe than sorry."

The waiter coughed softly beside our table and we looked up at him.

"Are you ready to order?" he asked, notebook on the ready.

"Sorry. Just give us another couple of minutes, if you can please?" Patrick replied.

"No problem."

"Martha, would you like to order some drinks now?"

I looked at Patrick. "Why not?"

"We'll have a look." Patrick handed me the wine list as he often used to do, though he was more particular about wine than me.

"Sorry, leave it with me please," I said to the waiter, opening the black leather-bound book. My eyes were fixed on the words but my thoughts were on Patrick. What was he thinking? What was he feeling? Were we on the same page in our feelings for each other or…?

"What do you feel like having?" Patrick asked.

Sex would have been the honest answer and the one I would have given back in the good old days but I looked down and flicked through the pages until I came to Spanish reds.

"Rioja Reserva?"

"Fine by me. It rarely lets us down. What about food?"

I quickly scanned the menu, too distracted to really read it.

"Scallops, followed by sea bass. And you?"

"Oh, I didn't think you liked scallops with black pudding."

"Sure. I'll give it a try this time. There's always a first!" I hadn't noticed the mention of black pudding.

"I think I'll have the chicken pieces rolled in sesame seeds with mixed greens and red-hot relish, followed by steak and horseradish mash."

"Sounds good," I said, wishing back to the days when we tasted each other's starters, then shared a fish course followed by a shared meat course. That way neither of us missed out and we savoured many a long and leisurely dinner out. Twenty-five plus years of living together and now it felt too awkward to suggest such a thing. My eyes welled up and I stood up and excused myself before the floodgates opened.

I looked in the bathroom mirror and brought my mind to what I was going to say about our financial situation. This helped to stop the flow of tears.

The waiter was pouring wine into our glasses as I sat down again. Through the window I saw darkness broken by the ghosts of two white swans gliding along the still, black waters of the canal.

"I hope you don't mind, I went ahead and ordered the Rioja while you were gone."

"Of course. Good idea. Thank you."

The waiter took our food order and we sipped the wine.

"Still reliable," I said savouring the familiar full flavour. We had promised ourselves a Spanish wine trip when we had traded our way out of austerity. The Rioja valley was to be top of our list. I wondered if he remembered. So much left undone. So much time wasted.

He opened his mouth about to say something but paused and seemed to change tack. "Kids are doing well," he said.

"Yes. I think so. But I find it hard to live up to Zara's high standards when it comes to saving the planet. I'm forever in trouble."

"Me too. I've got used to emptying the bins before she comes over and inspects them for evidence of my sins against the environment! There is no brown bin in the apartments so I'm supposed to eat everything or save it for her to bring home to compost!"

"Try living with her! It's not always possible to get organic rapeseed oil in the local supermarkets, for example. I said to Matt the other day that if I buy anything else other than organic she wants my guts for garters. He said that sounded completely in keeping with her recycling policy and probably was exactly what she would do with my guts when the time comes!"

"Guts to garters. Now, would that be upcycling or recycling?"

"Guts," I said poking myself in my stomach. "To garters," I added, slapping my thigh. "Down-cycling maybe?"

We laughed. "Maybe recycled guts could be used to replace all that single-use plastic."

"Good idea. You must suggest it to her."

"Dad, you're doing it again. If I can't convince my family to take the plastic issue seriously what hope have I with the rest of the world?" he said putting on a high-pitched voice, doing a poor, but recognisable, imitation of Zara.

"Sounds too familiar." I laughed. "Mind you, she has a point. But the only thing that will make a real difference is government policy and new laws, gradually banning single-use plastic or other non-recyclable or non-compostable items, starting with straws, coffee cups, wipes, cotton buds…"

The waiter arrived with our starters and placed them in front of us.

"Thank you," we chorused, smiling down at the dishes.

In the middle of a large blue, hand-turned ceramic plate was a small pile of rocket from which small rich red slivers of roast peppers pointed outwards towards a circle of scallops alternating with medallions of black pudding. The rich aroma from the pudding reached my taste buds and reminded me that I was hungry. But before putting my fork to my plate, I admired Patrick's starter which was served on a slightly larger and paler blue ceramic plate. A long oval-shaped slice of bread had been oven dried into a tubular shape and mixed green and purple leaves were spilling out of it. Around the base of the tube was a red circle of relish. Beside that were four generous sesame-seed coated chicken pieces, sliced to reveal soft succulent meat inside their crispy exterior.

"Looks good," I said, nodding at his plate, wondering if he'd offer me a taste.

"Yours too," he said.

We ate in silence, my mind too occupied to really appreciate the food. We needed to talk finances. That was why we were there. Or was it just an excuse to meet him and test how I felt about him and he about me. The silence hung like a veil between us, a reminder of all the things left unsaid that should have been said.

The waiter cleared our plates and we both declared the food lovely and reverted to silence. One of us needed to speak.

"Patrick."

"Yes."

"About your Affidavit of Means…"

He swallowed hard and I watched his Adam's apple again protrude from his neck. He spoke in a measured tone. "I am very sorry, Martha. I know you told me not to touch those apartments in Ballydermot, not with a forty-foot barge pole…I have no excuse."

"Yes, that is only part of it. Patrick, you didn't tell me. You never told me. Was I that bad that you couldn't bring yourself to tell me?"

"No. It wasn't that. It was going to be one gamble. Just one. Get in quick. Get out fast. As soon as I did it, I was going to tell you but then Trish took ill. I thought that I would wait until she was better. But then she wasn't going to get better. I thought I'd wait until after you had time to grieve. But there was no time to grieve. We had to save the business…"

"Yes. But after that. When things started to turn around? What about then…?" I brought my hand up across the sweat of my forehead and rubbed it down the side of my face to rest under my chin. "By then I was too much of a menopausal anti-Christ, wasn't I?"

"That wasn't the issue, Martha. That wasn't it at all. It was the longer I left it to tell you, the harder it got. I am so sorry. So very sorry. But there always seemed to be something: Matt going into a downer after failing his first-year exams; Fiona dealing with that stalker from the hockey team; our demanding, ageing parents…We were in a bad place with it all but still you kept saying, we will get there, together we will. And then you would say 'Thank God, we didn't do worse than buying those three houses' – and the more you said, the worse I felt and the harder it was to tell you. It sounds pathetic now, given all we had been through together over the years. And all you went through growing up…" As he spoke his hands were in front of his mouth and he was twirling his wedding ring around on his finger. He was still wearing it. I had considered taking mine off many times but I never could bring myself to.

"I'm sorry too. I should have made sure that we talked but I was stuck wallowing in bad humour and pools of sweat…I should have…"

"It was my fault not yours, Martha. I thought I could solve it without telling you. But I made things worse when I turned to Isabel for help." His hands were up over his nose and mouth at this stage, a gesture he had always had. The more uncomfortable he was with what he had to say, the more he hid behind his hands. I gently reached across and with both my hands I brought his down onto the table and held them there.

"Those were hard times, Patrick. For both of us. We both made mistakes." I had talked this through with my counsellor. I didn't blame Patrick. I was working on not blaming myself. "Someone is not always to blame. Circumstances can conspire to create an avalanche and we don't always see it coming or have the wherewithal to get out of its way. We can get caught in the path of devastation…and be lucky to come out of it alive." I was thinking of Joey…

He looked straight at me. His eyes and mouth open. His mind considering my words. His face expressing both compassion and sorrow. Or were those my feelings? Was I projecting them onto him? In hope of a connection. I didn't know. I hadn't planned on this conversation. I was going to talk finances. I had jumped ahead of myself. I was scared I was rushing things and in doing so putting any hopes of reconciliation in jeopardy.

He pulled his hands from under mine.

"Martha, I think that you are being too kind to me. I screwed up when I invested in that apartment development…" He spoke quietly but emphatically.

"It is only money, Patrick. Only money…perhaps I am being too kind to myself…putting a spin on it that suits me…" I spoke to the fork that I was fiddling with and then looked up to see his face filled with frustration, ready to spill words out that I wasn't sure I wanted to hear.

"Martha, listen to me. I went against your expressed and reasonable wishes when I signed up to that development…"

"I know. I know…I forgive you…if that is what you need, I sincerely forgive you. In time I hope to forgive myself too for not making the time and energy to talk and be there for us," I whispered and put my hand on top of his on the table. He pulled his away again.

"Listen to me, Martha…you know that I did worse. You said it yourself. I went to Isabel for help out of the mess…I knew she had experience of these situations but—" His voice was pleading.

"I know, of course, I know." I did not want to hear him spell it out. Isabel had experience alright, more than of a financial nature.

"We met up a few times to see how I might get out of the mess. She thought it better to meet in the privacy of a hotel room, where we wouldn't be seen or heard…there was a golf outing that she was at. I got drunk, really drunk and…and I slept with her. It is the most stupid thing that I've ever done. Every day since then I have wished that I could undo it, that I could roll back the clock and not get drunk, not…I didn't see her again after that night. Honestly, not until the dinner party." He shook his head, trying to disown himself.

He had said it and though I knew it, I did not know it absolutely until he said it. I swallowed hard gulping down the words 'I slept with her'. He slept with her. I didn't want to think any more about that. He had said 'one night', one night did not make an affair, a betrayal yes. But not a reoccurring deliberate affair. I had thought about this.

"You slept with her *once*? You were drunk?" I almost whispered these words for fear they were not true. Had it only been one night? I didn't want to make excuses for what he had done but I did want to make it smaller, less insurmountable. A slight feeling of relief washed over me. But my whisper must have been louder than I thought because the couple at the table behind Patrick were both staring at us, their eyes and mouths open wide. I nodded at them and kept my face straight. They pretended not to see me but I saw them exchange knowing smiles. I felt like I was watching us too. From an observer's point of view I could appreciate their amusement. But this was my life. My husband. My marriage. I turned my attention back to Patrick. "One night?" I asked. If there had been previous lesser acts of intimacy, I had decided that I did not want to know about them, not yet anyway.

"Yes, Martha. One stupid night. And I will regret it and all that goes with it until the day I die."

"You regret it. Why do you regret it?" It was a harsh question but I needed to hear his answer.

"Look what I've done to you...to us. If I had just told you about the doomed development...we could have worked it out, like we did all the other stuff we worked out together over the years. I broke your trust...the rock on which our relationship was built. That is what you said when you said yes to marrying me. And I broke it. I broke it. And I broke it with her, of all people." His hands were back in front of his mouth. His voice was thick with suppressed sobbing. His eyes and face were wet but he didn't wipe away the tears.

"It is not that simple, Patrick. I know that now. I didn't make it easy for you. When Trish died and there wasn't time to grieve, my shutters started to go down. Then, when my hormones went awry, I reverted to self-preservation mode. The one I mastered as a little girl when I felt unloved and unwanted by my family. But I wasn't unloved and unwanted, I just couldn't cope and Trish wasn't there to help me and then you weren't there because of the business and..." I was squeezing the words out thick with tears.

"It is my fault not yours, Martha."

234

"Patrick, is assigning fault to someone the answer? If we are looking for *things* to blame then the list is long. I have been thinking back over the last eight to ten years and remembering the onslaught we have suffered. When we were dealing with the fallout from the boom times, we had no time or energy left for ourselves or each other. One wave after the other hit us. Trish dying, no paying clients, no money, Fiona wondering if being nice to that guy when they were both drunk gave him the right to stalk her, knowing that he could have raped her if her friend Lucy hadn't checked on her. Matt thinking he'd failed us because instead of working to pay his way that summer of first year, he had to study to get his repeats. My thyroid going on permanent strike, my menopause horror-show or as Zara would call it my near-permanent hysteria. Celine being beaten and trying to face the reality of all that…the list is long. Too long. And there may have been a bit too much golf in there towards the end of it, but that was minor in the scheme of things!" I paused and found that my hands were on the table and I was twisting my everything ring around and around and around…I was about to look up to see Patrick's reaction but…

"Excuse me, madam, your fish." The way the waiter spoke I suspected he had been waiting for the right moment for a while and had eventually just dived in before the fish got cold.

"Sorry," I said as he put a speckled green plate down in front of me with what looked like a perfectly cooked piece of pan-fried sea bass, beautifully served on top of a neat pile of chard and a small green buttery juice pool gently touching a side of floury potatoes.

Rather than make eye contact with the waiter, I looked over at Patrick's dish, a medium-rare steak, sitting also in a small green pool of juice, with a narrow pile of chard arranged in a C-shape around it. His side of horseradish mash was presented in an oval bowl hand-painted with the long dock-like leaves of a horseradish plant. In the past, I'd have been oohing and aahing about such things.

"Looks lovely. Thank you," I said, putting my hand on our surprisingly empty bottle.

"Another bottle please," Patrick said to the waiter who seemed in an indecent hurry to scurry away. I would be no different if I were in his shoes.

I looked at what was before me and I wondered how I could fit in food when I already felt over full with emotion.

I used my fork to take a nibble of fish up to my mouth. It was fresh and moist with a perfect firm texture. I picked at some chard too and it was rich and dense with a slight crunch in its yellow stalk. I put my knife and fork down, wrapped my hands around my glass of iced water and then put my open hands over my cheeks, giving myself time to digest what had been said. I felt overwhelmed but at the same time I felt hope. I needed time and breathing space. I suspected that Patrick probably needed the same.

"Patrick," I said. "I didn't plan on...on having that conversation. It's maybe too much too soon to say more. I'm trying to work things out, slowly. You probably are too. But...but I think I'm glad we did..."

"Me too. But perhaps it is all too much and too painful. I'm sorry, Martha."

"I'm sorry too. But right now, I need to hit pause to allow myself to catch up." If there was one thing the counsellor and Celine had drilled into me it was to pause and think about what I was feeling, think about what was going on for me. Pause Martha. I lifted my hand up to my forehead and felt drops of sweat on it. I dabbed it with my serviette and felt the sweat sting the patches of psoriasis in my eyebrows and at the corners of my eyes. When I brought my hand back down to the table Patrick brought his hand down from his face and placed it on mine. I looked at his tired face and I knew that I wanted to fall asleep beside it.

"I understand. I didn't plan this either. I thought that we were going to discuss finances and you were going to fill me in on Barry's thoughts on how I should proceed."

"That was the plan…I'm comfortable at talking finances most of the time. I can struggle with anything else!" I half smiled.

"I'm nearly as brutal as ever at talking personal stuff, even finances. Martha, I have tried to make good by you financially, despite everything else…"

"I know. Too much so. It worries me. Patrick, I don't need so much…as long as the kids are sorted. I'll be fine."

"Me too."

"Barry said, as Barry would, and in his usual deadpan tone of course, that it might be helpful if we stayed separated…at least until you've settled with Vespers." I spoke very quietly and looked to Patrick for his response. His mouth and nose were hidden back behind his praying hands. His eyes, if they were saying anything, seemed to ask me to say more. But I left the words hang in the air.

"And how did you respond to Barry?" he eventually asked.

"One word only. Noted." I smiled and nodded, remembering that my mental response to Barry's words had been 'pity'. But I had verbalised 'noted'.

"Okay so. Noted." He smiled and nodded too. I experienced the thrill of a possible shared private joke. Were his thoughts my thoughts? Another flicker of hope made an appearance and it felt good. But I stopped myself latching onto it and uncertainty filled the void. How could I ever again presume to tune into his frequency and he into mine when for so long we had been operating in entirely different bandwidths? And the affair, where was I really with that? It shook off my dreamy notions. I paused, and reverted to my comfort zone, our finances.

"Important question so. Where are things at currently with Vespers?"

"They have stopped piling on the interest but are pushing for full repayment. They want me to immediately sell the three houses and hand over any equity to them. Then they want me to sell off any other assets or borrow against them to repay the debt. I don't know how far they will push at this stage. But Joey lost his farm. It all got too much for him…a neighbour found his body…" Patrick gulped a deep breath and his eyes moistened again. Behind his hands I imagined that he was biting his lip. My heart reached to him and I mourned for his dead friend and for the old Patrick and me who would have been there for each other, facing Joey's death together.

"I'm sorry, Patrick. I only heard when I met Barry. How awful. They lost everything. How are poor Catriona and the children doing?"

"I heard that she and the girls moved back to Castlebar to her mother's for now. They were all devastated at the funeral as you can imagine. Catriona was still in shock. She said to me that she told him they would be fine, she could go back to nursing. But the farm was his life and was all that he really knew…"

"Isn't that the sheer tragedy of it?" I sighed. "Joey and half of the rest of us got distracted by the mores of the Celtic Tiger when we should have stuck to what we knew and were perfectly happy with."

"Don't I know that, Martha? I know it too well!"

"Sorry. I didn't mean it as a swipe at you. Honestly. All I'm saying is that it was hard not to get sucked in. There are no doubt others suffering like Catriona because…"

"Because of greed. Because of wanting more, when we already had enough. Because we couldn't see what was in front of our eyes because we were going so fast, bang." He slammed his right fist at speed into the open palm of his left hand. "Debris everywhere!"

The man at the table behind him jumped and turned to look at us again.

I think my mouth hung open and I looked from Patrick to the man. I might have given the man another none-of-your-business look because he turned back around fast. Sweat beads burst out on my forehead and my hands. I practised focusing on my breath, inhaling slowly and deeply, exhaling to the count of ten. I closed my eyes and reminded myself to say nothing. Whatever I said would be wrong. When I opened my eye lids, my eyes met Patrick's. His response was to close his eyes, curl up his mouth and bend his head down slightly. He looked like a bold dog who knew he was in trouble. A part of me wanted to pat his curly head and laugh but I knew that would be fuel to the fire.

"I hate everything about that Celtic Tiger," he said, as if needing to explain his outburst.

"I do too. But it is over. We are where we are and we have to start from there. Or here, I think I mean."

"And where might that be?"

I paused, knowing that his question was open to many interpretations. "Financially speaking, we are in a bit of a hole, but I think we can, with Barry's help, dig ourselves out of it and be back at having enough, or more than enough relative to what others have." *Financially speaking…we* can…dig *ourselves*…I chose my words carefully and I wondered if he was picking up on it.

"And what is the two accountants' view of said hole and how *WE* might dig ourselves out of it?"

"Well what assets do Vespers think you have to borrow against?"

"My share of the equity in those houses and the practice. I've told them I have nothing else."

"And they believe you?"

"I have spelt it all out for them including that we are separated. I am happy that the other assets are safely in your name. The transfers to you are solid and were timely."

There was something in what Patrick said and the way he said it that unsettled me. Little ripples of anxious excitement raised through my veins, tripping the switch that brought on the inevitable sweat which duly ran down into my eyebrows and stung the already angry patches of psoriasis. The stinging hit a nerve in my brain. Had Patrick had a fling so that I would push for a separation and our assets would be protected, out of reach of the vultures? Had he had a drunken or a deliberate fling? With Isabel, the serial temptress, the be-sparkled bitch on heels? If Patrick was to choose to have a fling, he would choose someone he could afford to have out of his life, someone who would not be devastated by the abrupt ending of it. Patrick was a man who played the long game. He was protective of me, at times to a fault. And sometimes these things can get thwarted and messed up. Perhaps I was getting carried away in my thinking. Perhaps not. Patrick interrupted my thoughts.

"So, are you going to tell me what you two eminent accountants think the answer is?"

"The answer?" I stalled, trying to get back into my role as accountant as opposed to confused wife.

"To how I should play Vespers."

Not for me to teach a granny how to suck eggs, I thought to myself. I shuffled in my seat and bent down to take my notes out of my bag. I spread them in front of me and scanned them, point by point, all neatly typed out as I would if Patrick was my client.

"We anticipated that Vespers might push for you to borrow against the business and so I looked at the likelihood of you being able to raise a loan based on the security that you could offer any lending institution, and on your ability to repay any loan. The business currently has a loan repayable over the next five years. In addition, it now has to pay rent to the landlord, me." I paused after the word me. "As landlord, and disgruntled wife, I am no longer going to waive the rent due but am going to insist immediately on payment of full market rent as set down in the lease of ten years ago. I will base the rent charged to the practice on the rent currently paid by Brideshead Insurances and on market figures. You can of course challenge it, if you see fit? But I should warn you…" I smiled.

"I'm hardly going to challenge it! Go on…"

I turned to a printout of a spreadsheet I had done showing projected figures for the practice for the next five years. "In conclusion," I continued, "based on projected cash flow and allowing for payment of market rent, the business is not, or by extension, you are not, in a position to take on any significant further debt. The bottom line is that no sane bank would lend to you."

Patrick brought his fingers up to his forehead and into his hairline and he massaged his temples with his thumbs. "Hmm. I hadn't thought of it like that. Where does that leave me so?"

"As Barry and I see it, it leaves you with a problem which we both agree could be the key to a solution."

"Go on."

"The problem is that you are, as you know, technically insolvent. If Vespers push you for full payment then you probably will have to file for bankruptcy…"

"I know. I would lose everything, my practice cert, my business and my only means of earning. I don't know what I would do. It would be awful. What would be the point?" A grey shadow came over Patrick's face and his grave tone almost foretold a death. It was chilling to listen to. His right hand went over his mouth and worked its way to kneading his chin and jaw. "It's hard to hear it said like that," he added.

I wanted to reassure him. To say what I had always said, together we will get through it. But I paused and said, "Patrick, it's unlikely things will come to that. Barry thinks that Vespers won't push for full payment because then they would get next to nothing from you, other than your share of the equity in the three rental houses and maybe something on your pension. There's no incentive for them to push you for full repayment."

"But they won't just walk away when they get my share of the equity in the houses either?"

"No. But that will be your starting position. Let Barry handle the negotiations. He's tough and trusted and it puts some distance between you and them. He will show them your Affidavit of Means. They will push for you to take on more debt. He will get an independent accountant's opinion that you don't have the capacity for much more debt. They will reject his first offer. They may threaten you with bankruptcy, but Barry will remind them of the implications of that...and eventually they will hopefully settle for your share of the equity in the three houses plus maybe a couple hundred thousand."

"And where would I come up with a *couple hundred thousand?*"

"From me. I've still got the remains of the fund that Dad left me and plenty of potential to raise some more immediate cash..."

"That fund is supposed to be for you. To go to college maybe some day. Or some other dream. You were never supposed to touch it for other than that..."

"It got us as a family through some tough times. I think my father would have been glad of that. I know I am."

"So, you used it already?" He gave his head a slight shake and his eyes blinked. "I didn't know."

"It's in the past, Patrick. As I said, I've got other cash coming to me too. I'm selling the bling back to the bling maker. Seemingly he can't keep up with the renewed demand for it on the Southside, in D4 and Foxrock in particular!"

Patrick smiled, a full broad smile all the way to his eyes. I read it as a smile of victory, that he felt victorious because the bling could do what it was supposed to do and be converted to cash. "You didn't like it!"

"Oh, but I did. I won't be without it. I'm having replicas made, in glass. I'm going to flash them wherever the likes of Isabel might see me!" I was speaking tongue in cheek and I think he was too.

"Really! I'm surprised at you."

"I'm being sarcastic, Patrick, as well you know. I'm less into bling than ever."

"That's a relief."

I instinctively touched his left hand with mine and our rings clinked quietly.

"I've come close, but I haven't totally lost it, not yet."

"No, you haven't." He raised his glass to mine. "May you never lose it, Martha."

"Whatever *it* might be," I whispered, feeling my breath catching as another rush of desire swept through me. Where had it been back when Patrick and I were still sharing the same bed? His face gave me no great hints as to what he was thinking other than it seemed to be less wrinkled than when he first arrived. But that could have been the wine. These thoughts were enough to turn on the sweat tap again and I was forced to mop my brow and face with my serviette. Post-menopause sweating has got to be one of the most tedious forms of low-grade torture imaginable. God is a man.

"Still no let up on the sweats?" Patrick asked as he refilled our wine glasses.

"Worse in some ways, better in others," I said, feeling an urge to lean across the table and whisper to him that yes, every stressful thought still brought on a sweat but being there with him was bringing on something more, much more…I smiled as I imagined his reaction. Oh, to be back flirting across the table with my own husband. Scandalous. Oscar Wilde would not approve. I thought it best if I excused myself to go to the bathroom.

"So, what do you think? Do you want Barry to negotiate for you?" I asked as my ageing bottom, whose fat pads had moved to my belly, hit the restaurant's hard chair again.

"Yes. Thank you. Tell him I appreciate it. I had been using O'Hare & Co. Hence the payments you saw going through the books, but I'd prefer Barry."

O'Hare and Co., the accountants Isabel used for her personal taxes. I shuddered. My face and my silence spoke my thoughts.

"I'm sorry," Patrick said.

"Yes," I said, aware that my deflation, even at this vague reference to Isabel, was palpable.

"Shall I ask for the bill?"

"It's done. I sorted it when I went to the bathroom."

"Oh! Thank you."

"No problem, you're welcome," I said, thinking that until a couple months previously it had made no difference who paid the bills as our credit cards had been on the one account. I had taken out a new credit card in my name then and I rarely used the joint card. Only the key household expenses and a few of the children-related living costs still came from our joint bank account.

We got our coats and Patrick insisted on using his phone to order me a taxi but he refused to share it to drop him off on the way.

"I'd prefer to walk. I can go some of the way along the canal," he said.

"I know it sounds silly, Patrick, but can you text me when you get safely home. Please," I said as I reluctantly opened the taxi door.

He smiled and nodded.

My heart tingled again. I'd have walked with him if he'd asked. I might have done more than walk. But he didn't ask. He didn't kiss me, not even on the cheek when we parted. All he said was, "Good night, Martha, and thank you," then he turned and walked away. My teary eyes looked after him. I buried myself in the newsfeed on my phone in the back of the taxi, trying to hide my sniffles.

"You gotta cold, miss?" the taxi driver asked. "There is a lot of 'em goin'."

"Yes, I think one is just starting. Hopefully you won't catch it," I lied rather than have to explain my tears.

"Don't worry about me. I'm tough as nails. I've survived everythin'."

"Everything?" I said.

"You bet. Bouts of heavy drinkin', drugs of all kinds, been homeless for ne'er on two years, on the streets for half that, I've done it all. A cold be nothin'."

"That sounds awful. I'm sorry." I leaned a little forward as I spoke and looked at him more closely. I saw a man in his mid-thirties, short, neat hair, clean shaven, respectably dressed, in a shirt and round neck sweater; a man who took pride in his appearance.

"We lost our home when the landlord decided to do it up like. Do it up, me ass."

I sighed at the well-known shenanigans of landlords finding their ways around rent restrictions. "You mean he got you out so he could up the rent?"

"You got it in one! Me, the missus and two young uns. They, the council like, put them in a shitty bed and breakfast and me in a bloody hostel. Drugs were flyin' round the place. And what was a man to do? No work, No home. No effin' place to hang with me family or nuttin'."

"Sounds shit. How did you ever get out of that hell?"

"The Simon got me a place, to detox like. Then temporary accommodation. Then Respond gave us all an apartment. You've no idea how good it is to have a gaff to call yer own. Just watching TV together feels grea'...I rent this taxi plate now but I'll get me own one soon enough."

"That's some doing. Fair play to you. Wow." How far he'd fallen and how he'd turned it all around. My problems were nothing.

"Fair play to the Simon and Respond, I say. They're massive. They are. If I was relyin' on them fuckin' politicians I'd have been found dead in the gutter...Sorry for the language, miss."

"No worries...I'm no innocent on that myself Ah the Simon, glad they're still doing good. I used to volunteer with them years ago. I did the soup-run every Wednesday night. The people I met were great, but their situations were awful."

"Simon're great. I tell ya."

"That's good. It's been twenty something years since I gave it up after I got pregnant with our eldest."

"They still do good work for sure, diggin' people like me outta trouble..."

"Sorry. Just here on the left please. Thanks. And thank you for telling me your story. You've made me think of going back volunteering with them or some other charity."

"I'm goin' doin' that meself. I might see ya there..." He pointed at the meter. It's on your card, Mrs, the fare like. Do you need a receipt?"

I didn't correct him to say it was on my husband's card. I just handed him a generous five euro note as a tip and said, "No receipt thanks. Have a good night."

"Thank you. You too. Good to talk to you, miss."

Wake up and smell other's harsh realities, Martha, I thought as I walked up the path to our front door. I saw Fiona and Zara through the bay window, in the sitting room watching television together. As I stepped into the hall, it was on the tip of my tongue to say to Zara, what are you doing watching TV and you with three assignments due. But I stopped myself.

"Hi Mum. You have a good night?" Fiona called from the sitting room. I heard her stand up and the television being turned down or off.

"Yes. Lovely. Thank you," I responded, still feeling the afterglow of my chat with the taxi driver. I hadn't told her I was meeting her dad but I suspected that he had. She had been unusually enthusiastic about checking what I was wearing and doing my eye make-up but she hadn't asked where I was going or with whom. And she was normally quite nosy on that front. But far be it for me to be nosy when the shoe is on the other foot.

"I was just about to make some chamomile and mint tea. Would you like some?" she said as she stepped into the hall.

"No thanks, pet." I gave her arm a warm squeeze and kissed her on the cheek. "It has been a long day. I think I'll head to bed if you don't mind," I said, walking straight up the stairs, taking my handbag with my phone in it with me. I usually left them downstairs in my office.

By the time I had changed for bed, brushed my teeth and had taken out my contact lenses, there was still no text from Patrick. I started to feel anxious. I picked up my book, *The Heart's Invisible Furies*. The family situation in it was far more complex than mine. I was at an exciting part of it, a violent scene in Amsterdam. But I couldn't concentrate. I kept checking my phone.

At one minute past midnight I got a text from Celine.

I know I promised that I would wait until Friday to find out how your night went and guess what: it's Friday now. So in as many words as you like, how was it? You can of course call me. Xx

I smiled because I would have bet on Celine not being able to wait to find out. She was a beautiful romantic at heart. I wasn't ready to talk about how the night had gone but I couldn't ignore her text. I realised that it was too difficult a question to answer even for myself right then. I needed to sleep on it, to internalise and process where the night had left me, where did 'we' stand, could Patrick and I ever again be 'us'? Just thinking about the evening with Patrick got my juices going. Or maybe that was the localised HRT! Either way, I was no longer ready to kill him. I was possibly ready to jump into bed with him. I had vaguely suspected something like this might be my feeling, but the reality surpassed my expectations and it was not something I was ever going to put in a text! I felt like a teenager again. Will he? Won't he? Should I? Would I?

I decided to kick for touch in my response to Celine.

Celine, I just knew you wouldn't last! Words that come to mind are: better than expected, challenging, a step in the right direction, hard to process, possibilities... Bottom line is I need to sleep on it and tell you more over a walk and coffee in the morning. Ok? XX

Celine texted straight back.

Ok. I guess I'll have to spend the night imagining all sorts! Sleep well. See you at 9. Xx

I texted back a winky face and then reminded myself that Celine's phone was still one from the dark ages so I sent another text:

Xx

And with that it was half twelve and a message from Patrick finally popped up.

Home safely. Thank you for tonight Martha. It was good to meet up and talk. I feel there is still so much left unsaid, yours Patrick xx

Now what did he mean by 'there is so much left unsaid'? Does he mean that we should meet up again? If so, why doesn't he just say so? And 'yours Patrick', that was a strange choice of sign off. Why did he choose that? It wouldn't look good in a court of law for a couple who are supposed to be unhappily separated! Feck that.

I typed:

Please explain your last text. Xx Martha.

But I deleted it. Then I typed:

I agree that it was good to meet up and talk and I too feel that there is so much left unsaid. Xx Martha

I considered it but I couldn't bring myself to type, *yours* Martha. We had a long way to go and a lot of talking to do before I might feel like I was his and he was mine. We wouldn't have been texting each other from opposite sides of the city if we hadn't broken our proven habit of making time for proper talking. Should I suggest in my text that we meet again soon? No that would give the wrong message. It would sound a bit desperate or something. You shouldn't rush these things. Anyway, this time he should be the one to suggest it.

Then Trish's voice came to me loud and clear inside my head.

"You fecking eejit, Martha. Are you going to make a habit of losing or nearly losing that man? Leave him guessing and play hard to get with your own husband, why don't you? When all you really want to do is jump into bed with him."

"But he slept with Isabel," the voice in my head protested.

"For Fuck's sake. He had sex with her once, Martha. Sex. Once. When he was drunk and troubled. Back when you two forgot how to talk. Back when sex wasn't available at home because you felt dried up and burnt out…"

"Oh, Trish, what am I going to do?"

"Text him, Martha."

"I will tomorrow."

Chapter 16

The Bastard

November 2018

Joseph Mary Murphy didn't make anything easy. I imagine that the judge's directions at the separation hearing had sent the controlling bastard into overdrive. I don't call people bastards lightly but this was the name that Celine's first counsellor had given him and it fitted the two-faced piece of lowlife that was Joseph Mary Murphy. When I was being measured about him, I called him JMM.

The images of my broken china doll friend, smashed and bruised at his hands, will always be with me. It disturbs me that men can do things like he did and still remain free to work in respectable jobs and go as they please with their heads held high. That they are greeted warmly by others and held up as pillars of society by more people again gives me a sensation that creeps like icy water through my veins, a sensation that starts at the back of my head and makes its way coldly down my spine. That they can get inside their children's heads and turn sons and daughters against good mothers such as Celine breaks my heart.

And this is only how I feel. I cannot imagine how to take these feelings to Celine's level. I cannot pretend to tread in her small but capable shoes. I can get angry on her behalf, but to what good? I can witness some of her physical pain as she turns her head on a cold day.

I can barely imagine her emotional pain with each day that her son does not acknowledge her very existence. But really, I am only dipping my toes into the waves as they reach the pebbled shore relative to the all-encompassing, tumultuous battering ocean that Celine's body and mind have been immersed in.

After that awful assault on Celine, Patrick had secured a new safety order, barring JMM from being within two kilometres of Celine's house. So much had happened in all our lives that it was hard to believe that was less than two years ago. There were still some years left to run on the order. Yet early in the mornings or in the evenings I kept thinking that I saw him. It might have been near the end of our road, outside the local church or outside the nearby Spar shop. All places frequented by Celine, be it to go for a walk, light a candle or buy a paper or some milk. The man I saw was of the bastard's build, tall and solid. He was wearing a big black raincoat and a baseball hat. I was sure that I could see the collar of a white shirt peeping out from the crack at the top of the jacket's zip. I never got to fully see his face but I could feel the menace of his presence, the feeling that someone was walking across the freshly dug grave of someone dear to me.

For a few weeks, I said nothing to Celine other than one time when we were out walking and I saw a young man in a baseball hat. I casually asked her what Joseph Mary Murphy's baseball hats had written on them.

"He never wore them," she said. "He hated them, said they were for drug dealers and other bollixes."

There seemed to be a certain irony to that comment but I didn't point it out to Celine because I was still hoping that the man I kept seeing in the baseball hat and big black raincoat wasn't her soon-to-be ex-husband. They should have been divorced already. Celine's solicitor had filed for divorce but JMM had disputed the dates of unbroken separation arguing that they hadn't lived apart for four out of the last five years, a requirement for divorce under Irish law. He claimed that they had slept together in that period. Does Irish law consider rape as sleeping together? Apart from that, there had been no sex between them, of that Celine was painfully adamant.

When Celine and I were together I had tended to steer her away from the church and Spar. I had found myself constantly unsettled and frequently convinced that I spotted him, back behind us or up in the distance. I got to the stage that I wondered if I got near enough to him would I be brave enough to take a photo. I was planning to take Patrick's advice and tell Celine and the Gardaí of my possible sightings.

The Saturday morning, two days after my dinner with Patrick, Fiona and I were walking near the church. It was lashing rain and we had crossed the road from the promenade to escape the wet wind and waves that swept over the sea wall, drenching everything that crossed it.

Patrick had sent me a text early on Friday morning while I was deep in sleep. Trish's voice must have been ringing in his head too.

Martha, our conversation tonight got me thinking. If we both agree there is so much still left unsaid, would it be reasonable to suggest that we have dinner together again soon? Xx Patrick

Patrick, you beat me to it. Where and when? Xx Martha

My place on Sunday late afternoon/early evening? I'll cook. I've discovered that I can still do a mean stir fry! Xx P

Perfect. Xx M

My face glowed at the thought of it. Just like in the early days when we were dating and we invited each other over for dinner. Dinner in my place or his place always meant dinner and more. I giggled at the memory of the first time. Another awkward first time was planned for Sunday. Who knows! We might rebuild our marriage by starting back where we first started from. I smiled. I had a date with my husband. Anything was possible. Everything was more possible.

Saturday morning's grim weather couldn't touch me. Fiona and I charged along the path with the hoods of our raincoats pulled around our faces, our arms linked, laughing together at the madness of the weather and us out in it, warm and dry in our raingear. I stopped, grabbing Fiona back by the elbow as I did so. JMM was standing at the church railings. I was certain this time.

"Shhh," I hissed, stepping in behind her and getting the camera on the phone ready. I peeped around her and took some rapid photos, paused, then zoomed in and took more. He looked our way as I was clicking. I dropped to the ground as if to tie my shoelace.

"Mum?"

"Shh, Fiona, shush."

Fiona looked down at me as I put my fingers to my lips. I stood up fast, feeling dizzy for doing so. I took her by the arm and led her into the church, keeping my head down for fear he would recognise me, even under all my raingear. I marched us a third of the way up the aisle and moved to sit in a pew. All the more conspicuous for not genuflecting, I thought with a smile. My hands and knees were shaking. I moved to the kneeler and brought my hands up in prayer – praying that he had not followed us.

"What was that about, Mum? What's wrong?" Fiona was more anxious than cross. I swivelled around in the tight space and surveyed the church. I didn't see anyone other than two women up at the altar changing flowers. I took my phone out of my jacket pocket.

"It was him. I'm sure that it was him."

"Who's him? For God's sake, Mum…"

"The bastard."

"Mum!" Fiona pointed towards the altar.

"Sorry God," I said, not meaning it one iota.

My phone wouldn't recognise my wet thumb print. I tried punching in my code to access the phone and photos. It took me three attempts. The last photos left no doubt as his face glared large and frightening, set clearly against the background of the church and its railings.

"It's Celine's husband, Fiona."

"So?"

"He's not allowed within two kilometres of her house. There's a Safety Order…"

"Oh my God, Mum. He's the bastard who battered and raped her!" I had told her much of the story with Celine's blessing. It made her more understanding of my dedication towards looking out for Celine.

"Yes."

"Fuck!"

I pointed at the altar. "God will understand," I said with an almost smile.

"What now?"

"I have to go to see Celine and tell her and then we need to go to the Gardaí. Will you come, as a witness?"

"I'll have to call Daniel and tell him I'll be late. He'll understand."

"He will. He's one of the good ones! I like him." Of course I do, I thought, he's a bit like your father, brains to burn at one level, especially when it came to the law, but totally naïve at another. Street wise he was not.

Fiona rang Daniel and I rang Celine from the church side-porch.

"Are you in?"

"Yes. Everything okay?"

"Fiona and I are just out for a walk and we want to call in to say hello. See you in two mins?"

"Sure."

I hung up and linked Fiona's arm as we ran the few hundred yards to Celine's house, both of us now in overdrive with anxiety.

Celine's kitchen felt warm and cosy relative to the first time I saw it. Months after the assault she had got me to move the bastard's big comfy chair, that she couldn't bring herself to sit on, out to the garage. Out of sight, out of mind, she had said. Then after the separation hearing she had found new energy and had repainted the whole kitchen in what she called a Mexican colour palette: blues, yellows and greens sang together in bold unison. When she had finished, to celebrate, I brought her a big vase of flowers from my garden. She had put them down on the table with a certain ceremony. "I hereby declare this kitchen officially mine," she had said.

As Fiona and I sat at the table I felt like I was about to undo some of that magic. I was trying to think of an easy way to tell her we had just seen *him* as Celine put a large pot of tea down on the table and sat down on a chair opposite me.

"Out with it, Martha. What wee thing's eatin' you?"

"It's *him*. The bastard's back."

"Here Martha he's what? He cannot be, he's barred."

"I know. But for the last couple of weeks, I kept thinking I saw him but I wasn't sure because I couldn't see his face under the baseball cap…"

"A baseball cap!" She brought a trembling hand up to her face. "That's why you asked…"

"Yes, it is. Today we saw him for sure. I took photos." I handed her my phone. "See it *is him*…I'm sorry, Celine, I'm so sorry."

Celine pushed my phone back across to me. "I thought I saw him with a baseball cap too," she whispered. "I thought it was PTSD and I was imagining my biggest fear – *him*!" She brought her knees up to her chest and rocked in her chair, her eyes closed tight. I watched her going back and forth, back and forth. Then, without further comment, she stopped, put her feet firmly back on the floor and stood up, straight to her full small height. "No, no, no," she said in a voice bigger than her size, "I will not give in to him. We will go to the guards and report him. Right now. They can arrest him for breach of the Safety Order." She made for the kitchen door. "Are you coming?"

I looked at the cup of tea that Fiona had just poured for me and I became aware of being thirsty, peckish and probably needing to catch my emotional breath. Celine followed my gaze to the tea.

"Just a few sips and we'll go. Okay?" I said, feeling sheepish.

"Of course," Celine said, turning on her heels and going straight into the hall and putting on her raincoat. I went after her and Fiona came after me. The tea would have to wait.

Two days later, the guards in their wisdom, or otherwise, went to JMM's place of work and arrested him for breach of the Safety Order. They told Celine that they thought that it would give him a fright and put manners on him. I thought they had a valid point. He was released on bail. Celine was up to ninety.

"They know nothing," she said. "It could make him more danger-ous than ever. You don't fuck with JMM's ego."

I stayed in her house with her for a few nights that week and then Jacinta came down to stay for the weekend, and stayed for a week. I hadn't seen Jacinta in a long time as Celine had been mostly going up North to visit her, rather than her coming down. Celine said the odd escape did her good. Jacinta was her usual plain-spoken self.

"There are only two possible solutions here and both have serious fucking risks. One is Celly follows through on the assault and rape case against the bastard and the other is that we bypass the system and or-ganise our own punishment for the wee bastard!" Jacinta declared one evening when Celine had gone to bed and she and I were alone in Celine's kitchen. Jacinta had produced a bottle of Paddy and poured two full tumblers of what she called liquid gold.

I took a few gulps and felt it go pinging around my brain. If I had much more of it, there was no knowing what I'd agree to.

257

"The first option puts Celine through a queer amount of shit and may still leave the wee bastard to walk free, and the second one will only work if we can get *him* to visit up North and we know when he'd be visiting…I've made some enquiries." She knocked back the last of the whiskey in her glass straight down her gullet and slapped the glass on the table demanding a refill.

I poured her a 'wee' measure, meaning I almost filled her glass.

"Don't hold back," she said.

"No problem. But I'll have mine with a bit of water, if you don't mind," I said getting up from the table and, with my back to her, I splashed some of my whiskey into the sink. I ran the tap until it was cold, then filled up my glass with water. Jacinta always made me on edge and with too much whiskey, I'd be sure to put my foot in it with her.

"Well, what do you think?" Jacinta demanded before I sat down again.

"Jacinta, perhaps I should give you a kind of synopsis of Celine's recently expressed thoughts on the Northern Ireland option," I said, feeling nervous about bursting Jacinta's take on the situation. I knew it needed to be said, I just wished that I didn't feel like I was putting myself on the firing line.

"Fuck it, Martha. Out with it?"

"Promise you won't shoot the messenger?"

Jacinta dismissed my question with an upward sweep of her head and a roll of her eyes.

"Okay." I swallowed hard and paused to make sure that the words came out in a way that caused the least offence.

"Martha!"

"I'm just trying to remember…it was something along the lines of it ain't gonna happen and we just need to accept that and move on from the thought of having him sorted the Northern way because if you do the crime, you've got to be willing to do the time, and she doesn't want you, or anyone else, doing time. Not even for that bastard." I gasped in some breath and watched Jacinta's face for her reaction. She poured herself another wee dram of whiskey. I was damned if I told her what Celine had actually said, which was that Jacinta was playing the tough Northerner and talking a load of bollix and the only way the bastard was ever going to lose his knee caps or any other part of him would be if she blew them off herself. And she wasn't going to prison *again* for that bastard. The 'again' referred to the previous prison of living in the same house as him! Anyway, where would her kids be with her if they thought for a minute that she had any hand, act or part in having something *done* to their father? She had been particularly angry that day because a judge had yet again handed out a suspended sentence to a man who'd viciously beaten his partner, leaving her with permanent scarring physically and mentally. The judge, in his presumed wisdom, decided that there was little chance of the defendant re-offending.

"Fuck it, I don't want to do time for that bastard either. We will just have to hope that the assault case will do the trick and that a bitteen of time in prison will see his sweet face rearranged."

"Jacinta, she hasn't told you?"

"Told me what?"

I brought my elbows up on to the table and my hands to my face, and rubbed my face slowly. I was giving myself time. I let out an involuntary sigh, wishing myself not to be sitting there with Jacinta poised and ready, waiting for me to speak.

"As you know, for a long time Celine's counsellor had her all fired up to push for a serious assault case and get the bastard off the streets. She was encouraged by her separation case. Two Gardaí were being wonderfully supportive. They took photos of her bedroom and said they would get forensics out to it. Things were looking good. Then

Celine started to google other such court cases. That's when she got really angry. On our walks she ranted non-stop about how few men were convicted and how they got short or non-existent sentences for stupid fucking reasons. After that she got deeply depressed." I remembered because I'd been in pretty shitty humour myself at that stage. I'd struggled to be there for her and keep her buoyed. I had tried to persuade her to go up North and spend time with Jacinta but she had refused. I think she was incapable of getting herself together to go.

"That's when you didn't see her for about a month," I continued, remembering that I was in the thick of my own struggles at the time, looking at the long months ahead, biding my time, waiting for Zara's Leaving Cert to be over. "At that time Celine just about left the house occasionally to go for a walk by the sea, but no further. There were times I couldn't persuade her to get out of bed. She said that even if he was found guilty, and that would be a big IF, he could still *fucking walk free*. There'd be a queue out the door to give him good character references – Father Joseph Daly, after whom he is named, would be first in the line! Sure, didn't he know JMM's family all his life and there is none like them, blah de blah de blah."

"Martha, the fucking evidence from Dr McCarthy would deal with that bullshit." Jacinta slammed her palm on the table in frustration. I shuddered as if feeling the impact of the slap.

"That's what the counsellor said and I thought so too. But it's not that simple, is it? Celine asked me straight out one night what would I do if it was me?" I took a slow deep breath, knocked back the rest of my glass of whiskey and seriously considered having another. I wondered what might be the least provocative thing to say to Jacinta.

"So, out with it, what'd you tell her?"

"Jacinta, I was stymied. Up against a man who plays the hail-fellow-well-met at every turn – outside of the house that is – what chance would she have against him? But, on the other hand, if a case wasn't taken where might it all end? If not for her, for someone else? There is no easy answer, on balance, I told her that I thought that I would go for a case, but I stressed that she really needed to decide for herself."

"And what did *she* fucking decide?"

"It took her a long time to decide. She talked to her doctor, her counsellor and the Rape Crisis Centre and decided that, with their support, she was up for it."

"Good. That's it so. We will all support her and—"

"And nothing. After that horrific case up North, she changed her mind again. When she saw how the girl was treated in that trial, she said there was no way she could go through with it."

"But Celine's case is so fucking different. There wouldn't be all those ugly barristers, ye don't allow the nosy-parker public in down here to sit in the court with their effing mouths open and some of them gooey eyed looking at the defendants as if they're hunks sent from heaven…"

"No, we don't let the public in but that's not the point. That very public trial up North highlighted the horrors of any rape or sexual assault trial, North or South, for all victims. You have to remember, the victim is a mere witness, there to be belittled by every barrister who sees fit. And mostly with no legal representation of their own and definitely with no say in what happens in the trial."

"You're too fucking right there!"

"His lawyer can make you feel like a piece of second-class shit – Celine's words, not mine. The bastard will be portrayed as a saint and Celine says that she will be painted as a binge-drinking lush who seeks hard sex when she's drunk and then falls over and bangs into things, hence her many injuries as recorded by the hospitals and by Dr McCarthy. He has the smooth tongue on him to say all that."

"Fuck it, Martha."

"Anyway, the verdict of that bloody trial came in just at the start of Easter weekend. I remember because Fiona had persuaded me to go away with her to Malaga and leave Patrick at home to keep an eye on Zara and Matt and make sure that they both did some proper study; Zara's Leaving Cert mocks hadn't gone too well given the points she was looking for! Fiona and I flew out on a Friday. And the case was all over the papers, social media, twitter, everywhere. It was impossible to avoid. It came up in conversation with every Irish woman we met, at the airport on the way out, on the way home, everywhere we went, women, and even men, were horrified by how that young woman was treated."

"It was the same up North, non-stop chatter about it. Only different opinions in different places!"

"And those WhatsApp messages those lads sent each other. I was shocked by them too but Matt said that lots of fellas he knows, not friends of his mind, do that sort of texting; boasting about how they scored and naming and shaming the women they scored with, as if they're nobodies, just points on a score card...and Fiona said we should see what some of the girls post on WhatsApp group chats about fellas! They're pretty bad, she says – nothing's fucking sacred!"

"I knew the world was fucked when *Fifty Shades of Grey* and whatever you're having yourself topped the bestsellers list for years."

"I'm with you there," I said with exasperation.

"But where does all that leave our Celly?" Jacinta always called Celine Celly, whenever she was in protective mood.

"Sorry but...when I think of that trial I always get worked up! On the Tuesday after Easter, I called as usual to her to go for a walk. Normally, she opens the door and lets me in while she puts on her coat or puts the lead on Chuckie. That day she left me waiting outside and then barely opened the door enough for Chuckie and her to slip out. The rancid smell of bleach hit me. I was left standing in its waft at her

262

door as she took off down the garden path as fast as her legs could carry her. I followed her and asked her where's my welcome home hug. You know, trying to make light of the situation. In the split-second hug that she barely gave me, I was knocked backwards with that same pungent bleach smell."

I remembered that my eyes had watered and I had started to sneeze.

"Our Celly? I've never seen her with a bottle of bleach in me life!"

"No. Me neither, until then. I asked her if she'd fallen down the toilet or something and she ignored me. Then I asked was it that she was expecting a visit from the Queen and had taken to giving the house a deep clean. They were stupid questions! She barked at me for mentioning the Queen. 'Aye,' she said, 'don't you know the Queen and I go back bleedin' years! It's more likely Gerry Adams I'd be expecting.'"

"Ach, you were showing your Protestant colours there, Martha!" Jacinta gave a raw snigger.

"Hey, I'm as Republican as the majority of people down here – just without the violence!" I laughed, more to relieve some tension within me than because I thought anything funny.

"But what was Celly cleaning?"

"She used the weekend to immerse her old bedroom in bleach – the main bedroom – the one which she hadn't so much as entered for the three years since that awful night that he assaulted her. She bleached out all the evidence of it. The fumes could have killed her! No less than four litres of bleach, she'd used. I know because I counted the bottles."

"I fucking didn't know any of that!" Jacinta exclaimed.

"Well, there you go. It happened and then she had my handyman, John, come in and load the furniture and contents from that bedroom, other than the paintings, thank God, into a skip together with the bastard's chair from this kitchen that I had previously been tasked with moving to the garage."

"Well good for wee Celly!"

"Yeah, but I asked her what about forensics? She said, 'Fuck forensics, what's forensics when you can repaint a scene to whatever seems appropriate in the eyes of the powers that be. They won't have to airbrush out the blood in my bedroom,' she said, 'I've bleached it all out myself!'…And with four litres of bleach she did a pretty thorough job." I sighed.

"Shit!" Jacinta said.

"It's called reclaiming my house. The whole thing was cathartic," Celine said from the kitchen door, her tone giving a certain affirmation of the correctness of her actions. Chuckie was sitting by her side, nudging his head against Celine's thigh for attention. I don't know how long they had been there. It can't have been long. Chuckie would have caught our attention or would have come over to me. Jacinta and I looked at her and at each other. Jacinta poured what was left of the bottle of Paddy into her glass and handed it to Celine. Celine knocked it back in one. "You could only smell bleach, Martha, but I smelt the brief whiff of freedom. And then this. Then the bastard reappears in the area, in total breach of the safety order. What do I do now, Jacinta?"

"Celine, you can still take a case. There's still a lot of compelling evidence. Dr McCarthy's, Martha's, the Gardaí…"

"Forget it. The bastard would twist everything. He will make up more effing stories and he'd have the best of bloody barristers on his side. He's already working on the kids. Karen said that he told Shane weird stuff already. Seemingly he apologised for having to tell Shane, but he thought that he should *know* the whole story. Did you hear any of that, Jacinta?"

"No Celly, I don't think I did." Jacinta spoke surprisingly quietly, as if fearing what Celine was about to tell her.

"Seemingly, he has alluded to me having some messed-up sexual relationship with my paint brushes and that's how I got injured down there! Sick, isn't it? But it would sound good in court, wouldn't it? Wouldn't it?"

"The fucking bastard." Jacinta spat the words out.

"I don't want him or his barrister making me out to be the problem. I'm not the problem. He is. He's a big fucking problem." Celine's voice filled the kitchen and all Jacinta and I could do was nod in lame agreement.

Celine continued. "And if he did, by some miracle, get put away, chances are it would be short and made shorter by his 'good behaviour'. What's good behaviour in jail got to do with what he did to me? It's a bleedin' joke."

"Fuck it, Celine, what are you going to do?" Jacinta asked.

"I'm going to paint and travel and after that who knows. But I'm not letting that bastard dictate my life anymore…it's my life and I'm going to live it."

"I believe you, Celly. I really do," I said and gave her a big hug.

She looked over at Jacinta.

"I fucking believe you too, Celine."

Celine's paintings became darker. She worked in various shades of grey, always with a splash of red screaming to be noticed. They were not likely to have mass appeal and be in high demand but their message was clear to those who wanted to hear it.

One painting was of a woman with a collar around her neck. A lead was attached to the collar and it was being held by many men. Another was of a woman locked in chains. The men who surrounded her held in their hands the keys to the locks. The details of the women's faces were precise; fine lines in their foreheads, light reflected in their eyes, the distinct arch of their eyebrows, the lines and shadows of their chins and noses. But their mouths were barely there. Their lips were mere suggestions.

Epilogue

I continued with my counselling and in time, Patrick and I had some sessions together. It was a long, emotional journey. We had both been fools at times. We had forgotten the importance of spending time together and of talking, really talking. I believe him when he says that he wanted to protect me but that he had confused protecting our assets with protecting me. To protect our assets, in his legal mind, he had worked out that it would be best if we separated. While I knew Patrick sometimes had his own version of events, I believed him when he said that in his heart, he didn't want us to separate. The night with Isabel was a drunken, emotional mistake and it horrified him that he had done it. I said I hoped it horrified him in more ways than one.

For the most part, we are learning to forgive ourselves and each other. We know that we must always make time to talk and be open and honest with each other. We agree that we are stronger together for all that we have been through; older and wiser, Matt says, with emphasis on the older. Financially poorer, emotionally richer, Patrick says. Vespers got their half-pound of flesh but we have more than enough, even with Fiona's wedding to pay for, I say. The bling is gone. We have sold more paintings. Soon I will move into a smaller house, with less stuff, with less housework and more time for the things that matter. We'd too much stuff anyway, Zara says, insisting we get eco paint for the walls of the new house. We are lucky. We are not ready to go back living together yet and part of me thinks there's a lot to be said for keeping separate homes. Patrick is now living in his father's house and when I move, we will still have a family home where we can eat, sleep, talk and argue without worrying about other people; not like the homeless people I see in increasing numbers on the streets of Dublin. Their daily struggles for any peace must be endless. I've promised myself I will go back volunteering with the Simon Community or some other homeless charity after Fiona's wedding and I'm settled in the new house; hopefully then life will be less busy and I'll be over the worst of the energy sapping, sweat-inducing menopause.

Last I heard, Gavin and Isabel's house was on the market and there were rumours of Isabel moving in with her solicitor. It may not be true. I have seen Gavin out in town a few times with an attractive grey-haired lady whom I recognised as one of the more active and vocal politicians for Dublin North. They looked good together. He seems to have given up wearing those garish waistcoats and is looking quite handsome with his short new hair style and designer glasses.

Celine and I didn't see JMM again and I've long since stopped looking over my shoulder for him. As promised, I treated Celine and myself to a trip to Bali. Before we left, she got Matt and Fiona to help her to sort out her house. She got them to move all her personal stuff into the garage. She stayed with us or Jacinta in the weeks before our trip while some cleaners and painters got her house in order. The auctioneer had the place rented and a family settled in before Patrick left Celine and me to the airport.

I came home after a wonderful three weeks and Celine stayed on, travelling in Bali, Vietnam, Thailand and wherever her spirit led her. She bought herself a smart phone before we left. I get regular WhatsApp messages from her, full of colour and smiling faces. I know it can't all be smiles. She is painting bright scenes and powerful portraits, mainly women and young children. She sends rolled-up canvases to me every couple of months. Opening each cylinder is exciting. I don't know what emotion I will see in the eyes that peer out at me from the canvas. There is a power in the ambiguity of some of the expressions. They say different things to different people. I get each one framed and pass them to her agent to sell. In galleries they sit beside some of the grey mouthless paintings. I tell her that her paintings are her voice and the voices of the women who cannot speak.

Patrick and I are going to visit Celine on her travels next year, if we can get her to commit to staying put for long enough for us to catch up with her. It will have to be outside of term time, for the next year, because I'm committed to doing paired reading with two fine young boys, in between walking Chuckie and keeping our finances and personal stuff on track. There will be bumps and maybe even potholes along the way but together we will get there: whatever *together* might mean; wherever *there* might be.

About the Author

After thirty years as a reluctant accountant, Vanessa retired from figures to focus on writing and over the last seven years has taken part in writing workshops at Bantry Literary Festivals, The Irish Writers Centre and The Big Smoke Writing Factory.

When not escaping to West Cork or further afield, the author lives in Clontarf, with her husband, three of their four children – one has flown the nest – her black dog Yoda and her black, epileptic cat named Cat.

Find her on Twitter @VanessaPearse1

Lightning Source UK Ltd.
Milton Keynes UK
UKHW010357251121
394507UK00001B/38